Lucilla Andrews, the second daughter of an
English father and Spanish mother, was born
in Suez in the twilight of the old British
Empire and was a teenager when World War 2
started. After 18 months as a VAD in
English military hospitals, she took her general
and then midwifery nursing training at
St Thomas' Hospital in London and acquired
an SRN, Part I SCM. She married a doctor
in 1947 and was widowed in 1954. She has
one daughter.

A House
For Sister Mary

Lucilla Andrews

CORGI BOOKS
A DIVISION OF TRANSWORLD PUBLISHERS LTD

A HOUSE FOR SISTER MARY

A CORGI BOOK 0 552 11384 0

Originally published in Great Britain
by George G. Harrap & Co. Ltd.

PRINTING HISTORY
George G. Harrap Edition published 1966
Corgi Edition published 1967
Corgi Edition reissued 1969
Corgi Edition reprinted 1973
Corgi Edition reissued 1979

This book is set in Times 10 pt.

Corgi Books are published by Transworld Publishers Ltd.,
Century House, 61–63 Uxbridge Road, Ealing, London, W5 5SA

Made and printed in Great Britain by
Richard Clay (The Chaucer Press), Ltd., Bungay, Suffolk.

CONTENTS

CHAPTER ONE

THE END OF AN ERA

THE apple blossom was in full bloom that morning, and the breeze sent pink fragments floating on to my apron skirt as I swung. They reminded me of confetti, so I brushed them off. I was all for being strong-minded, but never could see any point in masochism.

The swing was hidden behind the great bank of rhododendrons that cut off the orchard from the formal part of the garden. In the pond beyond the rhododendrons the water-lilies had opened in the sunshine. Beside the pond was a small and very hideous sleeping stone gnome known as 'Old Trypo' to a whole generation of Barny's pupil midwives and midwifery clerks. 'Trypo' was short for 'Trypanosomiasis'.

When David first told me about 'Old Trypo' I had been too junior to know 'trypanosomiasis' was sleeping-sickness. David had explained that along with a good many other things, including why we must be intelligent and wait until after his pre-registration year for our marriage. Then he decided it would be even more intelligent if he got Membership and I collected a midder qualification. A few weeks after I started midwifery he drove down to the Maternity Unit Annexe to give me an equally intelligent reason for ending our engagement. He now had a good job in Canada. His wife worked in the same hospital.

His wife had not been one of our girls. I was glad about that and that David had left Barny's. He had been the last of his original student-set in the hospital, so I should not have to avoid his or her old pals around the place when I got back to the general side on Monday, and there would be no-one to feel his name had to be avoided with me. Barny's was so big that few people knew more than their own small circle of friends really well, and once anyone moved out, as I had done when I branched into midder a year after my own set of nurses, they quickly lost touch and became almost a stranger in their own hospital. Once that might have bothered me—now it suited me well. Despite my personal problems I had enjoyed midder but was well pleased about returning to general nursing, which I much preferred. Of course, there was a chance one or two of David's friends might turn up for Sister Mary's party tonight, but with luck I would not have to talk to them, and even if I did we could always discuss the weather. In any case, a party only lasted one night. I hoped my new job in Observation Ward would last around two years.

In the little wood at the back of the orchard the chestnut candles were red and white, and the new oak-leaves were still more golden than green. Frank, our gardener, paused on his way from the wood to say summer would be real warm, as the oak was out before the ash. He looked towards the house. 'All gone, eh, Nurse?'

'All.' I stopped swinging. 'It's so odd.'

'Aye.' He removed then replaced his cap, as if saluting the end of an era. 'Be real queer working here without the old Sister and all her ladies. Don't seem right—seeing you nurses taking it easy, like, of a mid-morning. The Sister calling on the old Guv'nor? I see her drive off with that Mrs Evans.'

'That's right.' I did not ask how he had seen as he had been in the wood most of the morning. Frank saw everything, knew what everyone in the Annexe was doing, and why. Our obstetric registrar had frequently remarked he often wondered why he bothered to ask Sister Labour Ward to let him know when his services would be required as Frank invariably gave him the necessary warning first. 'Best get up there sharpish, Doctor!' or 'Reckon you can have your tea first, Doctor,' he would announce gloomily. He never smiled, and only looked mildly cheerful when bearing bad news. He seldom talked much to nurses, and never at all to our patients, but there were few things he enjoyed more than a good funeral, and he had on his funeral expression at the moment.

Sister Mary was paying her final visit to old Mr Norris, the former owner of Wylden House, who had given the house and grounds to the hospital when the old Mary

8

Block in London had been wrecked by a flying bomb in the Second World War. The house stood two miles from Wylden village. Mr Norris, now in his eighties, lived in a large Georgian house in Astead, our nearest market town. He was a very wealthy man, a childless widower, and owned a great deal of property in London as well as Astead. He had once been a patient in Barny's for a few weeks as a young man. His gift had come as a total but very welcome surprise to the hospital.

I asked now, 'Frank, you worked for Mr Norris. What was he like? And is it true he's never come near this place after handing it over?'

Frank hitched his cap up an inch.

'He was a good guv'nor. And what'd he want to come back for? Seeing as he wasn't living here no more?'

I shrugged. 'To see what it looked like.'

'Reckon he reckoned as that weren't his business.' His tone showed it wasn't mine either. 'So the old Sister's moving in along of that Mr Martin's cottage up the village?'

'Just as soon as Mr Martin marries and moves out.'

Frank sighed. 'I can see as I'll have to keep an eye on that garden for her. Them weeds! Higher than me lupins they are! Need to take a scythe to the lot and then dig it over two spits deep. You seen that garden, Nurse? In a cruel state, it is!'

'And not only the garden, Frank. The whole cottage needs redecorating.'

'Reckon that'll please the old lady. She'll not want to sit by and fold her hands, even if they have given her her cards. Shame.' He sighed again. 'Don't like to think of her gone, but we all got to go.' He ambled on, leaving me plunged in gloom for Sister Mary.

Sister Mary was Miss Maud Bush. She had been in her forties when she opened the St Barnabas' Hospital Maternity Unit Annexe in Wylden House two days after that flying bomb landed. She had then expected to be back in London inside of a year as the war with Germany was ending, but before it ended two more flying bombs and one rocket hit Barny's. The massive rebuilding needed years of planning. In the interval the Mat. Unit Annexe

9

had become a great success, and its closing date was shelved.

Years ago ward extensions had been added to the house; an obstetric theatre had been built into the Labour Ward floor; a large flat had been made over the stables for the obstetric registrar and two housemen; and the stables converted into dormitories for the male midder clerks (medical students doing their midwifery training). The huge attic floor of the house had been converted into a miniature nurses' home, and the girl students shared rooms along our corridor. Our Professor of Obstetrics had bought a house in the village and commuted between the Annexe and Barny's proper.

Our London mothers had enjoyed having their babies in the country, and the families and friends had equally enjoyed the regular coach service laid on for them between Barny's and Wylden. An ambulance convoy had gone to and fro thrice weekly; a hospital van came down daily; and an emergency ambulance had been kept ready at Barny's to make the trip at any hour of the day or night. Surprisingly few babies had been born in that ambulance. The last ambulance convoy had left us yesterday afternoon. This morning the Annexe had closed for ever after twenty years. This week-end Sister Mary, the oldest and most senior sister in the hospital, was leaving her profession after forty-five years' nursing.

When Matron spent a week-end with us last month to announce our closing date in person, she had asked for three volunteer nurses to stay behind for the last week-end to clear up, clean, and then close with Sister Mary. The whole nursing staff volunteered. Matron had chosen the only three of us not returning to midder in London. Jill Collins, the first staff midwife, was becoming Sister Elizabeth Ward; Harriet Jones and I were returning to Barny's as senior staff nurses, Harriet to Casualty and myself to the Observation Ward.

The Annexe was shortly reopening as a holiday home for invalid children. By then Sister Mary should have moved into the cottage in Wylden she was buying from one Mr Martin, a retired art-master, who had shocked and enchanted the village by getting engaged to an Australian lady he had known only a few weeks, about a week after his sixty-sixth birthday. His future wife was a widow with a grown-up family in Australia. She had persuaded Mr Martin to sell up and move back to Perth with her. They were due to marry and sail in the next few weeks.

Their belated romance had been a godsend to Sister Mary. Until Mr Martin offered her his cottage there had been nothing in the neighbourhood she could afford. Wylden was sixty miles from London, but the hourly train service from Astead was so good that all the local villages round Astead were now much-prized commuter territory. Anything for sale sold instantly, at prices way above Sister's savings. We were getting desperate when Mr Martin made his offer because he liked Sister Mary, asked a moderate price for a quick sale, and wanted to deal with someone he could trust to be kind to the tits that nested each spring in the letter-box on his front gate.

From the morning Mr Martin had arrived in the middle of one of the Professor's teaching rounds demanding a word with old Miss Whatsit the Matron-lady, Sister Mary had looked years younger. The bed-sitting-room in the seaside guest-house for retired nurses had been cancelled. That room had upset us all, though we had all praised it when Sister Mary was around.

'Just imagine the poor old bags sitting round swopping horror stories,' said Harriet, 'and shaking their heads when one of them has a cough or a twinge of rheumatism. They'll all have seen a fatal case that started just like that—and they'll give the details! Then think how clean it'll be! No-one'll dare squash a cushion!'

'Apart from all that,' I said, 'what will Sister Mary have to do? When she's used to being hectically busy.'

The prospect of owning a cottage plus the first stages of closing the Annexe had left Sister Mary without one spare moment since Mr Martin's visit. The usual slow official negotiations had been started, and Sister had begun adding to the few possessions she already had in store. Never having owned so much as a two-roomed flat before, she found the idea of choosing her own furniture, curtains, and colour schemes as exciting as any young bride. The cottage could not stop her regretting the end of her career, but by giving her such an interest it was making this week-end more bearable for her.

I remember now how she had looked when that last ambulance disappeared yesterday, how she had gone on watching the empty drive, and then turned slowly to look back at the empty Annexe. A lifetime's habit of self-control had produced a firm little smile. 'Well, my dears! That's that! Now, back to work! We have a great deal to do to make this place fit for our guests tomorrow evening!'

Harriet and I had thought up this party when Matron said we could stay on. We had put it to Jill Collins. Jill consulted with Mrs Evans, our cook, then asked Matron. Matron had approved: 'If Sister Mary agrees.'

We had approached Sister Mary in a bunch.

'A party? For me? My dears, we will then be empty. Who would want to come so far?'

'You send out those open invitations to all ex-Annexe and ex-old Mary Block staff, Sister, and you'll be surprised!'

It had taken us some time to persuade her that it would not be too much work for Mrs Evans and ourselves, and that her guests really would come thick and fast. Eventually she gave in and the invitations went off to Barny's. The grapevine did the rest. The news of Sister Mary's farewell party spread far beyond the hospital via the visiting G.P.s who called in to see old colleagues or discuss a case when in London. They had spread the word to other old Barny's men in their areas, and Sister Mary had been swamped with letters from all over the country. Our local postman had grumbled, 'Every day's Christmas, seem'ly.'

This morning's post had taken our guest list over the hundred mark, and as no-one could guess how many last-minute guests would drive down from Barny's proper, Mrs Evans had driven Sister Mary into Astead to stack up more party food while Sister Mary spent her fifteen minutes with Mr Norris. As Sister had insisted we all take an hour off while she was out, Jill Collins was washing her hair, Harriet had gone into Wylden on her scooter to fetch some shoes from the cobbler, and I was having a swing.

'Frank said you were here, Rowe.' Collins, her head

12

in a towel, came through the bushes. She stepped carefully to avoid squashing the primroses.

I jumped off. 'Time to work again?'

'Not yet. Jones isn't back, and I must set my hair. I came out to ask your views on the hall decorations. We need more flowers, but I daren't ask Frank again. He nearly wept when he brought in the last lot. So I've been thinking—what about ferns and cow parsley?'

'Brilliant, Nurse! There's masses of both growing wild, and Frank'll love you! He calls them something weeds.' I said 'something' instead of Frank's favourite expression intentionally. I liked old Jill Collins, but she was a very senior staff midwife, and, though a nice person, she was not one of those seniors who enjoy being all girls together with their juniors. 'Shall I get them, Nurse?'

'Would you, my child? Then I can get back to my rollers.' She turned, then spun round on one foot. 'How lucky you are to have red hair that isn't ginger or sandy and never looks like damp string, or frizzes, even after wearing a theatre turban. No matter what I do, my hair always looks as if it's been cut with the garden shears and combed with a rake! Ah, me! Life is very unfair.'

Her nickname was 'Hurricane Jill'. She knew it, of course, though no-one ever made the mistake of calling her that to her face. When I began midder I had found her high-powered efficiency and passion for platitudes very off-putting, but had since grown too fond of her to object to either. She was thirty-one, eight years older than Harriet and myself, and as first staff midwife she ranked as a junior sister. She was a very professional nurse, and the sight of her in a uniform dress with the sleeves rolled up and that damp towel round her head in the Annexe grounds in mid-morning showed, more than anything else could have shown me, that we were briefly between two worlds. Jill Collins was the type of nurse who felt undressed without her cap, and would never, even in a midwifery department—and midder standards of etiquette were far less stringent than those in Barny's general wards—consider addressing Sister Mary or any doctor from registrar upward without her cuffs on.

The winter had been long and wet. Spring and summer

13

had arrived together a couple of weeks ago. There were bluebells, cowslips, milkmaids, and primroses growing on the bank leading to the little wood, and the delicate white lace veil of the cow parsley was omnipresent. I left as much as I thought we could use in the shade under an apple-tree and went into the wood for the ferns.

It had been getting hot in the orchard, but the wood was cool and green. Stepping out of the sun into the dimmer light was rather like swimming underwater. The occasional shaft of sunlight filtered through the thick young leaves overhead, illuminating the patches of primroses, making the ferns more blue than green, and transforming the decaying stump of a dead tree into grey velvet.

The ground was thick with old leaves that crackled as I walked. I disturbed a squirrel but not the birds chatting to each other in the interwoven trees. At present that wood was alive with birds, and at night the nightingales sang in chorus. Last night I had dragged Harriet from the television set to hear them, and counted six different singers before her conversation silenced them.

I picked an armful of ferns, then sat on a half-buried log in a small clearing listening to the birds, sorting out the species, and thinking how strange it was not to be able to share moments like now and last night with a man. I had grown so accustomed to sharing with David, and though I had got over him I still missed having a man around. A specific man. I had been dated by other men since David. I had quite enjoyed their company, but had always been relieved when the dates ended. Harriet said I had lost my nerve about men. She could be right. Certainly I seemed to have lost more than David when he backed out of my life.

The village church clock chimed the half-hour and reminded me I should get back to the house. I stood up reluctantly, clutching the ferns. It was so pleasant in that wood.

'Hey! No! You can't move yet! I haven't finished!' protested a man's voice.

'Who's that?' I demanded in astonishment, having heard no footsteps. 'Where are you?' But as I was looking round wildly I saw him before I finished speaking. 'What do you

14

think you are doing in that tree?' I added.

A fair-haired man was sitting along a lower branch of a large oak a few yards from my log roughly ten feet above the ground. He wore a dark brown sweater and faded grey jeans and was leaning against the trunk as he sketched. The colour of his clothes was a good camouflage in that light, but I had not seen him mainly because I had not been looking his way. 'Hi, there!' He waved his pencil. 'Good morning. What am I doing? Can I be corny and say bird-watching? Or honest, and say sketching you?'

'But you didn't come here to sketch me. And you shouldn't be here at all. This wood's private.'

'Going to run me in for trespassing, Nursie?' He was smiling. 'You'll have to come up and get me first—which does not, if you press, strike me as such a bad idea. If that doesn't appeal, can we make a deal? You sit down for five little minutes and let me finish my picture, and then I'll go quietly. What do you say?'

'Sorry. I haven't the time to waste.'

'Who said anything about wasting time? You're giving me inspiration. How do you know I'm not another Picasso? One day this could be worth thousands. Do sit down!'

'Are you another Picasso?' I was now much less surprised by his presence because of that sketching pad. Wylden, being a very attractive and remarkably unspoilt village, was a pet haunt of amateur artists. The members of the Astead Art Society came over in herds on most fine Saturdays and sat around the village drawing pretty pictures.

'That's not what they called me in art school—go on, Nursie—sit down! My intentions are strictly honourable, if that's what's worrying you. If it'll make you feel any happier I'll promise not to come down from the tree until you say the word. How about that?'

I sat down. 'No more than five minutes.'

'Heaven will reward you even if I don't. Now, get those ferns in your lap and look down as before. Not that way— turn your head—that's it.'

His sudden businesslike air amused me. 'Do you always climb trees to sketch?'

'Sure. Call me Tarzan. Are you Jane?'

'No.'

'No smiling!' he said sternly. 'You weren't smiling before. Brood on him again.'

'On whom?' I asked, without looking up.

'How would I know his name? I don't even know yours. I never take my crystal ball up trees. But obviously you were brooding about some man.'

'Why "obviously"?'

'Hey! Don't look up! Keep still! Why obviously? My dear girl, don't pretend to be dumb—you haven't a dumb face. You can look in a mirror. You must know you've got a lovely face and glorious hair. When a girl who looks like you sits around sighing, it's a hundred to one she's sighing about some man. What's the problem?'

I said, 'I thought I was posing for a picture, not on a psychiatrist's couch. Are you a Barny's man?'

'No. I'm no medic. And I'm sorry if I've been talking out of turn. Forgive me?'

'Forget it.' I liked his quick apology. 'Much longer?'

'Nearly done.' A couple of minutes later he said I could move. 'I haven't got you. This is bloody bad.'

'May I see?'

'Sure. Catch. May I come down?'

'If you like,' I said absently, studying his sketch. I had expected it to be rough and amateurish, but it seemed to me to be the reverse. 'This is very good! So good—are you a professional artist?'

He stood in front of me, his head tilted to one side, his hands in his pockets. He was taller, broader, and a little older than I had previously guessed, since he had been behaving like one of the midder boys. His clothes, carriage, and voice was purely English, but his build, colouring, and features were Scandinavian. That physical type was not uncommon round Wylden. Every invader from the Phoenicians to the Normans had come to trade, burn down, or settle in that part of the county, and it was still easy to trace their descendants by looking at the local faces.

He said a professional artist was not what they called him down at the Labour Exchange. 'I wanted to be one once. I even grew a beard and got into an art school by shamelessly pulling strings. Unfortunately, I like to eat. So

16

I had to get out and get me a job. I just sketch in my spare time.' He took back the pad and put it under his arm. 'And what do you do with your spare time? Apart from gathering ferns.'

'Me? Oh—I pick cow parsley.'

'My, my,' he said, 'but you know how to live!' and we both laughed as if he had made a brilliantly witty observation.

David had been fairish, but not nearly so good-looking. Even so, I stopped laughing. 'I must go. I should be working.'

'What at? You've no patients left.'

'How do you know that?'

'Heard it in the village. Everyone knows this place has closed.'

'You live in Wylden?'

'Just down for the week-end.' He watched me closely. 'Don't go yet. Please.'

I hesitated only briefly, remembering not what my mother told me about picking up strange men in woods, but that the way I was suddenly feeling was exactly the way I had once felt with David. I knew nothing about this man, and I did not want to know more, even though I was badly missing having a man in my life. A man-less existence might be dull—at least it did not hurt. 'I honestly must go. I've left some cow parsley under a tree in the orchard, and if it doesn't get into water soon it'll die.'

He grinned. 'I'll say this for you, Nurse, you give a man the brush-off in the cutest way. May I walk you to the orchard? I do know the way. I have been here before.'

I turned prim. 'Doesn't the fact that it's private property bother you?'

'Only one thing bothers me. May I tell you what that is?'

It was one of the oldest lines in the book. I had heard it a dozen times from a dozen men. I reacted like a Victorian maiden threatened with outrage. 'Not this morning, thanks—must save that cow parsley,' and I literally fled. I was through the rhododendron bushes before I was able to laugh to myself or look back. He had not followed me.

I walked more slowly up the path between the terraced

flower-beds. The first roses were out, the lupins were every shade of blue, pink, and purple, and the hydrangeas flanking the stone-flagged terrace at the back of the house were covered with flowers. The garden looked so gay and so unnaturally quiet. The three long white ward extensions stretched out from the house like empty arms. All the ward windows were open. There was no movement within. The beds were stripped to their bare mattresses; the ward tables were piled with pillows; the lockers we had scrubbed earlier this morning stood in lines outside the wards drying in the sun. The mattresses and pillows were going to be stoved on Monday before returning to Barny's. The beds, tables, and lockers were remaining for the children.

The empty terrace seemed much bigger and as strange as the silent wards. On such a fine morning the beds of the Caesar patients in Ward One would have been out in a row. There would have been up-patients in housecoats or smocks strolling along the paths or sitting on the low wall that edged the terrace. Their voices would have floated up to the nurseries on the first floor of the house. The nursery windows were wide. The folding and cradle cots had already gone to the new Mary Block in a hospital van this morning. The disconnected incubators remained until the firm that specialised in shifting heavy mechanical equipment arrived for them on Monday.

Indoors I had to resist the urge to walk on tiptoe as I helped myself to jugs in the vast kitchen, and was delighted when Harriet's scooter spluttered into the stable yard. She came in, unstrapped her skid-lid. 'Sorry I'm late. My heel wasn't ready. I had to wait, then old Martin came in and kept me talking. Is Hurricane Jill mad at me?'

'She's still setting her hair.'

'She is?' Harriet looked up as there was a muffled thud overhead. 'Then who's busy up there?'

'She must be starting alone.' There was another thud. 'That's higher than the nurseries. She must be on the isol. floor. We'd better join her.'

'Not before I've done something about my gastric juices.' She helped herself to a bridge roll. 'I'm starving.'

Harriet was a small, very plump, and very pretty brunette. In our general training she had been two sets my

18

junior, and though we had seen each other around, we had not met until we started midder in the same set. We were now great friends. She admired my wild flowers, asked what else I had been doing, and before I could answer went on talking about her trip to the village. 'Old Martin's worse than me! He waffled on and on about some nephew turning up unexpectedly and blood being thicker than water and how was he to know the boy wanted the cottage and did I agree he was letting it go for an absurd price and if I did what did I think he should do about it?'

'A nephew's turned up?' An obvious thought hit me. I dismissed it, momentarily, being more concerned for Sister Mary's future. 'Harriet! Martin's not thinking of backing out of his deal with Sister?'

'He can't.' She took another roll. 'It's all settled.'

'It wasn't at breakfast. Don't you remember? Oh, no, you were late. Well, before you got down, Sister said she hoped the final contracts would be signed early next week. She had hoped to have everything taped by this week-end, but Martin's solicitor is away on business till Monday afternoon.'

'Lor'!' She choked on her roll. 'The old boy may be having second thoughts! He said something about the solicitor-whatsit's absence being highly inconvenient. I wasn't paying much attention. I took it as his usual hot air. Surely it must be? Sister's paid a deposit! He must sell to her!'

'I don't know that he must even with a deposit. Buying a house is a tricky business. My eldest brother and his wife thought they had one tied up last year, and they'd paid a deposit, but a better offer came along at the last moment, and they lost it. Legally.'

'Anna! What'll Sister do? Shall we warn her?'

I considered this, then shook my head. 'There's nothing anyone can do without the solicitor, and to say anything today would wreck Sister's party.' I sat on the table. 'If Martin is trying to back out we'll have to stop him.'

'How? And when? The rest of today we'll need for getting ready for the party. Tomorrow we'll still have the overnight guests and the clearing and packing. Monday's going to be hell, shifting the last things out and then shifting ourselves.' She chewed reflectively. 'If he's had a better offer the only way to stop him accepting it would be to outbid it—which neither Sister Mary nor we can do.'

I thought of that man in the wood. 'Maybe we can go to work on the nephew? He may not appreciate how important that cottage is to Sister. Just what did Martin say about him?'

'That he had suddenly turned up for the week-end, hasn't been down for ages, didn't say he was coming, or even know the old boy was selling up. He seems to be in medicine, but I don't know his name or line. Martin said the boy worked in that hospital place, St Whatsit's.'

'Typical!' I was rather disturbed to discover that, though in one way pleased to be wrong, in another I was sorry. 'One thing, he won't be a Barny's man. None of our men would hurt Sister Mary.' There was a louder thud overhead. 'Oh, dear! We'd better get up them stairs.'

Harriet said she must have coffee first. 'You going to pass all this on to Hurricane Jill?'

'Why not? She's good at bright ideas, and we may need one—fast.'

She shrugged. She did not like Collins. 'Then don't be surprised if all you get is a bawling out for listening to gossip! We all know her anti-gossip fixation! Old Martin could just be having another of his brainstorms. Remember the state he was in when he decided the new motorway was coming through Wylden? When there was never any question of its coming within eight miles of the village? But if this time he is serious and she rushes into battle for Sister Mary, as she will treat all men like small boys, ten to one she'll rub Martin and his nephew up the wrong way. Perhaps you and I can soft-talk him—Collins can only talk baby-talk! And though she can organise,' she added calmly, 'she does it with the finesse of a bulldozer.'

'That's true. Right. Let's keep this between us.'

The second floor had been converted into single-bedded wards for the few mothers who produced raised temperatures or some rare complication like eclampsia, but were more frequently occupied by the many patients we had sent to us with known obstetric complications who were expected to have difficult deliveries. As we were a teaching hospital, with a particularly good Obstetric Department, we had taken a much higher than average number of problem patients than would be found in any normal non-teaching maternity hospital. Tonight we were turning two of those small wards into cloakrooms, and the rest were going to house our more exalted overnight guests. At breakfast Jill Collins had ordained that the two cloakroom beds must go down to the nursery floor. We were not yet clear how many guests would be staying the night but, if necessary, the nurseries were to be female dormitories. The younger men were having Ward Two. Ward One was our temporary stock-room. Ward Three was the dance hall. When I reached the isolation landing two dismembered beds and one mattress were stacked by the stairs. Another rolled mattress appeared in an open doorway.

I hurried forward. 'Nurse Collins, you shouldn't have done all this lifting alone! Why didn't you call——' I had grabbed the mattress before noticing that the encircling arms wore shirt-sleeves and the legs below trousers. Surprised, I let go jolting the mattress. I then dived for the pair of dark-rimmed glasses that landed unbroken at my feet. 'So sorry——' I gasped. When I saw who had lowered the mattress I nearly dropped the glasses again. 'Oh. It's you.'

His name was Robert Gordon. 'And I should have known it was you, Anna,' he remarked, as if it was five minutes and not over two years since we last met. He replaced his glasses. 'You never did look where you were going.'

I made no pretence of being pleased to see him either. 'Rob! What on earth are you doing here?'

'Toting a mattress.' He heaved it on to his shoulder. 'If you'll get out of my way I'll put this with the other things.'

'I'm not blind!' I retorted peevishly. 'I meant—what are you doing here? In the Mat. Unit?'

'I called to see Sister Mary. Jill Collins said she was out and asked me to shift these things. Excuse me.' He went on down the corridor just as he had walked on down the theatre corridor and disappeared into the surgeons' room on his last evening in Barny's. Then he had not troubled to say 'Goodbye'. Now he had skipped the 'Hallo'.

I leant against the nearest wall. I needed it. If I had listed the people I least wanted to see again Robert Gordon would have been out on top in a class of his own. He was David's oldest friend. They had met in Oxford and come on to Barny's together. Long ago, as he was David's friend, I had tried to like him. I had never succeeded. David had been my shadow for three years, and during all those years Robert Gordon had been a disapproving presence somewhere in the background. It had not been hard to guess he resented my relationship with David, but that also I had tried to overlook until the evening when David was rather drunk and told me Robert had given him a stern warning about getting too involved with me. 'Poor old Robbie nearly did his nut when I said that it was too late as I've asked you to marry me and you've said yes. Bit of a giggle, eh, love?'

For David's sake I had pretended it was a huge giggle. It was not a joke I cared to remember or had been able to forget. I almost enjoyed thinking of it again now. Now David had gone I no longer had to deal with his old pal Robbie with both hands tied behind my back.

I waited until he deposited the mattress. 'I thought you were working in Glasgow?'

'Edinburgh.' He draped himself against the opposite wall. He was much the same height as that man in the wood, but far less sturdily built. He had very dark hair and a pale, long-jawed face. I had known girls who thought him attractive. I did not.

'A long way from Wylden.'

'Four hundred and thirty-five miles.'

'And you've come down for Sister Mary's party? Well, well. I never thought you liked parties.'

'I don't. I do like Sister Mary, but her party isn't my only reason for being in Wylden. I'm spending this weekend with a relative. I walked up to call on Sister Mary in case I can't make her party. I'm pretty booked up for the rest of the day, and that may happen.'

I smiled politely. 'Sister Mary'll understand. You'll obviously be much happier curling up with a nice cosy copy of *Gray's Anatomy*.'

'Not on a Saturday night, Anna.' His voice, as always, irritated me by being so good. It was both deep and gentle. 'On Saturday nights I prefer James Bond.' He smiled as

22

Jill Collins bounded up the stairs. 'I've shifted those beds, Jill. What's next?'

'You good boy!' She sounded as if he was eight, not twenty-eight. 'I think—Ward Three next. I want everything out! Ah! Come along, my child!' Harriet had joined us. 'All hands to the pump!'

Harriet ignored her and beamed at Robert. 'Robbie! Hallo, there! Are you our first party guest? What fun! How are you? How long have you been here? And why didn't anyone tell me you were here?' She held out both hands to him. 'It's ages since you left!'

'Two years. It's good to see you again, Harriet. How have you enjoyed midder?' he asked, smiling.

'Need you ask?' beamed Jill heartily. 'How does the child look? A picture of health!'

'Picture—Heavens—I forgot!' Harriet turned to me. 'Anna, that man must still be hanging on. In Sister Mary's office. He says he wants to talk to you about some picture.'

'A man? Wants to talk to me? What's his name?'

'I don't know. Forgot to ask. He said he wanted to talk to Miss Anna Rowe about some picture. Isn't that enough?'

'Yes,' I said, 'yes. Thanks.' I felt most peculiar. It was not an unpleasant sensation. It just made me wonder how my legs were going to carry me downstairs.

My hand was still shaking when I raised the receiver. 'Anna Rowe speaking.'

'Anna suits you better than Jane,' said a voice I recognised. 'How do you do, Anna? I'm Nicholas Dexter. You can call me Nick—I hope.'

'How did you find out my name?'

'You mustn't expect me to divulge my sources of information.' From the sound of his voice he was smiling. 'But, having tapped them, I thought I would ring to introduce myself and ask you one question. What colour dress are you wearing tonight?'

I was too surprised for anything but the truth. 'White.'

'What material?'

'Lace. Why? What's all this about?'

'I like to know these things.'

I had met a good many opening gambits, but this was a new one on me. 'Are you in the rag trade?'

23

'No. I'll tell you my job tonight.'

'Tonight?' I came down to earth, remembering mentioning the party to him. 'Don't you dare gatecrash!'

'Perish the thought. I'm invited.'

'Oh, nonsense! That's impossible—unless you really are a Barny's man?'

He said pleasantly, 'I'm neither a Barny's man nor a liar. I have in my hand at this moment an invitation from a Miss Maud Bush to her party tonight. As I have a noble and understanding nature, I'll forgive your dark thoughts. And I want to see you again, Anna. Do we have a date tonight? Or are you already booked?'

I wanted to see him again. I wanted that so badly that I nearly lost my nerve a second time and invented an absent boy friend to whom I had to be faithful. Then I remembered Robert Gordon. If he did get back for the party he would expect to see me lamenting David. I said, 'I'm not booked.'

'You are now,' said Nick Dexter. 'See you, Anna. Thank you very much.'

CHAPTER TWO

A PARTY FOR SISTER MARY

HARRIET watched me pin the orchids to my left shoulder.

'Why is it that when I take a walk in our wood the only man I meet is Frank? I've never even been this close to orchids before!'

'Nor me.' Together we admired my reflection in our long glass. 'Think I should wear them? I don't want to give him ideas.'

'Any man who sends a girl orchids already has all the ideas you know plus a few you've never thought of, duckie. Relax.' She examined the florist's box. 'Special delivery from Astead. I thought you said he was staying in Wylden?'

'That's what he said.'

She put down the box and began wriggling herself into the particular foundation garment she called her armour. Being so plump, she had quite a struggle.

24

'His invitation was from Miss Maud Bush—not Sister Mary?'

'Yes.'

I saw what she was getting at. I should have seen it before had I not been feeling slightly drunk all afternoon. All Barny's and Wylden village knew Sister Mary as 'Sister Mary'. As far as we knew all her invitations had gone out under her official title. 'How could he know her name?'

Harriet gasped. 'Give me a heave first, Anna.' We both heaved, and by the time we had her properly in her armour and the back zip up we were both red in the face. 'There's one person who always calls her Miss Bush'—Harriet was still gasping—'old Norris.' She faced me. 'Your new boy friend must be one of his many godchildren. He's got a godson with him this week-end.'

'How do you know that?'

'I was helping Sister Mary with her post this morning when she rang to ask if it would be all right to call on the old boy, as she always does, knowing he can't abide casual callers. The housekeeper went off to sound him, and came back saying he'd be pleased to see Miss Bush at eleven-fifteen, and was sorry she would miss his godson as the young gentleman had already gone out for the morning. And where'd he gone? Into our wood!'

I was amused but unconvinced. 'Of course. That settles it!'

'Why not? From your description Nick Dexter's the right age. He could have known our wood as a small boy. He must have heard we were closed from old Norris.'

'He could just as easily have heard in the village—as he said.'

She refused to allow me to pick holes in her theory. 'He probably said that not to embarrass you with his connection with our wealthy benefactor.' She dropped a curtsy. 'Also, maybe he wants to be loved for himself and not his lolly—in which case, he shouldn't dish out orchids to hard-working nurses!'

'It won't be his lolly——'

'He may have to share a few million quid with three or four co-godchildren. That'll be tough!' She stepped into her dress. 'Am I going to make this?'

'Hold on. Ready?' Again we heaved together. 'That's it.' I stood back. 'You may not be able to sit down.'

She studied herself. 'Tomorrow I diet.'

'You do that,' I agreed tactlessly, my mind on her theory. 'Why should Sister Mary invite him? The old man's not coming.'

'Only because he's allergic to stepping outside his front door and so aged. Otherwise he'd be our guest of honour. Think what Barny's owes him—blah, blah, blah. But once Sister heard he'd got this godson staying, naturally she'd ask him. I'll bet she left an invitation card with the old boy, and that's how this Dexter had it in his hand when he rang you.'

'And how did he get my name?'

'Have you forgotten the old boy's housekeeper is our Taffy's cousin?' I had. 'And that you've been the only redhead here for months.'

That was true, but I was still not wholly convinced. I let it go, as once Harriet made up her mind nothing could shift her, and there was something else on my mind. 'Harriet, how long has Mr Martin lived in Wylden?'

'About five years.' She peered into the mirror to fix on false eyelashes. 'Why? Still brooding about him changing his mind?'

'Yes. Aren't you?'

She reminded me she was not the brooding type. 'That's why I'm so fat. I've tried worrying to get some weight off. It's no good. I keep forgetting my worry.' She had on the eyelashes and was busy with the mascara. 'Maybe he was just having another of his rushes of blood to the head this morning.'

'Hope so. Where did he come from before he settled in Wylden?'

'He was teaching up north. Not sure where. Why are you interested?'

'Robert Gordon.'

'What?' She glanced round. 'Since when have you been interested in Robbie Gordon? I thought you hated his guts.'

'I do. But I've just remembered something I had forgotten.' I went on to explain how David had once told

26

me Robert was spending a week-end near the Mat. Unit with some relation. 'This was ages ago, before I knew Wylden. I only remember it because at the time I had thought all Robert's family lived in Caithness or the Orkneys or some other outlandish spot.'

She was surprised. 'I thought he had no family?'

'No parents. He was raised by some cousins of his father. I wonder—do you know if his mother was English?' She shook her head. 'Then Martin could be his uncle.'

'You're not serious?' She saw I was. 'Anna, there are three hundred and fourteen people in Wylden. Why pick on Martin?'

'Because we know most of the people in the village and have heard of those we don't know. If anyone but Mr Martin had a nephew at Barny's we'd have been told. The village has adopted Barny's. We're their pet hospital. Anyone but old Martin would have buttonholed each one of us every trip we made into Wylden to ask if we knew the dear boy. You know all outsiders assume we all know each other. Mr Martin wouldn't do that, as he never remembers anyone's name, and I'm sure still doesn't know which hospital owned the Mat. Unit.' She did not say anything. 'But he did tell you this morning his nephew was doing medicine.'

That roused her. 'And you said he couldn't be one of our men because he was trying to spoil things for Sister Mary.'

'When I said that I had forgotten Robert Gordon. He wouldn't hesitate to spoil anything for anyone—if it suited him.'

She said, 'Anna, aren't you picking on the wrong man? It was David, not Robert, who asked for his ring back.'

'I haven't forgotten,' I said dryly. 'There's nothing like a good, clean jilt for lingering in a girl's memory. Not that I now blame David for that. As he had discovered he was in love with someone else, it was the only possible thing to do. Yes—I know—he should have told me sooner, but he only put it off because he hated hurting me. David was like that.'

She shrugged. 'I never knew David Somers. I just saw him around. But Robbie I knew quite well. I've never rubbed that in as his name always gets you to flash-point

27

in record time, but when you've talked about him I've always felt we must be talking about two different men. I like Robbie Gordon. Sorry, but I do.'

'Which just goes to show you don't know him quite as well as I do.'

'Come on, girls!' Jill Collins put her head round the door. 'Stop wasting time trying to make yourselves beautiful. Sister's waiting.'

Sister Mary and Mrs Evans were in our front hall. Our cook was superb in black satin. Sister Mary was wearing a long grey velvet dress, and she looked smaller, slimmer, and oddly defenceless without her uniform. And tonight she looked her age.

I had known she was elderly, but had never until now realised she was old. Now she reminded me of my grandmother's friends, and it gave me quite a shock to realise she belonged in their generation. She must have been a very pretty girl in much the same style as Harriet, and one of the thousands of pretty girls left unmarried by the First World War. I knew she had loved her life at Barny's, and she had probably been too busy to be aware of the side of life she had missed. After Monday she would begin to remember. I thought about my grandmother. She lived alone, and was a fiercely independent and active lady with three great passions: her grandchildren, hats, and sitting on committees. Sister Mary could indulge in the two latter, but as a human being she was going to be very alone. She had no family alive, and, apart from Barny's, the only friends she had had time to make lived in Wylden. As if to underline my thoughts, having thanked us all for the work we had done in preparing the party, she said how delighted she was to be retiring locally. 'I feel I won't be losing touch with you all. I am going to keep you dear girls to your promise to come down and help me with the decorating once I move in. Now, don't forget—any time you want a quiet week-end in Wylden just drop me a card. You will be more than welcome.'

I glanced at Harriet, feeling like Judas. She did not notice. She was discussing the supper menu with Taffy Evans.

Jill Collins had organised the party as she would have

organised a ward-list. She had even drawn up a list. She had put herself down to look after our most senior guests; I was to escort the others to the various cloakrooms. It was Harriet's job to stay in the hall with Sister Mary and move the crowd on into the reception-rooms. Professor Ferguson, our specific pundit, was running the bar with the help of his two teenage sons and any students as soon as they arrived.

Jill was in bronze silk, but bustled round so professionally that one forgot she was not in uniform and could almost hear the crackle of starch. She handled the two ex-Matrons, aged senior sisters, the consultants and their wives, with the brisk good humour with which she handled the patients and staff on duty. The patients had loved her and been only amused by her tactlessness, as she was very kind and extremely efficient. The patients felt safe when she was around; but, like every patient I ever met, they rated kindness as the top qualification in their doctors and nurses. 'That Nurse Collins is a born nurse,' they would say, and in Jill's case—which was by no means the general rule—they were right. She never could have been anything but a nurse; her job was her hobby as well as her profession; she had no outside interests. Harriet said Jill Collins was not just uninterested in being a woman—she had not yet discovered the fact.

I often wished I had her one-track mind. I loved my job, but it had never been enough to fill the gaps left by David. When our guests began to arrive and I found myself looking at every fair man with a new interest, I felt as if I had suddenly come alive again.

The party got off the ground instantly. Each new guest sensed the atmosphere, shed a few inhibitions, and added to the general high spirits. Girls I hardly knew fell on my neck like long-lost sisters and gave me the latest hospital gossip as I took them upstairs. 'Have you heard about Sister Florence and the S.M.O.? My dear, they've already changed the date three times, and they say . . .'

Three girls with whom Harriet and I had started midder came back from the new Mary Block. 'Haven't you seen it since it was finished? Anna, it's a dream! It's got the lot! Spherical, air-conditioned theatres, four-bedded wards that look like five-star hotel rooms, mums' lecture-rooms, fathers' lecture-rooms, thermostatically controlled nurseries, and, of course, incubators, and absolutely fab decorations —there are plants climbing every other wall! The mums can't believe their eyes when they come in! And the waiting fathers are having a ball amongst the potted plants and crafty little push-button machines that produce hot coffee, tea, and iced milk in their waiting hall. Did you hear the block has won some high-powered international architectural prize? The man who thought it up has gone off to Italy to collect it!'

'Sounds great. What's the new Sister Mary like?'

'Sweet. Didn't you know her as Sister Elizabeth?'

I said not. 'I've never worked in Elizabeth.'

They exchanged glances. 'Then you won't have worked with Sabby Wardell, as she was senior staff in Elizabeth for four years before Matron gave her Observation.'

'No. All I know about Wardell is that she's the best-looking girl in Barny's. What's she like, girls?'

' "Miss" Wardell, if you please, Nurse Rowe.'

I laughed. 'God! Like that, eh? Thanks for the tip. Any others you can give me?'

One girl said, 'I worked with Wardell in Elizabeth. She wasn't too bitchy then, and I'll say this for her: she knows her stuff.'

'She'll need to in Observation,' said another.

I asked, 'Is she now bitchy all the time, or just some of the time?'

'That depends on——' The speaker broke off as Jill bounded in.

Jill Collins and Sabina Wardell, my future ward sister, had started training in the same set. When the girls had removed themselves Jill told me she had lost one of her ex-Matrons. 'You seen one up here, Rowe?'

'Sorry, Nurse, no. I've been too busy gossiping about Observation.'

'Of course, you're going there. You'll like it. Sabby Wardell's making a very good job there as sister, I hear. We used to be great pals—though I never quite understood why. Much as I like her, we've so little in common. Where is my Matron?'

I was rather amused and rather relieved to get her version on this. On balance, I was inclined to back her opinion against that of the girls. Sabby Wardell was so very good-looking that she was bound to be judged harshly by her fellow-females, unless they happened to know her well, which Jill did. I was not worried by her being occasionally bitchy. All ward sisters had to be sometimes, or they made rotten ward sisters. I should infinitely prefer to work under a tough who knew her job than under a gentle soul who tried to please her nurses and then looked the other way when something went wrong. We had had a few sisters like that at Barny's. They never lasted long. While they lasted their nurses nearly had nervous breakdowns.

Jill chased up and down the corridor, looking in empty rooms. I cantered after her. 'Where did you lose her, Nurse?'

'On this floor. I had to abandon her to cope with a phone call from Mr Martin.'

'What did he want? Forgotten the date? Sister said she'd asked him.'

'He's not coming. He's got some meeting on in the village hall. That wasn't why he rang, though. He wanted to speak to Robert Gordon.' She misunderstood my reaction. 'Don't tell me he's here? I said he hadn't shown up.'

'I haven't seen him. But why did Martin want him?'

'Didn't ask, my child. I said I couldn't oblige, and he rang off.' She leant over the banisters. 'Where has the child Jones got to? Half those people down there have nothing in their hands. Thank God! Clerks!' She ran downstairs and pounced on a quartet of final-year students. 'Boys, we need you!'

They leered hopefully. 'And we need you, ladies!'

That sailed over Jill's head. 'Go and help the Prof. in the bar like good lads!' She waved them off and slapped my arm. 'Wake up, Rowe! Here's another car and, so help me—a coach!'

I had to push my thoughts about Robert and that telephone call to the back of my mind as the Rugger Club coach drew up at the front door. A stream of students swept out. 'Sorry we're late, Sister Mary. We had a puncture.'

Jill muttered, 'Taffy'll have a coronary! We expected a few clerks, not half the final year. I'll warn her.'

A few minutes later I saw Nick Dexter with Sister Mary. He had not yet seen me. I was glad about that. Seeing him had such an effect on me that I deliberately reminded myself of David. And then I thought, to hell with David and went on watching Nick Dexter.

He looked even better in a suit than he had in casual clothes. The way he held himself was a joy to me after working for years among Barny's men with their beloved and affected medical stoop. He looked large even in the middle of all those rugger-playing students, but he managed to look elegant at the same time, which was something no student I had come across had ever achieved. His dark suit accentuated his fairness, but his colouring was neither anaemic nor the type that would turn ruddy. He was the only man I had seen who, as a man, equalled for looks Sabina Wardell's looks as a woman. His face was sensitive and good-humoured. And he had sent me orchids. I touched them to make sure they were there.

Sister Mary was greeting all her guests warmly, but seemed to be greeting him with extra warmth. I thought of Harriet's theory, and then I saw him coming towards me and stopped thinking.

We shook hands, and he thanked me for wearing his orchids. 'I hoped you would, but I wasn't sure.' He looked me over, still hanging on to my hand. 'May I say I like your dress? And that you look very lovely?'

'Thank you—and for the flowers.' I moved my hand and took a mental grip. It was necessary. I asked if he had met Sister Mary previously.

'Yes.' He smiled. 'We are old pals.'

'Why didn't you tell me so this morning?'

'You didn't give me much time, did you?'

Jill appeared at my elbow. 'Doctor, you must forgive me, but I need Nurse Rowe. What? No drink? Rowe, my child, why haven't you looked after the poor man better?'

Nick said, 'The lady is a girl after my own heart, Anna.'

I introduced them. Jill pumped his hand briskly. 'So you're not a Barny's man, Mr Dexter? You must feel a fish out of water. How do you come to be here?'

He was amused. 'That's quite a story, Nurse. When you've three days to spare I'll tell you it.'

Professor Ferguson came out of the sitting-room wearing a short houseman's coat. 'Ah, Dexter!' He pushed through the crowd. 'Good evening to you! I didn't expect to see you here. Naturally I should have done! Where would the Obstetric Department of St Barnabas' Hospital be without you, eh? And how did you enjoy Rome? Have a good time? Come and have a drink and tell me all about it. I'm barman, so I'm the man you want to know tonight!'

'Dexter! Of course!' Jill said to herself as the Professor removed Nick. 'Rowe, Taffy's having a crisis. Go and cope, and if you see that wretch Jones, tell her to get back to her job. Hurry!' She gave me a shove to be on my way.

I met Harriet in the kitchen corridor. She had come out of the scullery with a tray of clean glasses. 'Your new boy friend shown up, Anna?'

'Yes. He's with the Prof. Harriet, I think your hunch was right.'

'Aren't I always right? Out of my way, girl! I must see this dreamboat.'

'Hold on, there's something else I want to tell you.' I lowered my voice as the sound of the sink being rinsed came from the scullery. 'Old Martin's been ringing Robert Gordon here. What do you make of that?'

'Nothing. I happen to know——'

I cut her short. 'I also happen to know him, dear. You'd be surprised how much inside information one picks up about a man when one runs around with his best friend for a few years. And men say girls yak! God! If you'd seen and heard as much about Robert Gordon as I have, you wouldn't put anything past him either!' She shook her head violently. My voice and trigger-temper rose together. 'All right! Be like that! Trust that smug, conceited, dead-crafty bastard! But I'll bet you anything you like he really is Martin's nephew, and this is one bet I'll win!' I swept round her and raced down the remaining corridor to the kitchen. 'What's the problem, Taffy?'

Mrs Evans had an apron tied round her black satin middle, a resigned expression on her face, and one of the cold turkeys scheduled for tomorrow's lunch on the table

33

before her. She was sharpening a carving-knife. 'There's four pairs of hands I need, Nurse, and there's my problem! Be a good girl and go find me a sensible man to help with my carving. No students, mind! I am not having my turkey dissected like a dogfish!'

'Shall I carve? I can.' She looked so horrified that I recovered my temper and laughed. 'Don't worry, Taffy dear. Leave it to me. I'll get you no less than a Fellow of the Royal College of Surgeons if I can't lay my hands on a Master of Surgery!'

'I'm no M.Ch.,' said Robert Gordon's voice behind me, 'but I've got a Fellowship. Any use?'

'There's enough work you've done already, Mr Gordon, with all the washing up you've done for Nurse Jones,' protested Taffy. 'Working your fingers to the bone, you are, and you in your fine suit. Nurse Rowe will be on her way to find me another man.'

Nurse Rowe was in no condition to be on her way anywhere. Robert had been in the scullery, and must have overheard most if not all of what I had said. Not that his expression gave anything away. but then it never did. Like most quick-tempered people, I was always instantly overwhelmed with guilt after an outburst, but on this occasion my guilt was very short-lived. He had had it coming to him. 'Before you do another good deed, Robert, you ought to ring a Mr Martin in Wylden. He rang you.'

'I know. He rang again. I've spoken to him.' He took the carving set from Taffy. 'How far do you want this to go, Mrs Evans?'

'As far as you can make it, Mr Gordon.' She raised her eyes to the ceiling. 'It's a mercy I'm used to catering for doctors and nurses. There's starving they always are? Now Nurse Collins tells me we have forty extra students, and starving they will all be! Nurse Rowe, love, will you go and count heads for me that I may know the worst?'

'Heads just for tonight? What about lunch tomorrow? Every other guest seems to want to stay the night.'

Taffy sighed. 'Wait then while I look in my larder for the list Nurse Collins gave me, then you can tell me the numbers for the two meals.' She handed me a dish and fork.

34

'You can be arranging the pieces for Mr Gordon while you wait.'

Robert said nothing when she disappeared into her vast larder. The atmosphere between us was so thick that I doubted even that the carving-knife could have got through it. I did not let it stifle me. I was determined to get the truth out of Robert, but had to be careful for Sister Mary's sake. Taffy was a dear, but a great talker, and the larder door was open. Sister Mary would be very upset if she heard I had a row with Robert during her party. At lunch she had described him as such a dear boy. If I was right, and I did not doubt that 'if', Sister Mary would do all she could to make allowances for him. I was in no humour to make any.

I studied him covertly, thinking up a way to begin, and was annoyed to notice he looked unrecognisably spruce. It was the first time I'd seen him in such a good suit, and it did a great deal for him, but nothing could make him as attractive as Nick Dexter—which thought made me feel much more cheerful. Robert's face was too thin and had too much jaw. He did not look as physically tough as Nick, but his face was tougher and totally lacking in that good-natured charm.

I said abruptly, 'I didn't know you knew Mr Martin.'

'Why should you?' He did not look up.

'Are you related to him?' He looked up then. 'Didn't you know he was selling his cottage to Sister Mary?'

He said, 'You've got the wrong tense there, Anna. And your facts wrong.'

I put down my fork. 'How do you mean?'

Taffy came back. 'Nurse Rowe, love, be a good girl and ask the young man your questions later. Here is my list. Count how many for supper and how many staying on, and put the figures on these two sides. Careful now. There's easy it would be to make a mistake with this crowd and count the same head twice.'

I had to go. 'I'll be careful, Taffy. I won't make any mistakes.'

Robert looked at my orchids, then at my face. 'Care for a wee bet?'

Had Taffy not been there, he would have had that turkey

at his head. His glasses would not have stopped me any more than my being a woman would have stopped his chucking it straight back at me. I went off, fuming, and did not cool down until Nick Dexter joined in my head-counting.

The Professor wanted to know why I was making our guest do sums. 'A useful assistant, eh, Nurse? Mathematics must number among your many talents, Dexter. As a matter of interest, how long did it take you to do all the sums necessary for all those complicated blueprints of my new block you showed me?'

'The new Mary, Professor?' I demanded, and turned on Nick. 'Did you design it?'

'It's all those regular meals,' he apologised. 'I told you I had to get a proper job.'

'But you are one of the architects working on our re-building?'

'The new boy. Very junior partner.'

'That's as may be!' boomed the Professor, who was in terrific form. 'But your most senior partner told me my new Mary came originally out of your head, my lad! Have another beer!'

'Later, thanks, sir.' Nick took my elbow, and we moved on. I was very impressed, and did not attempt to hide it. He suggested I just call him a genius and have done. 'At least you now know how I got my invitation.'

'Yes.' Sister Mary had said she was inviting our architects. 'So you were coming?'

'I was not. Until I met you. I forgot all about this party when I decided to come down to Wylden for the week-end yesterday. I'm staying at the pub. It's a good pub. I discovered it when I first had to come down here to talk to Ferguson three years ago. That's when I met your Miss Bush. She said I could use your grounds when I was in the village. What's the joke?'

He laughed at Harriet's theory. He had heard of Mr Norris, but never met him.

'Let's get this job finished, Anna. I want to dance with you.'

The red night-lights down the centre of Ward Three were switched on, and as the long May twilight faded outside the crimson glow deepened. It was as mild a night as it had been a warm day. The air genuinely smelt of roses and lilac and new-cut grass, but even if it had not that was how it would have seemed to me as we danced dance after dance. Nick was not the only man to ask me to dance, but because he was making such an obvious play for me and was an outsider, I had many more offers than I should have had without him—there being nothing like having one man openly admiring a girl to make all other men present sit up and take notice. Had Nick been a Barny's man they might have taken notice, but would have left me strictly alone, as Barny's men played the game to their own rules. Only a few knew Nick's job—it did not bring him into the fold. He did not look as if he objected to my being such a success story with the boys, but each time I danced with someone else he was waiting for me when the music stopped. I always went back to him.

I was dancing with him when the strap of my left sandal snapped. He said, 'Let's sit this one out while you fix it.'

It was now dark outside. He had already tried twice to get me outside, and twice I had refused. My nerve was coming back, but it was not yet wholly back. 'I'll get another pair first. Why don't you'—I looked round—'finish this dance with Jill Collins? Over there, by the radiogram. I did introduce you.'

He did not look round. He looked hard at me. 'In case you're interested, my sweet. I have never yet kissed a girl who didn't want me to kiss her. You don't have to run out on me again.' He was smiling. 'Don't look so scared. I don't mind hanging around while you change your shoes, though, as you must know, I would much rather we took a little walk round the garden.'

'Nick, I'm sorry. You must think me crazy.'

He shrugged amiably. 'Maybe. Maybe I'm crazy too, to let you get away with this. Why worry? Just a couple of nuts, that's us. Don't be too long.'

I looked back when I was out of the nearest french window and saw him walking towards Jill. She smiled uncertainly, then something he said made her laugh. He was still dancing with her when I got down from my room, and as my feet were reminding me I had been on them all day,

I went back to the terrace and sat on the low wall, wondering if I ought to get my head examined, what I had done to deserve my luck in meeting Nick Dexter, and whether it would last if I went on behaving like this.

It was queer to see dancers and not the outlines of beds and sleeping mothers in that ward; to hear the music and voices and not to have to worry about the noise disturbing the babies or the ill mothers on the isol. floor. I glanced casually back at the house. My head stayed over my shoulder when I saw who had come out of the staff sitting-room. 'Robert,' I said accusingly, 'I thought you had gone.'

He had been handing things round at supper, but had not appeared since in the dance ward, and I had been enjoying myself too much to remember his existence and that conversation Taffy had curtailed. I had not given another thought to Sister Mary's future. That now made me annoyed with myself, and doubly annoyed with him for being the fundamental cause of my annoyance.

'I had to go into Wylden. I'm just back.' He sat on the wall a little away from me. 'Someone getting you a drink?'

'No. I'm resting my feet.'

'Want a drink?'

'No, thanks. As you're here, there's something I do want to know. About that cottage——'

'Not that nonsense again!'

'Is it nonsense?' I sat sideways to face him. 'Is Sister Mary going to buy that cottage from Martin? Yes or no?' He was silent. 'Robert, I asked you a question.'

'Does the fact of asking automatically give a right to an answer?' There was enough light from the house to illuminate his slight smile. 'Life might be even more amusing than it is if that was so.'

'Don't be evasive, please.' I spoke quietly. I did not want to lose my temper again, as he never lost his. Consequently, in our previous arguments he had invariably won the point, as I had equally invariably ended up too angry to talk sense. 'You know what I'm getting at.'

'I don't know anything. I can guess that you seem to have some fixation about Sister Mary's future plans, but why you should assume they concern me I don't follow.'

'You're not involved in them?' Again he was silent.

'Then why did you say earlier I was using the wrong tense about that cottage? I know Sister Mary can't have bought it yet. Has it been sold? And why have I got my facts wrong? Aren't you Mr Martin's nephew?'

'How do you work that one out? I'd be interested to know.' He folded his arms and settled his legs in a more comfortable position. 'The way your mind works always used to fascinate me, Anna. Are you still incapable of using your intelligence when not wearing a uniform? Do you still use your emotions as stepping-stones to all non-professional conclusions? Or have you reached this specific conclusion by a process that has actually involved a certain amount of thought?'

I knew he was trying to rouse me. It amused him. It always had. He had succeeded in the past. He was succeeding now. I also knew he was hedging. 'Why won't you answer my questions?'

'Is there any reason why I should assuage your very feminine curiosity?'

That did it. 'Don't be so damn silly, man!' I snapped. 'I'm not being girlish! I don't want a good gossip with you! I'm asking because what happens to Sister Mary matters to me—though, knowing your utter indifference to other people's feelings, I can't expect you to understand that! And if you don't want me to ask you more questions, why did you make those remarks in the kitchen?'

'Why, indeed?' he queried dryly. 'I slipped up. Even Homer sometimes nods.'

'But not you, Robert!' I jeered. 'David always said you never spoke without thinking! Incidentally, if you want to know how I guessed you were Martin's nephew, it was from something he once said. Of course, I can understand why you don't want to talk about it. Here we are surrounded by half Barny's, and, though you've left, you are, unfortunately, an old Barny's man and——'

'I haven't left Barny's. I was away for two years. I've been back these last six weeks. And, having cleared that up, we may as well deal with another minor detail——' and there he had to stop, as Sister Mary came out of the sitting-room.

'Dear boy, there you are! I've been looking for you

everywhere to thank you.' She did not notice me until she took both his hands. 'May I tell Nurse Rowe? I know how interested and delighted for me she will be. Dearie such excitement . . .' and without waiting for his permission she explained how this morning Mr Norris had warned her he had heard from his housekeeper the local rumour that Mr Martin had had a better offer for his cottage. 'I thought it was bound to come to me, but Mr Norris said there was a legal loophole. And what do you think he did? Dearies, he sent this dear boy to act for him and outbid any offer Mr Martin might have had. You remember Mr Martin's solicitor was away? At Mr Norris's particular request he returned this afternoon. Do you know what the position is now?' She patted my hand. 'Mr Norris now owns that cottage and is selling it to me on Monday morning! I declare I am in quite a little daze what with all these complicated business arrangements, and so very grateful to this dear boy for his busy day on my behalf, and to his most kind and generous godfather. But I must not keep you young people talking any longer. Off you go and dance!'

'Sister Mary,' said Robert, 'can't I persuade you to dance with me first?'

'Dear boy, thank you, but not at my age! I shall enjoy watching you. Come along!'

There was nothing we could do but return to Ward Three with her. She smiled fondly on us as we moved on to the floor. The students running the radiogram chose that moment to put on one of our very few waltz L.P.s I waited until we were well away from Sister Mary.

'Robert, I don't know what to say.'

'I'd be obliged if you didn't say anything. My godfather dislikes having his affairs discussed, and so do I.'

'I didn't mean about that. I won't spread it around.' I looked up. 'Oh, hell, Robert, you know very well I'm trying to say I'm sorry.'

The corners of his mouth turned down in a derisive smile. 'I expect you are. No-one likes making a fool of himself.'

Having asked for that, I had to take it. We finished our dance in silence. Nick came over directly the music stopped, and Robert took himself off.

A little later I told Nick about the nightingales in our wood, and he instantly insisted I took him down to hear them, which I did. He did not ask why I had changed my mind, and I did not tell him. But when he began to kiss me I suddenly realised Robert had indirectly done us both a good turn. Then, as Nick kissed very well, I stopped thinking about anything else for quite some time.

CHAPTER THREE

OBSERVATION RIVALS THE UNITED NATIONS

THE train from Astead raced past apple and cherry orchards covered in blossom and hop gardens that were still forests of bare poles, the brown earth newly hoed and the young hops invisible. The bricks of the oast-houses were orange in the late afternoon sunshine, and in the fields beyond the orchards the ewes were half asleep with one eye on their lambs. The lambs were chasing each other round in circles. The pylons straddling the county from the downs ahead to the coast behind us looked like petrified giants carrying milk-pails.

We had the carriage to ourselves, but only Harriet had done much talking. Our taxi had dropped Sister Mary at the Fergusons' house in Wylden before taking us on to Astead. Jill Collins had in her handbag for Matron the main set of Mat. Unit keys newly labelled Wylden House. The spare front- and back-door keys had been left with Frank.

We were in the outer suburbs before Jill roused herself to discuss our future plans for Sister Mary's cottage. Jill produced a list of the many people who had offered their help as decorators. 'We'd better form a committee. Right?' I nodded and Harriet grunted. 'If only a third of these people join us we should be able to get that place perfect without it costing Sister Mary more than the price of paint and brushes. But it'll need spring-cleaning before any painting can start. Mr Martin marries in three weeks, and Sister hopes to move in the week after. There should be a week-end in between. How would it be if we three made a fixed date now to get down and clean up that week-end?'

'Suits me, Nurse, if I'm off.' I said, expecting Harriet to echo this, as it was an idea that had already occurred to us and we had roughly agreed on.

Harriet was vague. She thought she might have to go home that particular week-end for some family celebration. 'May I let you know, Nurse?'

'Any time.' Jill made a note in her diary.

Home Sister came down our front steps as our taxi drew up. 'Welcome back, Nurses! That is, I should have said, "Welcome back, Sister Elizabeth and Nurses!"'

Jill looked startled, as if, like myself, she had forgotten her promotion. Home Sister gave Harriet and myself our room numbers, then escorted Jill to the Sisters' Home next door.

'There goes your chum "Hurricane Jill", and a chum no longer, mate. We are back in St Barnabas' Hospital, London.' Harriet looked at the assorted blocks across the road. 'Democracy may have raised its naïve head in the Mat. Unit, but it's still a dirty word up here.'

'I can't see Collins allowing the fact that she's now a member of the upper classes go to her head.' I put down my bags to study the new Mary. I had seen it going up without bothering to look at it properly. I felt now as if it belonged to me. 'Imagine, Harriet, that came out of Nick's head. Isn't it wonderful? It seems to be floating.'

'Hasn't he rather overdone the glass? And why did he have to put it on legs?'

'So that the ambulances can drive right in.'

She said she supposed that was a point, but she was not sure she would like to be up on that top floor when the east wind was blowing up river. 'What's that hideous mass of scaffolding over there? Another of your golden wonder boy's dream children?'

'Yes. The new kids' block.'

'That going to keep him around the old firm?'

'Yes.' I smiled at my thoughts. 'Let's get our keys.'

The portress was new to us. 'Nurse H. H. Jones? I thought Home Sister said Nurse A. H. Jones?'

I read the many notices in our hall while Harriet was

sorting this out. One particularly drew my attention. 'Harriet, isn't the Cricket Club dance the week-end you have to go home?'

'Had you forgotten?' She turned, smiling.

'Yes. Not that it matters. I'm not dated. You?'

'I haven't a date for it yet. I will have. That's why I wasn't tying myself down to a jolly scrubbing week-end. I adore Sister Mary and would do anything for her, but there are limits!'

The portress finally produced our keys and a sheath of yellow roses.

'You Nurse Anna Rowe, Nurse? Then these come for you.'

Harriet read Nick's card over my shoulder. 'Ringing tomorrow evening to find out your off-duty, eh? A fast worker,' she murmured, 'and smooth. Very smooth.'

We had not yet had time for a private post-mortem on Saturday night. During the party I had managed to tell her Nick was nothing to do with Mr Norris, which had rather annoyed her, as she said quite honestly that she detested being wrong. Going up in the lift, I suggested we unpacked quickly and had a good natter before supper and meeting up with the other girls.

'Sorry, Anna. I've got a date.'

I was curious. 'Who with? And why didn't you tell me before?'

'Forgot. Charles Devon. He's one of Blakelock's housemen. He was down on Saturday, and I danced with him quite a bit. I don't expect you noticed,' she added, not unkindly. 'You were not exactly with us that night. By the way, how did you enjoy the nightingales?'

'Very much.' We laughed at each other. 'You heard them too?'

'Duckie,' said Harriet, 'you know me! I don't need nightingales.' The lift stopped. 'Must fly or I'll be late. See you at breakfast.'

'Sure. Have a good time.'

'I always do.'

That was true. Harriet, despite or possibly because of her comfortable curves, had more dates than any other girl I knew, and enjoyed them all with equal enthusiasm.

43

I should have guessed she would fix up something for her first evening back, and as I had Nick's roses for company I was perfectly happy to potter on with my unpacking and then go over to supper alone. There were a few girls I knew by sight, but not one I had ever worked with, at the senior table in the nurses' dining-room. The girls asked politely if I had enjoyed midder and where I was now working, then chatted among themselves. I felt nearly as strange as when I was a new junior out of the P.T.S., but much more alone, as in those days I had my whole set of fellow-juniors to support me. Only three of my original set now remained in the hospital; two were at present on holiday, and the third was on night duty.

I walked all round the outside of the hospital after supper. Having admired the new Mary from all external angles, I felt much happier and strong enough to go into Casualty and read through the massive residents' list on the porter's lodge outer wall. As we had approximately ninety consultants and each one had at least two and often four attached residents, the list took some reading. Robert Gordon was one of Mr Blakelock's registrars. Mr Blakelock was a consultant general surgeon. I was delighted to see that his list of wards did not include Observation.

My first reaction on seeing Sabina Wardell at close quarters next morning was to wonder if all our men were blind. She was tall, slim, and blonde, with regular features and a perfect skin. Next I wondered why she had taken so long to be made a sister. Jill Collins had taken longer, but that had been from her own choice. She had consistently refused promotion until the Mat. Unit closed. I had not heard of Wardell's turning down any other sister's job, and those things generally got round. She might have been waiting for a plum post like Observation, and her now having it showed Matron had a high opinion of her. Yet, though I had not troubled to think on it before, it did strike me as odd she should have spent four years senior staffing in Elizabeth, and when Matron wanted a new Sister Elizabeth she had offered the position to Jill. Certainly Elizabeth was a gynae ward, where Jill's long midder experience would be invaluable, but, as Wardell must have known the ward inside out, I should have thought her the ideal person for the job. Very odd, I decided, watching Wardell's lovely, composed face as she listened to the night girl. Some time I must ask someone about this.

Sister ignored me until the report was over. She raised one eyebrow.

'I understand you were junior staff nurse in Florence Ward before doing your midwifery, Nurse Rowe.'

'Yes, Sister.'

Her large grey eyes considered me impassively. 'I have read your reports from Sister Florence and the former Sister Mary.' She paused. I waited, expecting some more comments. None came.

I said, 'Yes, Sister.'

She looked at a file on her desk. 'You will be my second staff nurse. Nurse Addy will be your senior, Nurse Trimmer your junior. You will work with your own team. Nurse Addy will explain your work and introduce you to your patients and team as I have now to see Matron.'

She handed me a detailed work-list, diagnosis, treatment, and team-list, the ward off-duty rota, and a copy of our twenty-four-hourly shift system without another word. She did not address a single non-professional remark to me for the next couple of weeks.

On my third day I asked Nurse Addy, 'Does Sister ever talk? Or is she just allergic to redheads?'

Addy I had worked with previously. She had been my senior on nights when I was night relief in Arthur Ward three years ago. She was in her second, and normally final, year as senior staff nurse. 'Don't ask me, love!' she retorted cheerfully. 'I haven't found out any of her likes or allergies yet. She's only been with us seven weeks.'

The Observation Ward occupied the top floor of the new medical block. Though technically a general ward, it was made up of two long rows of single-bedded small wards lying off a centre corridor. The twenty-eight rooms were divided among us three staff nurses, and each patient was nursed only by his or her nursing team. As Addy took over the ward in Sister's off-day, my team had the extra room. Our rooms were One to Ten, Trimmer's Eleven to Nineteen, Addy's the rest. Observation had a larger nursing staff than any other ward or department in the hospital, but no first-year students were included among the nurses.

The ward had been open eighteen months, and was the first Barny's ward built and equipped to treat patients under near-sterile conditions. There was not one unrounded corner in the entire ward and not one window that could be opened. We worked in purified air provided by our own highly complicated air-conditioner, and the temperature was always early summer in the rooms and spring in the corridors and outhouses. We wore gowns, masks, special shoes that never stepped beyond the ward, and often sterile gloves, all day. Every time we went from one patient to another we changed our gowns. On a normal week's laundry list the Observation nurses' gowns numbered around five hundred. Often the figure was higher. One cupboard that in another ward would have been a full-sized linen-room was devoted to gowns alone.

There was not a broom, brush, dustpan, mop, or duster in the place. All the cleaning was done with vacuum cleaners of varying sizes; every bedpan and bottle was sterilised after use. The sluices had as many huge sterilisers as our theatres. The washing-up machines in the ward kitchen were set to boil for twenty minutes after each meal.

On my first morning Addy said, 'There's just one thing to remember: whatever it is, it's got to be boiled before and after use.'

We did not admit infectious patients, the whole idea being to prevent our patients being infected by any stray bug floating in on the air, on or from their nurses and doctors, the very few and carefully vetted medical students allowed near them, or their own visitors. Addy warned me, 'If you only think you are getting a cold or a septic finger for God's sake report it, and don't come near us until you are cleared, or you'll get chucked out of Observation so fast you won't know what's hit you. And watch your team, and above all your visitors. You'll have to be ruthless, but you'll have everyone from old Julius downwards to back you up. No bugs are allowed in Observation, and that is official.'

We had patients of both sexes, including children from eight upward, officially from every firm in the hospital,

46

but mainly, for obvious reasons, from the surgical side. Addy said the three men who kept us most busy were Sir Julius Charing, our senior consultant surgeon and one of the pioneers in kidney grafts; Mr Browne, our top cranial surgeon; and Mr Bunney, a thoracic surgeon. Sir Julius and Mr Bunney were contemporaries. Mr Browne, known throughout Barny's as Brown-plus-E, had once been one of their students. He was in his forties, though he looked much older, and along with another younger pundit, Mr Muir, head of our Ophthalmic Department, he had first demanded the Observation Ward several years ago. Messrs Browne and Muir were great friends and determined men. They had talked, lectured, coaxed, bullied, and eventually swung the great Sir Julius to their side. Even Sir Julius had had a tough time with his more conservative colleagues, and was reputed to have said later that he understood how Lister must have felt when he first suggested his carbolic spray. 'After all I have had to listen to about our having excellent results without all this a-sterile nonsense, I'm only surprised I've not had a lecture on laudable pus!'

Inevitably, once Observation had been open long enough to show the excellent results that could be obtained by the new technique, every pundit in Barny's and a good many outside, wanted our rooms. Addy said, 'The United Nations had nothing on us. Your Mr Mulligan in Room One had a lung out last week. He's a Brazilian, despite his name. They flew him to us from Buenos Aires. Mrs Lee, the head tumour in Fourteen, is Chinese. From Singapore. And my little Tina—the nice little kid in twenty-eight—and her mum in twenty-seven are New Australians. They were Poles. They settled in some small town in Queensland, and when it was found Tina had to have a new kidney the whole town clubbed together to pay all their fares. Dad's come along too. He's in our flat. Mum's donating her left kidney. I've got that on this afternoon.'

All our patients had one thing in common. In hospital language, they were ill—which meant very ill indeed. A scarlet D.I.L. (Dangerously Ill List) label on the outside of a door was the rule, not the exception. And as the close relatives of any Barny's D.I.L. patient could stay in the hospital throughout the danger period, Observation had

47

its own 'relatives' flat' at the far end of the corridor beyond the lifts and stairwell. The relatives had their own gowns, masks, and overshoes. None of their flat windows could be opened since shock and worry makes people cold, in that flat the temperature was always set at midsummer.

'Well?' asked Addy one evening at the end of my first week. 'What do you think of it now?'

'Fascinating and frightening.'

'I know. After eighteen months I've got used to living on the edge of the next crisis. All I've not got used to is not being able to open a window.'

That was still bothering me. 'Not that the air doesn't smell fresh. I keep smelling the sea. Are they pumping in ozone along with our nice aseptic air?'

'Something like that. Must be very health-giving as the sickness rate of Observation nurses is nil. You finished? It's time for report.'

Sister did no actual nursing, as all her time was occupied with administrating her very complex ward, dealing with the consultant medical rounds, and with the many relatives and their problems. But from her very detailed reports she knew everything about every single patient, and, though her attitude appeared so detached and her manner so reserved, her professional insight and computer-like memory were most impressive.

I mentioned this to Nick when he rang me for the second time since my return to London.

'Your ward sister is a pal of Jill Collins?' he queried, and before I could answer, went on, 'Anna, my sweet, you'll have to take that girl in hand!'

'Jill? Why?'

'I've been remembering that bronze outfit she wore the other night. The line was fine, but the colour was impossible for her.'

'Nick,' I said, amused, 'with your interest in fashion you ought to try dress-designing.'

'I wouldn't be any good at that, darling!'

'Why not? When you're so keen on colours?' He said sadly, 'I have another weakness that would stop me from getting to first base. You'll keep this to yourself—but I have strong, but strong, heterosexual inclinations.'

'Which, of course, you do your best to keep under control.'

'Care to make a small bet?'

That rang a bell. I only placed it after we had discussed which show we wanted to see on my next free evening and he rang off. I went slowly back to my room, thinking of Robert in the kitchen that party evening.

Harriet was waiting with tea. 'Why so glum? The golden boy had to call off your next date?'

'No.' I exclaimed, thinking of Robert.

She laughed. 'Charles says Blakelock has no patients in Observation. Just as well.'

'I'll say. And how is Charles?'

'Dandy! He's dated me for the Cricket Club dance. You going to get the golden boy to take you?'

I hesitated, not wanting to sound smug. The Cricket Club dance might be amusing but it was nothing special, and if I had that week-end off I did want to go down to Wylden. I said evasively, 'It's an idea. I'll think about it.'

'Do! Then the four of us can have a ball!' She refilled her cup. 'The golden boy does seem gone on you. How do you really feel about him?'

'I dunno.' I thought it over. 'Yes, I do! I feel good!'

I went on feeling good for the rest of that night, and was still on top of the world when I got on duty next morning, but then my new job was so interesting, as well as so demanding, that I forgot Nick's existence. Mrs Bird, in Room Three, was due for a major abdominal operation during the morning. Mr Sands, in Five, was in his thirty-fifth day of unconsciousness after a head injury, and was to have his temperature artificially lowered still further, which would entail his being specialled constantly all day; the patient in Ten was returning to a general ward, and a new man, Mr Elkroyd, was coming in to take his place. Of my seven other patients five were on the D.I.L., and one of those five was unlikely to live more than a few hours. She had had a pulmonary embolus just before breakfast, and when I saw her her pulse was untakeable. Up to last night she had been doing quite well. As she was a Roman Catholic, before I did anything else I had to contact Father Gough, the R.C. chaplain.

'Miss Miles, Nurse? You don't tell me! The poor girl was up and walking when I saw her yesterday.'

'I know, Father. This happened as she was getting back to bed for breakfast. She was going back to a general ward tomorrow. I'm sorry, but she's not at all well now.'

He had worked in Barny's for years. He knew I was telling him Miss Miles was dying. 'I will be over to see her this instant, Nurse.'

The telephone rang directly I put it down. The caller was Mr Turner's registrar. Mr Turner was the abdominal surgeon who was going to operate on Mrs Bird. 'She's to have blood and a drip before we have her down, Nurse. I'm coming up now with a houseman.'

My team-leader was a fourth-year. She took over Miss Miles as I had to attend to Mrs Bird.

Mrs Bird was fifty-five and so thin that her bones looked too big for her. She was a widow with two married sons. She had returned to full-time teaching four years ago after her youngest son's marriage. She had carcinoma of the stomach.

Her subject and hobby was history. Her pet period, the Norman Conquest. While I helped the registrar set up the drip, and my third-year helped the houseman with the transfusion that was to be inserted in her other ankle, she gave us a blow-by-blow account of the battle of Hastings. 'Harold would have won without doubt had he had a trained army. But'—her gesture had both sets of apparatus swaying—'though his men fought as men only fight for their homeland, there was no discipline. And William was the real soldier.'

Outside her room, when the drip and transfusion were running well, the houseman said he was now a walking mine of information on the Normans. 'I couldn't get any history out of the old girl until I'd agreed William Rufus was a much maligned man. The poor old bag's a nut!'

The registrar was more experienced. 'Only a superficial nut, chum. She's got guts. She knows what's going on all right.'

I asked, 'What's your prognosis, Mr Romford?' He looked at the closed door, shrugged. 'She's left it pretty late. I can't stick my neck out. I do know, in her shoes, I wouldn't want to waste breath talking about the future, either.'

When the men had removed their gowns and themselves the third-year asked, 'Do you think she really does know, Nurse Rowe? She's never said anything about it to me.'

'Nor me, but she's an intelligent woman. She's probably too intelligent to have looked up her symptoms in some medical textbook, but you've only got to open a paper or turn on the telly these days to have the works about carcinoma thrust down your throat. She knows.' I thought a moment. 'She doesn't strike me as scared. I wish I knew her better. You think she's scared?'

'Surely she must be.'

We had to leave it there as we had a lot to do. Miss Miles, in an oxygen tent, went into a coma that was as deep as Frank Sands's. Mr Jenkins, in Room Two, another lung carcinoma, had to have a shorter tracheotomy tube inserted, and Brown-plus-E arrived with his registrars and housemen—he had two of each—to see Frank Sands. My team-leader gave Mrs Bird her premedication with a second-year as witness. When I got back to Mrs Bird she was growing drowsy.

I took her pulse, checked the drip and transfusion. 'Comfortable, dear?'

She had known so much pain for so long that her face was now normally tense. It was beginning to relax. 'Very comfortable, thank you, Nurse. Having a busy morning?'

'Fairly busy.' With some patients that question would have meant, can't you stay with me? I did not get that impression from her. I felt she was not only happy to be alone, but wanted me to go. I did not want to disturb her, but she was worrying me. I asked about Harold Godwin. 'You make him sound a most interesting character, Mrs Bird. How can you square his being such an upright citizen with his backing out of his promise to William?'

She was drowsy, but her eyes were shrewd. 'Poor Nurse! How I must have bored you all with my stories!'

'You haven't bored us at all! Honestly! You tell them so well.' I tried another angle. 'Did you tell them to your sons when they were small? I'll bet they shone at history at school.'

'They did well. Naturally I had taught them a fair amount. They seemed to like my history bedtime stories.' She looked at the vacolitre of blood as if it was a long way away. 'They are good boys. They've married good girls. They'll be all right.' She sighed deeply as the drug took a stronger hold. 'I'm glad this didn't have to happen until now. It doesn't matter now. They'll be all right.'

It was then I knew why she worried me. She was not frightened, but, what was far more dangerous, she was resigned to dying.

'You've no grandchildren yet? What fun you'll have when they arrive! They'll love your stories, too.'

She said slowly, 'I would have liked grandchildren. I am sorry to miss them.'

The injection was knocking away the barriers of her resistance. It was not going to knock her right out, but it was going to put her into a light sleep. There was no time left for choosing tactful words.

'You're not going to miss them, Mrs Bird. You'll be a new woman after this operation. You wait and see.'

Her smile was sleepy and indulgent. As if I was a nice child. 'I'm too tired, Nurse.'

'That's your injection.'

She actually laughed. Weakly, but it was a laugh. 'Oh, no, my dear. It isn't that kind of tiredness. It isn't all the pain. That was just the finishing touch. I've been tired for years. As tired as only someone who has done the job of being both parents for twenty years could understand.' She paused, but I kept quiet intentionally, and after a few seconds she went on, 'My husband was a farmer. He was a good man, but he wasn't a good farmer. He was thirty-two when he was killed by an overturning tractor. Everything had to be sold, and when everything had been paid there was twenty-six pounds left.'

'Did you go back to teaching then?'

'No. I couldn't earn enough for the three of us at it in those days. We moved into the village, and I worked first for our local doctor. Then I taught myself shorthand and typing and did extra work for anyone who needed a part-

52

time secretary. Later I did part-time teaching and had pupils in the evening.'

I said, 'You must have been so lonely.'

'My dear, there was no time to feel lonely—at least, not in the day. The nights were bad—and the coldness of a double bed alone. But I got round that by using the night. I did all our cooking, cleaning, and washing at night. I got so used to being up when the world was asleep, the night became my friend instead of my enemy. And I had streaks of great good luck. We all kept healthy. Somehow, and looking back I'm not sure how, we always managed to have our own home, even if it was just a couple of rooms. We had a lot of fun. I got used to living with a pile of bills, and I learnt never to think about the future, much less let it worry me. Life is so much more simple when you only live one day at a time. And the boys were so good. Of course, they had their moody days. So did I. But they never gave me any trouble. People used to say, "How can you manage teenage boys alone? A woman?" I don't know how I managed. I just did. People kept saying, "You ought to marry again." I would like to have done— and I was quite good-looking—but I never had time. And though the boys missed their father, they would have hated any other man who tried to take his place as my husband. Children'—her voice was fading—'can grow as possessive about a parent as a parent about children. They had lost so much. They needed all I could give them, and they've more than given me it all back. They'll be all right,' she said for the third time.

I said, 'My dear, you can't be sure your job's done. They may well still need you to fight for them, and that's why you must still fight for yourself.' I heard the door open and ignored it. 'I'd say your job is nothing like finished yet. Think of those grandchildren you are bound to have. Grandmothers are probably more important now than they were. I know that from my own family. My sister and sister-in-law both have babies. They couldn't begin to cope without the grannies. They'd be lost if they couldn't shout for Grandmother when someone gets flu or they have another baby. Who can afford nannies? And think of all your stories,' I insisted. 'You shouldn't keep them to yourself.

I know you teach, but couldn't you also write some of them? A children's book, perhaps. It would be something to do while you are getting over your operation.'

'Funny you should say that. That's something I've always wanted to do.' Her eyes closed. 'No time.'

'There will be time after your operation.'

I did not think she had heard. Then she said, without opening her eyes, 'Might be amusing ... amusing.... I'll have to think about it ... later.'

Sister had been standing just inside the door. She came forward, put a hand on Mrs Bird's forehead, checked the drip and transfusion, looked at me without any expression in her eyes above her mask, and went out again. I had no idea whether she approved or was annoyed by my ignoring her presence at that particular moment. I did not wish to offend her, but, as I would not have interrupted my conversation even had I been convinced she was fuming with impatience behind me, I did not let the matter bother me. I was far too bothered about Mrs Bird.

The third-year came into stay with Mrs Bird until the theatre trolley arrived. Sister was waiting for me in the corridor. 'Miss Miles has died without regaining consciousness, Nurse Rowe. Mr Elkroyd has arrived in Room Ten from Henry Ward.'

'Thank you Sister.' I looked from one closed door to another as I took off my gown and hung it on the senior nurse's peg outside Mrs Bird's room. 'I'm very sorry about Miss Miles. She was far too young to die.'

She said unemotionally, 'A pulmonary embolus is no respecter of age.'

'No, Sister.' Her reserve chilled me. But Miss Miles was my first death in her ward, and there was a question I had to ask. 'Sister, do you like me to do Last Offices with one of my juniors?'

'I would prefer you to leave that to your team-leader. As the most senior nurse in your team, your work is with the living who still need you.'

Of course she was right. It was just her way of putting it that jarred. 'Yes, Sister. I'll see to Mr Elkroyd.' I stood aside for her to walk on to her duty-room.

She did not move. 'I will suggest to Mrs Bird's sons that

54

they encourage their mother to follow your advice in her convalescence. Your idea could be excellent occupational therapy for her.' She looked at the name-card in her hand that she had already removed from Miss Miles's door. 'A pity. She was a nice woman. Mr Bunney will be distressed.' And then, just as I had decided she was human, she added, 'This will affect his statistics.'

She walked on. Addy appeared beside me as I washed my hands at one of the corridor sinks. 'Sorry about that girl. Sister's just told me.'

I said bitterly, 'She also tell you it's such a pity as it'll upset old Bunney's statistics?'

'She did. Don't take it too hard. It's not her fault she can't unbend. I often feel she'd like to, but is afraid that would be unprofessional. She's scared stiff of being that. She's going to prove she's the best sister ever—if it kills her! She'll go to the stake rather than admit that, or how much she must have hated being the most senior staff nurse bar none in Barny's, while girls years junior to her turned into sisters, but it must have rankled.'

'Why did Matron wait so long? It's not as if Wardell isn't efficient, plus, plus, plus—damn her!'

'Do you need to ask? Now?' It seemed she thought I did. 'Any sister running a normal general ward needs a strong streak of the common touch. Here what we mainly need is a good administrator. Which is what we've got. At times I feel quite sorry for her.'

'You're a lot nicer than me. What I feel for her right now is not sorry!' I dried my hands, put on a clean gown, and went in to meet Mr Elkroyd.

CHAPTER FOUR

DINNER WITH NICK

MR ELKROYD looked round his room with a deliberation that could have been a natural characteristic, but could also have been one of the symptoms that brought him into the Observation Ward.

'What's this, then? Private patient, am I?'

He had been in Henry three weeks. I said, 'Didn't Sister Henry explain all our beds in this ward are in separate rooms, and why we are all dressed up like this?'

'Oh, aye.' He looked me over just as he had done his room. 'I thought as you'd have me in a cubicle. Not all this class.'

'All our rooms are identical. They are rather nice.'

'Oh, aye,' said Mr Elkroyd.

He was a fairish young man, well built, and with a square face. His blue eyes reminded me of Nick and instantly disposed me to like him.

I said, 'I expect Mr Browne thought you might enjoy a little quiet as you have these headaches.' He said nothing. 'I hope you don't mind being alone?'

'Have to put up with it, won't I, then?'

He was a bricklayer. He worked for a large firm of building contractors in Liverpool, and after having an unblemished work record for years had begun having a series of minor accidents at work in the last few months. The firm's doctor was an old Barny's man. He had examined Tom Elkroyd and then written to Mr Browne.

I asked, 'Have you been to London before, Mr Elkroyd?'

'Nah. I'd not have come such for this lot but for my Betty,' he added, not rudely, but just stating a fact. 'She's a mind of her own, has my Betty. Aye. That'll be her with kids.'

I admired the coloured photograph of his wife and four children on his bed-table. 'Your wife is very pretty.'

'She's all right, then.'

I asked about his headaches. He said they could be worse. His notes said they were getting worse.

One of my team juniors had been unpacking his belongings. She stopped by me later as I was re-reading his notes in the corridor. 'He looks so fit, Nurse. Why are they wasting one of our beds on him?'

'Mr Browne must think he needs the bed.'

'Does that mean he's got a head tumour?'

'I don't know. He hasn't been diagnosed yet.'

'Wouldn't they have spotted that in Henry? They've had three weeks.'

'Some aren't as easy to spot as others.'

She was only a second-year and very shaken over Miss Miles, so I did not choose that moment to enlarge on the dangers of deep-seated cranial growths. They were very present in my mind as I hung up the notes. Tom Elkroyd was a young man, a husband and father. Brown-plus-E seldom, if ever, was wrong about a patient.

Mrs Bird's sons moved into our flat that day. When she returned from the theatre and came round they took it in turns to spend the next five days and nights sitting by her bed, looking like spare housemen in their gowns, caps, and masks. They behaved so sensibly we forgot they were there. Their mother was aware of the fact, and most of the time one or other of them was holding her hand.

Her operation had been even more extensive than anticipated. Mr Turner, a naturally gloomy man, shook his head every time he looked at her notes. His registrar, Mr Romford, drew me some private pictures on the back of an envelope. 'We hacked out the whole stomach and a good six inches of this.' He shaded the area. 'She's got a massive growth. How she walked around with that thing inside her, only God knows.'

'No wonder she had all that pain, poor dear.' I studied his illustration. 'You joined up here to here?'

'Yep. The boss did a very neat end-to-end anastomosis. If it holds——'

'You think it'll give?'

He shrugged. 'You should have seen the stuff we had to work on. Wasn't much to play with.'

'And if it does hold?'

'She may have a few more years. We couldn't find any secondaries, but with the thing that size ...' He left his sentence unfinished.

I had a date with Nick that night. I told him about Tom Elkroyd, but I was too worried over Mrs Bird to discuss her with anyone outside of Observation. It was now her fourth post-op. day. The first five after her specific operation were always crucial. We had given her constant transfusions of whole blood. I had left her looking yellow and shrunken and more like eighty-five than fifty-five, with Bill Romford about to give her another transfusion. For a short while after she would be less yellow, and then, on past showing, she would look shrivelled and yellow again. It was not the yellow of jaundice; it was not caused by the transfusions themselves, which could happen; and, though countless tests were being made, there was nothing anyone could yet find wrong with her liver or gall-bladder. Another pathologist had arrived to take another drop of her blood before Bill Romford gave her that transfusion as I was going off duty. I had to leave her, but even though I had this date with Nick, if I could have stayed on, I would have done so.

I had not intended talking shop, as Nick was an outsider, but he had brought up the subject of Observation and asked if I had any interesting patients. 'Is this Elkroyd one of our chaps?'

'On your buildings? No. He's from the North. A honey of a man. He talks as little as Sister. They should get on well.'

'And do they?'

'My dear man, don't ask me! I work for a problem Sister. I'm not sure yet which she's made of—ice or iron. And Tom Elkroyd hasn't been in long enough for me to have found out yet what's on the other side.'

'What's wrong with him? Or shouldn't I ask? I know how you nurses feel about professional ethics.'

He did not know that from me, as I had never mentioned the subject to him, but as he had been in and out of Barny's for three years it was a reasonable assumption that he had had another girl friend on our staff, and possibly several. No-one had yet told me about her, or them, probably because I had not yet discussed him with anyone but Harriet. If I was right, it was only a question of time before someone took me on one side and said she didn't want to worry me, but she thought I ought to know . . .

I said, 'I can't tell you what's wrong with him as I honestly don't know. He's in for observation.'

'Who's he under?'

'A pundit called Browne.'

'Brown-plus E?' He tapped his head. 'Trouble up here?' I nodded. 'Poor chap. I saw Browne today, making for your block when I was talking to your hearty pal with the lamentable colour sense. Jill Thing. I ran into her in the park.' He grimaced. 'Why does she have to wear old sacks? And if she must, why no ashes?'

I smiled. 'She's a trained nurse. Too hygienic.'

'God! It oughtn't to be allowed! And if her clothes weren't enough to wreck my day, she showed me some curtain patterns she had got for your old Sister Mary. Pretty little pastels! Ugh! She'll ruin that cottage!' He emptied the wine-bottle between our glasses. 'You'll have to stop that, Anna.'

'How can I? Sister Mary thinks a lot of Jill, and she may like pretty little pastels. Even if she doesn't, I can't stop Jill. I never see her now she's a Sister. I wish I did. I miss old Jill.'

'Then why don't we have another party? Do you know a man called Peter Graveny?'

'Vaguely.' Peter Graveny was a paediatric registrar. 'Friend of yours?'

He nodded. 'I'll get hold of Peter, and you can contact Jill. Then we can both go to work on her colour sense. Or is that out on the ethics count, too?'

'Officially, yes.' He had obviously had another girl friend in Barny's. 'I doubt that'd bother Jill so long as the party takes place outside Barny's. Why don't you ask her yourself? I think she'd prefer to have it from you.'

He seemed surprised. 'Would that be all right with you, sweetie?'

'Fine.' Not only a nurse, I thought, but possessive. 'Any time.'

'Then I'll talk to Peter and let you know.'

His conversation was telling me so much about his former girl friend (or friends) that I wondered how much mine told him about David. I suddenly realised this was the first occasion I had remembered David since returning to London, despite the many opportunities for recalling the past that must have presented themselves to my sub-conscious down every hospital corridor, in the canteen, the park, on the riverside terrace, or even crossing the road from the Home. David used to admire the view from Casualty yard in our early days, and then happen to cross the road when he saw me coming down our front steps.

Later he waited on the steps. Later still in our front hall. Yet I had forgotten it all.

It now astonished me that a man who had played such a vital part in my life for so long should have vanished as finally and as easily as a stone in a pond. There had been ripples at first, and the first ripple had seemed a tidal wave. Had it really been that? Or had I not only allowed, but encouraged self-pity and pique to distort the truth? I did not know the answer. I did know that I owed a great deal to Nick, and felt a great rush of gratitude and affection for him. 'It's sweet of you to organise this party.'

'Darling, I could have an ulterior motive. You are less likely to run out on me from a quartet. Do you truthfully have to be back by midnight tonight?'

'Yes. I told you, I haven't a key.'

'Why not? You're senior enough to get late leave for the asking. Who are you really afraid of, Anna? Me? Or yourself?'

I said, 'You may not believe this, Nick, but I was late off and in such a hurry to get a bath and change that I forgot.'

He was briefly put out, and then he laughed. 'I believe you, darling. Don't ask me why, but I do.' He dropped his hand over mine on the table-top. His touch was light, but that contact was enough to have us both more relaxed and at the same time more aware of each other. 'I think I'm in love with you, darling. I'm not sure, but I think I am. How about you?'

His honesty did not offend me. On the contrary, I liked it. 'I'm not sure either, Nick.'

'I suppose you wouldn't care to find out?'

'No,' I said, 'no thank you. Sorry.'

He did not let go of my hand. 'I didn't think you would. You don't, do you?'

'No.' Again I thought of David and the rows we had over this. It was a relief to know this time the fight was not going to start. 'How did you know that?'

'My sweet, I've been around. For the record, why won't you? Because you're a nurse? Or does it go deeper?'

I had to think. 'Probably a bit of both. Before I started nursing I never used to understand why people had to leap into bed for kicks. You don't have to get drunk to

60

enjoy a drink. If you do finish the bottle in a hurry you end up being sick all over the floor. And I've known much the same happen to other girls a few mornings after a night in the wrong bed.'

'It doesn't have to happen——'

'Nick, dear, save your breath if you are going to start talking contraceptives to me. I've just finished midder, remember? The Pill aside—and in my book that hasn't been in use long enough for anyone to be dead certain what it does or doesn't do—I don't just think there's no such thing as one hundred per cent safety—I know. Ask any midwife or obstetrician. You should hear the number of girls we hear and their pathetic "But, Nurse, we were so careful!"' I paused. 'I don't suppose you've seen a baby being born?'

He shook his head, watching me intently. 'Go on.'

'Some women have a moderately easy time, which means it only hurts like hell for a little while. Some, a lot, have it tough. It hurts like hell for hours, and in bad cases days. That's hard enough when a baby's wanted, and, remember, it comes after nine months which aren't exactly a joy-ride. Few normal women enjoy the steady thickening of their figures, the nausea—if it's no worse—of the early months, the weight and fatigue of the final months. But, if the baby is wanted and normal, once it arrives the situation more than evens up. Women are realists, perhaps because they have to be. They don't expect something as good as a baby for nothing.' I smiled involuntarily. 'You should see the face of a woman when she has her first baby in her arms for the first time. She practically glows with happiness. But when the baby is unwanted—and I've seen dozens—then the whole business is unadulterated hell. Childbirth turns degrading as well as agonising and when the baby's there an even worse hell starts. I know lots of babies get adopted,' I went on, now grimly, 'and I've seen how mothers look when they sign the adoption forms. Maybe they are doing the only right thing, and people say they forget. I wonder. How can you ever forget the child that has grown inside you for those nine months? The pain? The holding it in your arms and seeing exactly what you've done?' He was silent. 'Then there's the other side. When I worked in Cas. we had about six women a week carried in after back-street abortions. They came in more dead than alive, and a good many died. Lots were my age and younger.' I drank some wine. 'A hell of a price to pay for a few kicks, but maybe you have to work in a hospital to know exactly what the bill for those kicks can look like. That makes it easier for a nurse to remember when a party hots up, or one is feeling glum, or the moon's shining and some man you are fond of comes out with the old blackmailing routine, "If you really loved me . . . blah, blah, blah." Of course there's just one answer: "If you really loved me you wouldn't ask me to risk it." But one seldom remembers that at the time, unless, as I say, you happen to be in my trade and have inside information.' Then I realised how long I had been talking. 'Nick, I'm sorry. You don't rate this outburst. Not that I don't mean it and it isn't true.'

'I wouldn't say I don't rate it, but we don't have to go into that. I don't mind your letting fly. I like it. You've been making a lot of sense.' He moved his hand at last and fiddled with his glass. 'Do other nurses feel as you do?'

'Expect so. Some, anyway. Why?'

He said deliberately, 'I don't hold with mixing the past and present any more than I have noticed you do. But as you are bound to hear this sooner or later, as you work with her, I'd rather you heard it from me.' He then intrigued, astonished, and did not wholly please me by telling me he had had an affair with Sabby Wardell last year.

My astonishment was short-lived. It was obvious that Nick's roving eye would have noticed her, and, having done so, of course he did something about it. Being such an extrovert, he had to unburden to me. He said, 'I call it an affair. To be honest, darling, that's only to salvage what's left of my ego. I didn't even get to first base. We ran around for quite a while, but'—he shrugged—'it didn't work out. I didn't know why not, then. You've just let in the light. Why couldn't she have done that?'

I kept silent. He didn't want an answer from me. He was chatting this out with himself.

He went on, 'You say you don't know if she's made of

62

ice or steel. Sweetie, you are not alone! I tried. I could not make contact. So I moved on. I didn't particularly want to, but there didn't seem anything else to do. I won't say she had me off my food'—his smile was self-derisive—'but it was another of those damned close-run things!'

'Poor old Nick!'

'I survived.' He sat back, watching me. 'Now you know her name, how about telling me his?'

I told him David's name. I did not enlarge on it.

'Just a couple of sitting ducks ripe for the rebound, darling.' He raised his glass to me. 'Will you weep on my bosom first or shall I weep on yours?'

I studied my Ward Sister with new interest next day, and though it was hard to credit any man could lose interest in her lovely face, the more I saw of her on duty and Nick off, the more I understood why their relationship had never got off the ground. Temperamentally they were totally dissimilar, and if Nick had tried to force the pace as he had with me I was not surprised she should have slapped him down hard. Then she probably took great umbrage. She took umbrage very easily on duty when she suspected a resident of not treating her with the respect she felt her position deserved. I suspected she had thought herself just another name in Nick's little black book and resented that fiercely. She might have been right about that. I didn't know. I did know she was a very determined young woman who knew how to say no, and did not hesitate to say it when she saw fit, at the risk of making herself unpopular. I was with her in her duty-room one evening when the Senior Medical Officer, our top resident, came in to announce we could in future expect double our usual number of medical students, as we had so many excellent teaching cases in the ward. Wardell flatly refused to allow even one more in Observation. 'I am sorry, Doctor. I will not have my patients disturbed. They are too ill.'

The S.M.O. said politely, 'I appreciate your concern, Sister, but we have to provide our students with the best training we can give them.'

They argued for twenty minutes. The argument was ended by Wardell's threatening to resign unless her wishes in her own ward were respected. She clearly meant it, and as Barny's sisters had considerable power in their own wards—good ward sisters were precious, and Wardell was a very good sister—the S.M.O. reluctantly stepped down. He walked off, very angry. Wardell showed no emotion at all as she turned to me, 'As I was saying, Nurse Rowe...'

Briefly I had thought of Nick's easygoing nature. I had already discovered he did not mind being pushed around by a woman, providing the pushing was done gently, but Wardell had no patience for velvet gloves. I thought of the S.M.O.'s expression just now, and could guess what he was saying to his colleagues. This was not the first scrap Wardell had had with a resident. It was then I finally understood how she had managed to remain unmarried despite her appearance. We all knew the men talked about us as much as we talked about them. Once any nurse got a reputation for bitchiness she might have her problems, but they would not include the problem with which Harriet battled non-stop, which was the how to get enough free evenings off duty to satisfy her many would-be dates.

I had not told anyone about my conversation with Nick, but as it became common knowledge in our Home that I was being dated by him and it was a safe bet Wardell had heard, I did wonder if it would have any effect on her attitude towards me in Observation.

If she had heard, she did not show it. She continued to treat me as politely and distantly as ever. She greeted my reports on my patients, whether good or bad, with an impassive, 'Thank you, Nurse Rowe.'

Mrs Bird was still alive, and that was about all we could say about her. On her fourteenth post-operative night, after expressing my anxiety, I asked, 'Why isn't she picking up, Sister? It's high time. And I do believe she now wants to live.'

'So it would seem, Nurse Rowe. Please continue.'

I had to go on. When I reached Mr Elkroyd I had more than usual to report. His condition was slowly deteriorating, and he had had a great deal of pain in his head that day. I ended, 'I don't like the look of that man, Sister. He seems to me to be going downhill fast.'

'Not very satisfactory,' she agreed. 'Is that all, Nurse? Thank you.'

Harriet was in her room and changing to go out when I got over to the Home. 'Wardell's not a woman!' I stormed. 'She's just a super-efficient nursing machine, and cold, cold as charity!'

'As she's running probably the most difficult ward in Barny's, dear, isn't it just as well she can keep a cool head. Sorry'—she opened the door—'must fly! Julian's waiting downstairs!'

'Which one's Julian?'

'My tame C.O. [Casualty Officer] who dates me on Tuesdays.' She stopped, one foot in the doorway. 'You fixed up the Cricket Club dance with Nick?'

'No. Remember I told you he's gone up North on business? And, actually——'

'So you did! Edinburgh or somewhere. He's building a hospital there. Won't he be back in time?'

'Yes, but——'

'You want to wait until he's back. Suit yourself. See you.' She shot off and down in the lift leaving me cursing myself for being a moral coward. I calmed my conscience by answering Nick's latest letter.

He had been away several days, and wrote me long, amusing letters almost daily. His friend Peter Graveny had been on holiday, so we had not had that party with Jill before Nick left town. In the letter I had had that morning he wrote that he had heard from Peter and about the Cricket Club dance. 'Peter says why don't we make a foursome for that dance and then go on elsewhere?'

I now knew my off duty for that week-end. I was free, but had not yet seen Jill to tell her. I had twice rung the Sisters' Home, and both times she had still been on duty. There was still plenty of time, so I had shelved things for the present. Of course, the obvious person to get a message to Jill was Harriet, as she worked in Cas. Cas. was the hub of the hospital, and there Harriet saw everyone. Observation was a closed little sterile world apart.

My letter to Nick explained why Jill and I would have to miss that dance, and having got that off my chest I felt much better until I began thinking about Mrs Bird and

Tom Elkroyd. Then I had to go and find Addy for consolation. She made cocoa, and we grumbled about Wardell and talked Observation until long after midnight.

I was about to leave when one of the theatre staff nurses put her head round Addy's door. 'Any cocoa going? I'm parched.'

She was on night call, and had already been called back twice since nine o'clock. 'Two perforated appendices. They'll find us a third.' She kicked off her shoes wearily. 'They always do.'

'Which firm?' I asked after we had sympathised with the tough life of the theatre girls.

'Blakelock's. He didn't come in. The S.S.O. did it with Robbie Gordon and a brand-new houseman who kept dropping things. The S.S.O. got so narked I thought he'd crown the lad with the other skin retractor. Wish he had, the ham-handed lout! Sister Theatre nearly had hysterics and the dressers were hysterical. They were laughing their silly heads off behind their masks.'

I said, 'And how did Robert Gordon take it?'

'He just looked over his glasses a couple of times and got on with the job. Someone had to. But, I say, girls—you're from Observation! Tell all! Is it true Sabby Wardell had a flaming row with the S.M.O.?'

Addy and I exchanged glances. We had had a fine time taking Wardell apart, but she was our ward sister. 'What about?' asked Addy. 'Anyone told you about this, Rowe?'

'No.' I was honest. 'No-one has said one word about this to me. You'd better tell us, Paddy.'

Robert was another person I had not seen since returning from the Mat. Unit. According to Addy, Mr Blakelock seldom, if ever, sent us patients, which gave me an additional personal reason for liking my new ward. I was more fascinated by my work than at any period in my nursing life, but, being still so new to the many new techniques we used in Observation, and to working under the strain of constant barrier-nursing, and having so many D.I.L. patients, I found my first month as physically tiring as my first training year, and far more tiring mentally. What my team and I did could most literally make the difference between life and death to our patients. I was in

66

charge; I had to watch the girls as well as myself. Sister, not unreasonably since she had three staff nurses, left the nursing in our three pairs of hands. She checked on our work, but the actual work was ours.

I was quite glad when Nick was away as he was a distraction, and at present I could not afford to be distracted. I was thinking this over at late lunch one day and wondering why my job alone should make me so content, when my team-leader came in looking worried. 'Did you give the ophthalmic registrar Mr Elkroyd's notes, Nurse?'

'Yes. This morning. For Mr Muir. Aren't they back? He promised he'd bring them straight back.'

She said, 'I don't think he got to Mr Muir, Nurse. He passed out in the corridor, and is now warded in Jude with an acute abdomen. Sister Jude rang Sister to say he's just remembered not returning those notes, and is feeling too ill to remember what he did with them. As Mr Browne has asked Mr Muir to have a consultation with him on Mr Elkroyd at two-thirty, Sister said I had better find you.'

'Oh, no! I mean, yes, thanks. Let's go.' We hurried from the dining-room and along the main ground-floor corridor towards our block. We had shot by Jill Collins talking to Robert before I realised it, but I could not spare the time for going back to say I would be spring-cleaning with her, so had to canter on.

In Observation, Sister was calm. 'Mr Elkroyd is your patient, Nurse Rowe. Those notes must be here for the consultant. Please find them immediately.'

'Yes, Sister.' I hesitated. 'Sister, have you any idea where the ophthalmic registrar went after leaving here this morning?'

'If I had, Nurse Rowe, I would have already telephoned the Sister in charge of that department.'

'Yes, Sister. Of course. I'm sorry. Thank you.'

Addy had arrived in our corridor as I was leaving. 'Good luck, chum.'

Barny's had ten blocks in use, dozens of wards and departments, literally miles of corridors, and I had less than half an hour. The staff lift was in use, so I galloped down the block stairs like a first-year. I tried the obvious first.

'They won't be here, Staff Nurse,' said Sister Casualty firmly. 'Any notes we find are returned instantly to their wards. Try General Out-Patients.'

Sister G.O.P. was annoyed. 'Ward patients' notes should never be mislaid! I never permitted my patients' notes to leave my ward when I was ward sister! I am surprised at Sister Observation allowing Mr Yates to remove them! However, I will look in my files. No. As I thought. You must look elsewhere, Staff Nurse.'

A G.O.P. staff nurse caught me on my way out. 'Try E.N.T., Rowe. One of their mastoid babies had grit in the eye this morning. I think Joe Yates went there from here.'

I thanked her, mentally cursed the unfortunate and itinerant ophthalmic registrar, and raced on.

The Ear, Nose, and Throat Department was having a post-tonsil clinic. The rows of waiting children were looking down each other's throats and swapping operation experiences as avidly as their elders on the Casualty benches. 'I'll bet you weren't sick as me! I was sick as sick all over my cot and the floor and the nurses and the doctor!'

'I'll bet I was sicker'n you, so there! An' I was sick blood! I had to have a whole blood transfusion! The doctor told the nurse I bled like a stuck pig, and I heard him! I had two pints!' The speaker was a plump little girl with pink cheeks. 'I'll bet you didn't even have plasma. Did she have plasma, Sister? Did she? Did she have plasma?'

Sister E.N.T. looked slightly wilted. 'One minute, dear. Yes, Nurse? Notes? They shouldn't be here, but by all means look for yourself.'

That wasted another five minutes. I tore on towards the Eye Department, taking the short cut between some secretaries' offices. I did not see the white coat coming out of one office until I had cannoned into the wearer. 'Sorry, Doctor,' I apologised mechanically, then looked up. 'Oh. It's you,'

Robert said, 'Forgive the awful pun, Anna, but do you have to run so true to form?'

'I do! It's not haemorrhage or fire, just the prospect of two irate pundits and one irate ward sister.' He was in my path. 'Do move, Robert. I must get to Eyes.'

He did not move. 'Why?'

68

'Joe Yates has lost one of my men's notes—do let me by!'

'A man called Elkroyd?' He had three sets of notes under his arm. He handed me one. 'This what you are looking for?'

'Yes!' I beamed on him in relief. Had he been anyone else I should have wanted to kiss him. 'What on earth are you doing with them?'

'I've just collected them from Muir's secretary. He left them with her to give to Joe. I was about to return them to Observation.'

'I'll save you the journey. Thanks a lot.'

'You're welcome.' We walked down the corridor. 'I'll have to come up to Observation after I've seen a girl with eyes in Elizabeth. Isn't Muir due for a consultation there at two-thirty?'

'Yes. But what's that to you?'

'I've been switched. My boss has lent me to Muir while Joe's off.'

'You? Why? How? It's an eye job. Have you done eyes?'

He looked at me over his glasses. 'For eighteen months, after leaving here.' He named the most famous eye hospital in England. 'I went from there to Edinburgh.'

'Of course! David told me you were doing eyes! I'd forgotten.'

He dug his hands in the bulging pockets of his limp white coat and hunched his shoulders. The flapping coat made him look longer and thinner than ever. 'Have you really such a bad memory? Or do you only remember the things it suits you to remember?'

I glanced at him. 'What's that supposed to mean?'

He waited until we crossed the main corridor and reached the foot of the medical-block stairs. 'I talked to Jill Collins today. She's having rather a tough time. She's got a new ward on her hands, and, in spite of all those promises, she now seems to be dealing single-handed with Sister Mary's affairs.'

I stopped on the first stair and faced him. 'Are you talking about the spring-cleaning week-end she's organising?'

'So you have remembered that? I hope you won't let it spoil the Cricket Club dance for you. I doubt you will.'

He looked at his watch. 'I must get to Elizabeth. You'll not forget to tell Sister Observation I'll be up in about ten minutes?'

'I won't, Robert.' I was as icy as Wardell at her most frigid. 'Thanks for these notes.'

'Not at all. See you later.'

'Yes. You will.' I went up the stairs as fast as I had come down, heaping more curses on Joe Yates's acute abdomen every step of the way. Then I remembered the wretched Joe was warded in Jude, and must be in a bad way to have passed out, which made me feel guilty instead of bad-tempered. It did not make me feel any better about the prospect of working with Robert again.

CHAPTER FIVE

A TALK WITH ROBERT

I RANG Jill again at the Sisters' Home that night, and that time she was in.

'You can join me? But Harriet Jones said you were booked for the dance and, I presumed, the match next day? You aren't after all? Splendid. Let's aim for the five-twenty down on Friday.'

I had to tell Harriet. I had to wait a few days as she was working a 6 a.m. to 2 p.m. shift in Casualty that week, and I was on the 1.30–9.30 p.m. in Observation. We did not meet until we arrived at the same tea on Thursday.

She said I must be crazy to chuck my golden boy for a jolly week-end scrubbing. 'Have you been working too hard, dear? Or are you playing hard to get? If you are, watch it! You may be playing with fire. Nick Dexter's quite a man, and no man likes being turned down. You'll be an awful fool if you let him slip through your fingers.'

I protested uncomfortably, 'Hell, Harriet—I did promise Jill first.'

'The more fool you, dear, for not taking my hint! Yes, I know we promised Sister Mary, but that was to interior-decorate, not spring-clean! And it isn't as if she's asked us to rally this week-end. It's all Collins' idea. But if you want to earn yourself a halo, you do that! I only hope you don't lose one very good boy friend in the process.'

'I don't see why I should. I heard from Nick again yesterday. He grumbled a bit, and says he's going to spend the week-end sulking, but he has asked me to dinner on Sunday night.'

'He has?' She was surprised. 'Well, well, well. Maybe he's more serious than I thought. When does he get back?'

'Some time today.'

'No wonder you were looking on top of the world!'

I was pleased about Nick, but his return was not the only reason for my feeling so cheerful. I had now been long enough in Observation to see some results, and most of those were very good. Mrs Bird had at last begun to do very well. She had come off the D.I.L. two days ago. Her sons now only appeared in the normal visiting hours, and that afternoon she had felt strong enough to sit propped up in her armchair instead of flopping weakly back when we lifted her out. She had even made a few notes for the book she had been planning in her mind.

Mr Jenkins was now breathing normally and without his tracheotomy tube. There was talk of moving him back to a general ward on Monday. Mr Mulligan was up and about, and sailing home to Brazil next week. He was the fourth generation of his family to be born in Buenos Aires, and had invited us all to call in any time we were in South America. He said his daughters would enjoy meeting the young English ladies who had been so kind to him, and his sons would have much pleasure in meeting so many beautiful young ladies with the skins of lilies and the gentleness of angels.

Mr Browne had done an unexpected round while I was at tea. I met him on the stairs with Mr Bunney. Mr Browne stopped to discuss Frank Sands. 'Still in that deep, frozen coma, poor lad. We'll just have to keep on, Nurse Rowe. Keep on. As for that lad Elkroyd.' He sighed. 'I'll have to think. Later, later.'

I should have liked to ask more, but Mr Bunney was waiting, and the two pundits went on together. Mr Elkroyd was now my most worrying patient, but he was a good patient. He accepted his innumerable spinal punctures, X-rays, and tests with a phlegmatic 'Oh, aye? Let's get on with it, then.' He never grumbled or complained. He endured the increasing pain in his head with the sort of courage more commonly found in the women's wards.

I had been off that morning. In my absence he had had what Wardell described in her midday report as an unpleasant headache. He was now on regular analgesic injections. During the afternoon—and a hospital afternoon stopped at five—he had been more comfortable, and, though his eyes were now giving trouble and his toleration of light was diminishing, he had asked to have his curtains drawn back. After supper he had the worst attack of head pain I had yet seen him suffer.

In my final report before going off duty I said, 'It wasn't a headache, Sister. He was in real pain.' She merely nodded. 'Sister, why are the surgeons still waiting? It's obviously growing.'

'Mr Browne and Mr Muir are well aware of that, Nurse. As you know, they consulted on him again this morning, and Mr Browne was back to see him this afternoon. Both those men are competent and experienced surgeons. They will operate when they see fit, and when there has been time to see the full result of this new drug therapy Elkroyd is receiving. You'll have to be patient, Nurse Rowe.'

'Yes, Sister.' I thought of Tom Elkroyd grunting and gasping with pain just now. The attack had come on shortly before his next injection was due. I had given it seven minutes inside the official limit.

Sister tapped the open Dangerous Drug book with one finger. 'I assume you were aware you gave this too early?'

'Yes, Sister. That's why I asked Mr Browne's houseman to witness for me.'

'I see.' She pressed her lips together. 'You gave it on the houseman's advice?'

'Officially, Sister.' I did not add I had bullied the houseman into being my witness, as she knew that as well as myself. I did add, 'It was my idea.'

She read me a little lecture on obeying the rules of the hospital, reminding me that I was a nurse and not a doctor, and that as a senior staff nurse I was expected to set an example to my juniors. 'Is that understood?'

'Yes, Sister. I'm sorry,' I lied.

'Thank you, Nurse. Good night.'

The senior night nurses came in to hear the full day report as I went out. Their juniors had their report from the senior night staff nurse later. They watched over the ward while the report was in progress.

I changed my shoes, collected my cloak, and was on my way out when a night junior came out of Tom Elkroyd's room.

I stopped. 'How is he now?'

'Asleep, Nurse. Flat out.'

I wanted to believe her. Experience prevented me. He had had an injection, not knock-out drops, and he was working up a resistance to those injections. Each one took longer to work and wore off sooner. I looked at my watch, the closed duty-room door, then, when the junior disappeared into Room Nine, I helped myself to a clean gown and mask, returned to change back into my ward shoes, and went quietly into Room Ten.

Outside it was a glorious midsummer evening, and the sky was pink. In his room it was dark. The curtains were closed, and the only light came from the red-shaded bedside lamp that was on the floor to prevent the rays disturbing him. There was a crimson pool of light round my feet as I stood by his bed.

I did not touch him or speak. He lay with one arm across his eyes, the other hanging over the side of his bed nearest me. He was breathing heavily, as men sometimes breathe in sleep, and often after immense physical effort. The rhythm, however, was too irregular for sleep, but he was doing his best to give the impression he was as flat out as that junior had thought.

As my eyes grew accustomed to the darkness I saw he had shifted the arm across his eyes enough to let him look at me. 'What's this, then?' he muttered between his teeth. 'Doing your overtime, are you?'

'That's right.' His dangling arm had reached for mine. His grip tightened. 'Still playing you up? Hasn't the injection helped?'

73

'Taking its time,' he grunted. 'The bugger keeps coming back—sorry, Nurse.'

'Don't mind me, Tom. I've heard the word.' I stroked his forehead with my free hand as that sometimes soothed him. 'Bad as before?'

'Aye. Oh—nurse—oh, dear—dear—dear . . .' His voice stopped like a tap being turned off as a fresh wave of pain overwhelmed him. First he twisted his head from side to side, but then as the pain increased the bedsprings creaked as his hefty body went rigid. He grabbed the head-rail with one hand, my right arm with the other. My right hand went numb, and the veins on my wrist stood out as if I was wearing a tourniquet.

His face was pouring with sweat and distorted in a grimace that pulled up his upper lip and exposed his gums. He was normally a good-looking man. He did not even look like a man now, and the strangled half-snort, half-scream he gave as the pain let go was animal, not human. Then he dropped his hands and lay exhausted, staring at me.

I did not say anything, At the best, words of sympathy would have been inadequate and at the worst, an insult. I wiped his wet face gently with his flannel, took his pulse, then held his hand in both mine and waited, as he was waiting.

We did not have long to wait. The next wave of pain was shorter and perhaps less violent, but his reserves had taken a terrible beating, and they were running out. Instead of relaxing when it passed, for the first time and for a few seconds he lost control. He tried to get out of bed, he tried to hit his head against the bed-rail, he tried to push me off. Though weakened by pain he was a strong man. It took all my strength and weight to save him from hurting himself.

'Tom! Stop it, at once!' I insisted, gasping. 'Hurting yourself won't help! It'll only bring the pain back! It'll bring it back! Stop fighting me!'

He had just wrenched off my hands from his chest when that got through. 'What's this, then? Am I off my rocker?' He flopped against me and dropped his head on my shoulder. By now I was sitting on his bed. 'Not hurt you, have I, luv?'

'Of course not.' I held him until his breathing grew less laboured, then helped him lie down again. 'You're not off your rocker. You've just had too much pain and a lot of dope.' I took his pulse again. 'It is working now.'

'Aye.' He closed his eyes. 'And time you clocked off.'

'I'm in no hurry.'

He began to cry weakly a few seconds later. I had never seen him in tears before. I did not enjoy the sight, but they were a good safety-valve, so I did not try to stop him. He did not hear the door open or notice Robert's masked face looking round and then backing out again. After he had wept he was able to sleep.

The senior night staff nurse was in the corridor when I let myself out of his room. 'Still here, Rowe? Sister said you had gone. She has.'

Her name was Hazel Carter. She was a nice girl and not one to bother over the ethics of a day nurse being around at night. In the changing room I explained what had happened. 'You might warn the men on their night rounds that if the surgeons are going to hang around much longer someone had better step up Tom's dope. Much more of things as they are and he'll go right off!'

'I tackled Henry Todd about stepping it up last night.' Henry Todd was Mr Browne's senior registrar. 'He said he'd already written Elkroyd up for the maximum inside the safety rule, and his boss didn't like being asked to break it. I could have killed the man! Who cares what a flaming consultant likes or doesn't like when it's a question of stopping pain? These men and their rules! Know what he asked me?' I shook my head. 'Was I prepared to turn Tom Elkroyd into a morphine addict?'

'What did you say?'

'That if we didn't do something fast to save his sanity as well as his life, he wouldn't have any future in which to be an addict. Then he threw this new stuff we are giving Tom at me. He said we must give it a chance.'

'Sister said I must be patient.'

Hazel's reply was unrepeatable. I repeated it to myself several times as I stormed down the block stairs. Robert was sitting on the windowsill nearest the foot of our stairs in the ground-floor corridor.

He got off and came up to me. 'How's Elkroyd now?'

'Asleep.'

'Good.'

'Yes,' I snapped bitterly, 'it is. He can use the sleep after having me practically sitting on his chest as the only way of keeping him from trying to bang his head against the wall. I'm not all that light—and nor was the pain he was in.'

'That I gathered from the state he was in when I looked round the door. I wanted another look at his eyes, but that can wait until my night round, and if he's still sleeping, tomorrow.'

Tom Elkroyd was Mr Muir's only patient in Observation, and, as Mr Muir had been called in by his colleague, Tom remained primarily Mr Browne's patient and in the general charge of the cranial residents. But Mr Muir was involved, which involved Robert. I had noticed he got on well with Henry Todd, and he was by a few months Henry's senior. Henry might pay more attention to him than he had to Hazel Carter, whom I guessed had rubbed him up the wrong way by demanding too openly that he write up that new script for Tom. In general it was possible to get our residents to order exactly what the nursing staff wanted, but it had to be done tactfully. Once any doctor, no matter how junior, suspected a nurse of teaching him his job, nothing would shift him. Admittedly I had bullied that houseman into being my witness, but there had been tears in my large blue eyes when he looked like refusing. He did not know that they were tears of rage, and I did not tell him. They got me what I wanted for Tom, and to help him more if necessary I would weep on Robert's shoulder.

I had first to swallow my fury with surgeons in general and dislike of Robert in particular. I asked meekly if he could spare me a few minutes. 'There's something I want to know about Tom Elkroyd.'

He looked at me thoughtfully, then up and down the long corridor. Two junior night nurses and a posse of white coats were some distance off but coming our way. 'We can't talk here. Let's go to Eyes.'

The Ophthalmic Department was closed at night but left unlocked in case it should be needed. Patients with eye injuries or ailments who came in during the night were first seen in Casualty.

He switched on the light in Sister Eyes' glass-walled office. 'We'll use this.' He put a second chair at the desk. 'Well, Anna? Do you really want to know something? Or am I right in suspecting you just want something?'

I hesitated, wondering what was the best approach. We had not worked together since I was too junior to have any direct dealings with the men. He was the only man on our staff I knew better out of as opposed to in a white coat. As a man he disliked frills. I cut them out. 'Both. Why has Brown-plus-E got this later, later, fixation? And if it's got to be later, why can't he be given enough dope to take the edge right off? I know that's going to mean stepping it up again and again. I know the rules. I've nursed addicts. I know they aren't pretty. But if you had come into Tom's room a few minutes earlier you wouldn't have seen a pretty sight either.' I told him briefly all that had happened. 'Quite apart from how much good is the memory of cracking once going to do his morale, how much good is all that thrashing about going to do his head? Can't he have more? Surely if the bosses say yes, no-one can question them?'

'No. They make the rules.' He took a clean ophthalmic chart from Sister Eyes' file and starting doing sums. 'Do you realise how much he's already having in the twenty-four hours?'

'Yes.' I gave the figure without having to look at his. 'But can't you set his age, weight, and general condition against that? And in any case, it just isn't enough.'

He said, 'There's talk of switching him to another line.'

I asked, 'Can anything touch the white poppy for pain-killing?'

He did not answer. He frowned at his figures, then took off his glasses. 'Was he truly maniacal?'

'Not truly. He went over the edge, but he did respond. Now it's happened once, he may lose his nerve. I'm worried about next time.'

'Yes. That could be a problem. I'll talk to Henry Todd. The move has to be his, as you know.' He replaced his glasses to look at me. 'Why haven't you discussed this with him?'

77

'No chance today. I did see Browne this afternoon, but he was in a hurry, and this hadn't happened then. And then you were there.'

'Yes. I was.' He drew a diagram of the brain on that blank chart-back and added the outline of a skull. 'You asked, "Why later, later?" The answer's simple. *Pro tem.* he's inoperable.'

'God! No!' Then I realised he had used that *pro tem.* 'Why?'

'It's sitting here.' He drew a tiny circle. 'See why?'

I could not say anything for a few moments. I stared at his drawing until the mist cleared. 'I knew it was deep, but not as deep as that. You're sure?'

'Afraid so. He's got the symptoms of one a little higher. That put everyone off the track at first. But it's way down here, and the only way to get to it is to go in this way'— he sketched an imaginary line with a finger—'slap through that.'

'That'll kill him.'

'Yes. Hence the hold-up. You know this new stuff he's having——'

'Which is doing sweet Fanny Adams——'

'Anna, no-one can be sure of that. He hasn't had it long enough. There is just a chance it may inhibit this specific growth.'

'An outside chance. I read it up.'

He glanced at me. 'How? It's too new to have reached the textbooks.'

'I discovered that. I asked Senior Sister Tutor. She got hold of some pamphlets for me. They said it had had a limited success, appeared harmless, and could be useful.'

He was watching me more keenly. 'That was very enterprising of you.'

I was too concerned by the main issue to bother to take umbrage at the implication behind that remark.

'I'm nursing him. I don't like giving patients drugs I know nothing about.'

'Reasonable. When you read it up did you read of its side-effects?'

'No. Far as I can remember, the pamphlets didn't give them. Why?'

'It seems to have one odd and apparently safe temporary effect. It toughens this.' He scribbled on his drawing. 'When—and if—that happens with him he'll start dropping things. Then he won't be able to grip anything. Then it may be safe to risk going in—and Brown-plus-E may take that risk. It'll still be a very dodgy business.'

'And he'll have to be told that.'

'He will. As he'll be conscious throughout, that means his co-operation as well as consent. Think he'll give it?'

I nodded heavily. 'He's expecting something like this. He's no fool. He knows we are not doing all these tests for fun. He's very worried about his family, and he misses them a lot. Not that he'll ever admit that. But when he has to be asked for consent I'll bet anything he'll say, "Oh, aye? Let's get on with it then."'

We were quiet for a little while, then I thanked him for explaining.

'Not at all. I would have done this before. I assumed you knew.'

'No. I've been meaning to ask Henry Todd, but he always has to rush away after rounds. It's been the same with Dick Richards [the houseman]. I can scarcely waylay Brown-plus-E.' I paused. 'Does Sister Observation know?'

'It was all discussed in front of her this morning.'

'Then why couldn't she tell me?'

'Possibly because all this is still mainly hypothetical, and Sabby Wardell has always preferred to deal in facts.' He stood up. 'We covered the lot? Then let's go.' As he switched off the light and followed me out he asked, 'Did Tom see me?'

'No.'

'Good. He'd not like that.'

I said, 'I am afraid he's not going to like my having been there. He's never let anyone see him weep before.'

'I doubt he'll mind your being with him. He likes you. He calls you "his Nurse Rowe".' We were back in the main corridor. 'I'll have that wee talk with Henry,' he said, and we went our separate ways.

Back in the Home a message in our rack said Mr Dexter had telephoned Nurse Rowe twice since 9 p.m. Nick rang again some time later. 'What train shall I meet on Sunday?'

'I honestly don't know. It'll depend on Jill Collins. We'll be coming back together.'

He grumbled, 'Three dinners instead of two! Back to the old drawing-board.'

I smiled reluctantly. I was glad to have him back in town, but not yet in a laughing mood. 'Nick, perhaps we should call this off. Jill may have other plans.'

He said, 'You wouldn't be trying to give me the brush-off again, my love?'

'Of course not! It's just that I can't answer for Jill. It's late to ring her now.'

'Then I must ring you over the week-end. What's the number?'

'I don't know. Sorry.'

'It'll be in the book, I guess, under Martin. Wasn't he the last owner? Right. I'll find it.'

'Nick,' I said, 'you are a dear.'

'I am not! I am a nut! I shouldn't be on speaking terms with you for standing me up for a scrubbing-brush! It's just that I hate eating alone. Ruins my digestion. But don't think I'm not cross with you, darling. I am raging,' he added cheerfully. 'I shall now ring off and try and cool down working out a nice new hyperbolic paraboloid roof.'

'A nice what?'

'A hyperbolic paraboloid roof. That's a roof that contains all the advantages of a double-curved surface like a dome, but is much simpler to construct, as straight beams can be incorporated. You follow me, of course?'

'Of course. Into the darkness.'

He laughed. 'Never mind, sweetie. I love you the way you are; though, after the way you treat me, God knows why! See you Sunday!'

I went back to my room, thinking I should be walking on air. It was not Nick's fault I was not. He did not know Tom Elkroyd, and even had he known about him he was unlikely to have been able to understand my present feelings about Tom. Had I attempted to explain my anxiety on the telephone, either Nick would have tried to laugh me out of it or he would have made some typically lay crack about Tom being responsible for my trying to avoid him. I doubted if anything would persuade him, or any other outsider, that it was possible to become emotionally involved with a patient without sex entering into it. I had felt as close to Mrs Bird, to dozens, if not hundreds, of other women and children, as well as to other men patients, as I now did to Tom. Perhaps, I thought, leaning out of my window and looking across to the lights in Observation, only another nurse or doctor could wholly understand how that could happen. It had made sense to Robert, and without either of us having to put it into words he had given me the impression that Tom Elkroyd mattered to him quite as much as he did to me. Nick might well have a word for that too, but it would have been too infantile—and off the mark—to be an insult. Robert, I decided, had been rather nice in Eyes. Perhaps his coming to Observation was not going to be such a bad thing after all. We did not have to see much of each other, and when we did there were invariably other people around. I had seen he was shaken by Tom's cracking. If he did manage to get something done to prevent that recurring I should be very grateful to him—which would certainly be a novel sensation.

Tom's injections were altered during that night. The new script was written, dated, and signed by Mr Browne. Tom was not told of his increased dose. He told me he had had a right good night and felt much better. I had not intended mentioning last night, until he apologised for playing me up like a right mug. 'Happen you'll be used to that?'

'I've known it happen, Tom. I won't say I'm used to it.'

'Soft, are you?' he grinned. 'Like my Betty.'

Sister came in. 'More comfortable, Mr Elkroyd? Good.' She turned to me. 'I'd like a word with you when you have finished in here, please, Nurse Rowe.'

After she had gone Tom asked, 'The Sister's not having you on the mat, Nurse?'

'I hope not. I don't think so. She probably wants to tell me something about one of my other patients.'

'You'll know your workmates, Nurse.'

He adjusted the dark glasses he had chosen to wear as

81

he wanted his curtains open. 'But the look the Sister just give you put me in mind of our foreman when he's of a mind to have one of the lads on mat.'

Robert was having coffee with Sister when I reached the duty-room. He lowered his cup. 'Am I in the way, Sister?'

'No, Mr Gordon. This won't take a moment. Come in and shut the door, please, Nurse Rowe.'

That, in mid-morning, was an ominous sign. It heralded bad news or a lecture. Robert stood up. 'I do have a lot to get through as it's my week-end off. Perhaps I should get on, Sister.'

'There's another message from Mr Browne I have to give you for Mr Muir.' She looked from him to me. 'Nurse Rowe, Mr Turner came in on his own to look at Mrs Bird while you were with Frank Sands. I did not call you. Mr Turner was very satisfied with Mrs Bird. He wishes her to remain with us for another week and then transfer to a general ward. Later he wants her to spend at least a month in our convalescent home. I have been in touch with Sister Matilda and reserved her a bed for next Friday. I have contacted the almoners and will let you know when they give me details about a convalescent bed.'

This was all good news. I was very pleased and said so.

'It is pleasing,' she agreed coldly. 'What did not please me was the condition of Mrs Bird's room. I do not expect to have to complain to a staff nurse of your seniority about untidiness, but I was appalled by the disgraceful state in which you have allowed your team to leave that room. I had to apologise to Mr Turner. I do not care to have to apologise for my nurses!'

I did not care to be scolded like a junior in front of a third person. There was only one thing I could say: 'I'm sorry, Sister.'

She inclined her head. 'Leave the door open as you go, Nurse.'

Robert was gazing at some notes. He did not look up as I let myself out. It was something that he knew how to behave, even if she did not.

I found Addy in the linen-room some minutes later. She made soothing noises while I exploded to her.

'Is Mrs Bird's room really untidy?'

'It is not! I've just checked. It's spotless, apart from a few notes spread over her bed-table and a few reference books on her locker. Old Turner wouldn't have objected —and it isn't even as if it's his morning for a round up here! I don't know why Wardell has to beef—and if she must, why couldn't she wait until she had me alone?'

'She never does,' said Addy, placidly refolding and then replacing a pillow-slip that had been put on the shelf the wrong way round. 'She's taken me apart in front of the girls, the men, and, once, even old Sir Julius. She's laid off us a bit lately, but you'll just have to get used to it when she is in one of her moods. I noticed she had the makings of one this morning. You done anything to upset her?'

'Don't think so.' Then I remembered last night. I explained to Addy. 'Would Robert Gordon have told her? If he has, why should she object?'

'Oh! Oh! That explains it.'

'It does? How? What's so wrong with my discussing one of my patients with one of his registrars in my own time?'

'There's nothing wrong with your discussing a patient, love, but there are those who would say you picked the wrong registrar.' She smiled at my expression. 'Hadn't you caught on?'

'Robert Gordon and Wardell—— No? Since when?'

'They do say since he came back to Barny's. They are always around together when they're off. Hadn't you heard?' I shook my head. 'Most people have. I haven't mentioned it before as Wardell's private life is none of our business, and as you are so patently allergic to Robert Gordon there was no need to warn you off. I'll tell you now it has struck me your attitude to him might be one reason why you have so far got on very well with Wardell.'

'I wouldn't say that——'

'I would. I've worked with her longer than you have, and I know what she's like when someone or something gets under her skin. We all suffer!' She dealt with another pillow-slip. 'Why do you suppose Frances Gilroy left this ward?'

Frances Gilroy was my predecessor. 'I thought because she wanted to go back to the theatre?' Addy was shaking her head. 'Wrong? Wardell?'

'Wardell. She didn't hit it off with Gilroy, and in a few weeks gave her such hell—and the rest of us—that Gilroy landed up in Matron's Office in tears, begging for a transfer. Matron smoothed that over by sending us Trimmer, smartly, but, as she was too junior to be second staff, she was temporary until you were free.'

I was intrigued and too amused to stay angry. 'I never thought the day would come when anyone would get het up about me and Robert Gordon! Are they that serious?'

'That I don't know. I know what I hear, but I never believe half I hear. What I do know is, Wardell has a very possessive streak. Haven't you noticed? *My* ward. *My* patients. *My* nurses. *My*. *My*. *My*. So—*my* man.'

'She can have him. Any day of the week and twice on Sundays, even though he has done *my* Mr Elkroyd a very good turn.'

'Robbie Gordon's a good doctor, love.' She was smiling. 'Or is that something else you haven't heard?'

The Elizabeth junior staff nurse was leaving the diningroom as I went into lunch. 'I hoped I'd see you, Rowe. Sister Elizabeth says could you look in on her as soon as possible?'

At lunch I looked out for Harriet, but she did not come in. I wanted to ask her why she was slipping. She heard every grapevine buzz in Cas., but had not said a word to me about Wardell and Robert. If, by some miracle, she had not heard either, I wanted to tell her.

As she did not turn up I left the dining-room a little early and went along to Elizabeth. Jill saw me in her duty-room. Her sleeves were up, her face was masked, and her eyes were troubled. She closed the door herself. 'Rowe, I have problems.'

She had five women on the D.I.L. and three major ops. coming off that afternoon. Her senior staff nurse was having the day off. 'My junior is a good child, but this is her first staffing job. I can't leave her to carry my ward alone as it is now. Sister Mary'll understand. My senior's on early tomorrow, so I'll get down to Wylden by an early train. Now'—she took a key from a desk drawer—'this is the cottage back-door. Sister Mary sent it up yesterday. She is going in today to light the boiler and make our beds, and then she's off to Hayhurst to visit one of her ex-Matrons. Where's that letter? Ah, here.' She scanned it. 'The Matron's got rheumatism. Hayhurst is forty miles from Wylden, and she'll be back on the evening coach. We will find food in the larder and are to help ourselves if we get there first.' She gave me the key. 'Rowe, I'm sorry about this. Will you cope alone? And rustle up supper for Sister Mary's return? Bless you, my child!'

When I got back to Observation I contrasted Jill's approach with Wardell's. Just to see Jill put me in a good humour. I had grown accustomed to Wardell's detachment, but for the rest of my time on duty that day she was not merely detached with me—she froze into a human iceberg whenever she saw me. She did not stop at freezing. Nothing I did was right.

Mr Muir came up with Robert and a houseman to have another look at Tom Elkroyd. It so happened Sister was occupied with Sir Julius Charing. We had the same off-duty for once because it was my free week-end. I took no chances, even in her absence. I smiled at Mr Muir and his houseman and ignored Robert, and if that seemed hard after last night I was sorry, but my instinct for self-preservation was strong.

Sister was free to join us after Mr Muir had finished his examination and was having a little chat with Tom about his wife and children. He surprised me and went up in my estimation by knowing all their names, ages, and interests. 'This the wee laddie, George, who already wants to become a doctor? That's grand. The country needs doctors.'

Robert had been ignoring me as I was him. When Sister escorted the men out he lingered to take a small chess-set from his pocket and lay it on the bed-table. Tom jerked a thumb upward and Robert nodded back.

I stayed to turn Tom's pillows and straighten his bed. 'I didn't know you liked chess. I'd have got you a set.'

'I've not played the game since I was a lad. My old Dad used to like it. Mr Gordon asked if I'd like to have a go when he come in late last night. I'd woken, like. Not for long. That Mr Gordon was sitting on my locker when I woke. Often comes in and sits of a night, he does.'

'I didn't know that. You have long chats?'

'Oh, aye. Times we'll chat, times he'll just sit. Puts me in mind of my mate Sid. Sid'll sup his beer all night and not say nowt. He's been a right good mate to me, has Sid. I miss him. A lad misses his mates,' he added apologetically.

'I'll bet he does. I hope you'll be back home with your mates very soon.'

'Oh, aye. See you Monday, then?'

'Yes.' I hated leaving him, even though I had a very good team and he liked all the girls. 'Have a good weekend—and take care of yourself.'

He grinned. 'I'll not have to do that, Nurse. I'll have half the doctors and nurses in this hospital on job for me! And you'll be going down to the country, then?'

'That's right.' I had told him about Sister Mary's cottage. 'Wylden's a lovely village.'

'That's what Mr Gordon said, like. He's off to visit his old grandad or summat in those parts. Happen you'll be seeing him down there?'

Oh, Lor', I thought, no! I said, 'I don't know. I'm not expecting to see him.'

'Oh, aye,' said Tom. 'No telling, is there then?'

CHAPTER SIX

A SUMMER EVENING IN THE COTTAGE

THE blossom had vanished from the apple and cherry orchards. In the hop gardens the young hops were beginning to climb their poles. The corn was still green and the hay was golden. The evening rush hour was on when I left London, but in the hayfields round Wylden the tractors and hay-balers were still busy, their drivers stripped to the waist and tanned as Latins. A few of the very young men had bare heads, their hair streaked by the sun and the hay-dust. The others wore old Army berets to a man, and the berets were so coated with dust that it was impossible to distinguish the original regimental colour underneath.

I was the only passenger to get off the Astead bus at Wylden. The village main street was deserted, and the whole place had a deceptively sleepy air. Deceptively, as Wylden was a very prosperous agricultural village, and June one of the hardest working months of the agricultural year. Work on the farms began at 7 a.m., if not earlier, and went on as long as the light lasted. A few old men were working in their gardens, and two were sitting on a bench outside The Swan talking to the middle-aged landlord. The door to the public bar was open—the bar was empty. The landlord was the only man under sixty-five in sight. He wished me a civil 'good evening' as I went by, and, even though I did not know him, called after me, 'Miss Bush should be back by seven-thirty on the Hayhurst coach, miss.'

'Thank you.' I was amused by this reminder of the efficiency of the Wylden grapevine. 'Lovely evening.'

The landlord agreed. One of the old men shook his head. 'Not doing the soft fruit much good.'

The street was wide. The old houses on either side leant companionably against each other, as if they had grown out of the land rather than been built. The square Norman tower of the church would have delighted Mrs Bird. It had been added to the church by one of the Conqueror's men, but it was still called 'the new tower'. The written records of the church went back one thousand years. The first records dated from one hundred years after the re-building of the church when the original building, itself old and wooden, had been burnt down by some itinerant Vikings.

It was difficult to believe I was less than sixty miles from London. Wylden was another world after the heat and noise of London today. The warmth of the evening sun was gentle, the pavements did not steam, the air was clean and smelt of hay, not exhaust and diesel fumes, and the whirr of tractors, combines, and balers in the background was as soothing as a drowsy bee.

In the rush to change, get my train, and then catch the cross-country bus, with two minutes to spare, I had had no time to realise that the new tension of falling out with Wardell today, coming on top of the general strain of working in Observation, had left me unusually tense and exhausted. I had gone to sleep in the bus, and the driver-conductor had obligingly woken me at the stop before Wylden. Sauntering towards Sister Mary's cottage, I felt myself consciously unwinding, and was suddenly very glad to have this opportunity to get right away from London and Nick for a week-end. I had recently discovered I was getting very confused about Nick Dexter, but had kept shelving the problem as something to think on when less busy. It had niggled at the back of my mind. I knew I found him attractive, so attractive that when I was in his presence I was incapable of thinking of anything else; yet when he was not around I kept forgetting he existed.

Had there been no David it would never have occurred to me to question whether or not I was in love. Previously I had leapt into a relationship first and thought it over afterwards. But, having had one man ask me for his ring back, I had no intention of allowing that scene to be repeated. As I would not sleep with Nick, from his letters and that last phone call I had the impression he was paving the way to ask me to marry him, and, being an impulsive type, it was not going to be long before matters came to a head. He was no man to hang around while a girl made up her mind, as his behaviour with Sabby Wardell showed. Another 'no' from me would finish things between us. Did I want to risk losing him? Could I bear to lose him? The thought of life without Nick nearly settled my problem, and then I began wondering about life with Nick. I reached Sister Mary's gate more confused than ever.

Frank must have scythed the small front garden in the last day or so. The grass heaped under the hedge was still fresh. The flower-beds against the cottage had been cleared of weeds and were filled with pinks, pansies, and an old lavender bush. The beds looked very nice and already typical of Sister Mary.

The cottage was very old, half-timbered, and built round a centre chimney. The roof tiles were a pale orange, and the lower brickwork was red-grey. The white paint on the timbered part was dirty and blistering, but the wood was good, and the tiles and bricks were in perfect condition. Sister Mary had been very lucky. A lot of people would have been willing to pay a lot of money for the place. I wondered how much extra old Mr Norris had paid. If Sister Mary knew, which I doubted, she had not told me. Then, inevitably, I thought of Robert the night of that party and how different he had seemed in Eyes last night. Last night while we talked about Tom I had forgotten the party, David, even how infuriated Robert had made me about this particular week-end. Now I had to see his point about that. I suddenly remembered all the people who had promised to help Sister Mary with this cottage, and how all but Jill and myself had now vanished. I felt more peeved than smug, and went round to the back to let myself in.

The back was to the weather side. The roof there was windowless and sloped down to a few inches above the kitchen door. As I put the key in the lock something crackled behind me. I glanced round incuriously. A mountain of weeds was smouldering on a bonfire—the obvious origin of that crackle. Frank had been as busy round the back as in the front. The nettles that had been knee-high under the wide old apple-tree had gone. The vegetable patch had been cleared and dug over. The back garden was bare, apart from the apple-tree. It was covered with leaves and minute pellets of apples.

An apple hit me on the shoulder as I opened the door. I looked round again. There was no wind, but the apple-leaves were stirring. I went closer to investigate, and gasped. 'Nick! What are you doing in that tree?'

He wore a London suit, but his smile as he swung himself down took me back to our first meeting.

'Darling, you know I am incapable of resisting trees and redheads! I've been waiting for you.' He looked round. 'Where's your bright and breezy pal? And where is old Miss Bush? I've looked in all the windows, but there's no sign of life within. Isn't the old lady expecting you?' He took my hands. 'Or is this just a convenient hide-out? Tell me the worst! What's his name? What's he got that I haven't got?'

His presence was having its habitual effect. I went weak at the knees and grinned like the Cheshire Cat while I explained. 'Now you tell me what you are doing here?'

'If you must know, my sweet, London had no charms without you. I felt lost. So, I thought, why not have a quiet week-end too? Nick the Nut has decided to go no more a-roving—at least, not till Monday. I rang to offer you a lift, but you had gone. So I got in the car and put my foot down.' He picked up my suitcase and followed me into the kitchen. 'I've got my old room at The Swan.'

'And the landlord didn't tell you Sister Mary's in Hayhurst? He told me!'

'The new chap across the way? No. He was heaving barrels in his cellar when I checked in. He said, "How do?" and I said "Ah!" Having been here before, as you will recollect, I speak the language.' He kissed me, then looked about him and shuddered. 'God! Look at these walls. Sepia! Ugh! In a slit of a room that faces due north. White's the only possible colour in here, picked out with —what? Orange, to attract every scrap of light. And as for those curtains ... The only thing to do with them is shove 'em straight on that bonfire!' He reached for the ceiling. 'This is far too low!'

'All old houses have low ceilings.'

'Not this low.' He tapped the ceiling, took out a penknife, and began scraping. 'I thought so. Some vandal has used plaster to hide the beams. There's good oak above this.'

'Hey! Stop that! You might be right, but this isn't my cottage, and Sister Mary may not like'—a telephone was ringing—'where's the phone?'

He found it under a pile of rugs in the microscopic front hall, and moaned with disgust at the dark-blue figured wallpaper as he handed me the receiver.

'What's this number?' I covered the mouthpiece. 'Shift those rugs, Nick. I can't read it.'

'Wylden 227,' he replied automatically. 'Looked it up.'

'Sensible man.' I gave it over the phone.

'Isn't that you, Nurse Rowe?' It was Sister Mary's voice. 'Dearie, is Miss Collins there? What's that? I can't hear you too clearly.'

I bellowed, 'I'm sorry, Sister. Miss Collins can't leave her ward until the morning.'

'You can't get her to leave what, dearie? Never mind.

90

You can give her a message.' She then explained her friend had summer flu in addition to chronic rheumatism. 'Dear Edith is too poorly to be left. I have asked her doctor to call either this evening or in the morning and must await events. I shall telephone you again tomorrow. I am very sorry to leave all my work to you dear girls, but I know you will understand how I am placed. Be sure and make yourselves quite at home; do what you think fit, but please do not work too hard. I must go now as dear Edith is calling.'

I replaced the receiver. 'Hear that?'

'Most.' He draped an arm round my shoulders, and we went into the sitting-room. 'Seems we've won the jackpot.'

'How do you make that out?' I asked unnecessarily, as it was obvious what he was getting at.

He rubbed his face against mine. 'You don't need me to spell that out, sweetie.'

I disentangled myself from him. 'Then maybe you need me to spell it out, dear. The answer is still no.'

Probably I should not have been surprised by his surprise, but I was. 'Hell, Anna! You can't pass up a break like this! We've this place to ourselves'—he caught my shoulders and drew me against him—'and I so want to love you. You know that.'

I moved my head back to look at him. It was not easy with the grip he had on me. 'I thought you never made a pass unless the girl was willing?'

'Don't pretend you aren't willing, darling. Not now I know how you feel about me.'

Until that moment possibly he had, and been right. Until that moment I had always been very scathing about the girls who let themselves get into much this situation and then complained when the inevitable happened. After this I would be far more charitable about my fellow-women.

'I'm fond of you, Nick, but——' and I could not go on as he was kissing me.

Eventually I freed my hands and caught his face. 'Nick, lay off! This isn't going to do you any good——'

'It's doing me a power of good!'

'No!' I pushed him away and took a few steps back. 'I'm serious about this, Nick! So cool down—or go.'

'Darling, don't be childish.' He grabbed at me. Only my training made me able to resist the overpowering urge to slap his face. But the truism that violence begets violence was engrained in me, and, as he was so much larger than myself, in any physical struggle I was bound to lose. That did not mean I was helpless, though it took me a few seconds to realise it. Then, as weeping was something I could do quite easily, provided I thought a distressing thought, I thought hard about Tom Elkroyd's future and the tears poured down my face.

As I had hoped, they acted on Nick like a cold shower. 'Oh, God.' He dropped his hands. 'Don't weep. I can't stand weeping women.'

'Sorry,' I wailed, 'can't help it.' As he had removed his shoulder I wept on the mantelpiece.

I was now feeling sorry for myself as well as for Tom, and almost as sorry for Nick. He was not a real wolf, or tears would not have stopped him. He merely had a very simple approach to women, and all that talk about understanding my attitude had only been part of the patter. He had assumed my talk was my patter. I clearly had him as much out of his depth now as Sabby Wardell had done. Being so attractive, he was not used to failure. He obviously had no idea what to do or say next. While I mopped my face he stared at the fireplace with an expression that was sulky, hurt, and puzzled.

'How could Gervase Martin live with that eyesore!' he muttered.

'It is hideous. It's not old, surely?'

'Only about fifty years old.' He tapped the fireside wall absently. 'The moronic vandal who shoved up that kitchen ceiling must have put in this wall. It's false.' He dug in his penknife. 'I've gone through. The original open fireplace must be behind it.' He noticed the smoke marks on the ceiling. 'No wonder this ruddy thing doesn't draw properly. How could it, with the main flue half choked?'

I said, 'I seem to remember Sister Mary asking about this and Mr Martin saying he hadn't had the chimney swept for years. Won't that clear it?'

'Doubt it.' He was less sulky and growing interested. 'How old do you think this is?'

'Two—three hundred years?'

'More like four or five.' He roamed the room, tapping the walls. 'The chaps who built it knew how to build, even though this is probably only standing on a few inches of foundations. But it's stood a few centuries. And they knew all about draughts and chimneys. Their chimneys work and don't smoke, provided no fool messes around with them. That's when the trouble starts. This wall'—he slapped it hard, and the sound was hollow—'should come down. Then this room'll be bigger and warmer.'

'Won't that cost a lot?'

'Not all that much. It generally costs as much to get a building wrong as right. As your old girl is starting from scratch'—he now slapped himself—'where's my pad? Just my luck! I left it in town.'

He was getting sulky again. I said quickly. 'Hang on. I've a writing-pad in my case. I thought I might have time to write home.' I fetched it. 'This do?'

'Have to. Got a pencil?'

I only had a pen. He had his own and used it. His calculations soothed him. He said more pleasantly, 'Looks as if I'm going to have that quiet week-end after all.'

That gave me another surprise. I had been expecting him to slam out and drive back to town. 'Nick, I'm sorry.'

'Hell,' he said, 'so am I—that you are such a pig-headed female. But I may as well stay on. I don't feel like driving back with this headache.'

'Headache?' He did not go in for ailments. 'I'm sorry. Taken anything for it?'

'Not bad enough. It's only the result of this.' He raised the hair above his right temple and exposed a small bump. 'I did this when I walked into a cupboard yesterday.'

I did not touch the bump as that did not seem a good idea. It looked purely superficial. 'Bad luck. Did you see anyone about it?'

'In Barny's? God, no! They'd just tell me to take more water with it.' He picked up the pad. 'Can I look around upstairs, or will you burst into tears again?'

Perhaps irrationally, perhaps not, I was now feeling guilty towards him. 'Go ahead. I'll make us some tea.'

'A typical nurse's reaction,' he said, and went upstairs.

I did not hurry with the tea. I heard him grumbling to himself above about vandals who called themselves builders, art-masters who called themselves artists, and nurses who called themselves women and behaved as if they were stuffed with straw. After a while he reserved his complaints for builders only.

He did not come down for about forty minutes. 'Where's that tea, love?'

'Coming up.' I switched on the kettle again. 'Sorry. It's gone off the boil.'

He looked at me crossly, then saw the funny side, and we both laughed. 'I suppose,' he said, 'you now expect me to stand you dinner at The Swan?'

'Some such notion did cross my mind. I crossed it off again.'

'Hungry? Serve you right!'

'Actually, I'm not. It's been too hot in town.' The kettle boiled. 'Are you?'

'Not now, dear,' he jeered, then laughed again. 'I'll never discover why I put up with you, Anna. We'll go over and eat later. This tea'll be just the job for my migraine.'

The atmosphere was less tense but still had a slight edge. We sat over tea for a long time, talking only occasionally. The silences were not unpleasant, but they were noticeable. With each silence we seemed to slide a little further apart.

I asked if he often had migraines.

'First I've had.'

'How do you know it's a migraine?' I yawned, and apologised. 'The country air.'

'If you had taken my advice and gone to bed early——'

'Nick tell me about your migraine! How do you know it's one?'

'God, you nurses! How? Hell, one of our draughtsmen get's 'em.' He fingered his right eye as if he had something in it. 'He told me today he always gets these flashing lights.'

'What flashing lights?' I stopped feeling sleepy. 'How long have you had 'em?'

'I dunno. Started yesterday. Quite a firework display. This chap in our office says he gets them in both eyes.'

'You've only got them in one? Which one?'

'Right.' He waved his hand above that eye. 'Round here.'

'Only lights? Anything else?'

He hesitated. 'Well—this'll sound daft——'

'Go on.'

'I seem to be having a special brand of migraine. I've got a sort of shadow. Here.' He waved his hand as before.

'Only a shadow? Can you see through it?'

'Over the top. It's rather like a black penny. I think it's your fault. It's only come on since you arrived. It seems to be moving up. Does it matter?'

I did not answer at once. I had to get my mental breath. I had worked four months in an ophthalmic ward in my third year. I recognised his symptoms very well.

'Nick,' I said evenly, 'I have to tell you something. Before I do you must promise to sit perfectly still while you listen. That's important. That black penny does matter. It matters so much that you have got to see a doctor and get to a hospital tonight.'

'Are you out of your mind?' He would have jumped up had I not leapt from my chair and held him in his by leaning on his shoulders. 'What is all this?'

'Ever heard of a detached retina?'

'Vaguely. So?'

I explained what that could entail without yet giving him the whole picture. Then I insisted he moved, without jerking, into the sitting-room and lay down on the still dust-covered sofa. 'That's it. Fine. You stay here while I get one of the local G.P.s. I can remember some names from the Mat. Unit. Then he'll get you into Astead General.'

'I am not going into Astead General!' Again but for my hands on his shoulders he would have bounced up. 'If I have to go to any hospital I'm going back to Barny's.'

'My dear, it's too far——'

'I got down in under two hours. I can get back in less now as there'll be less traffic. By the time you've rustled up a local G.P. and he's rustled up an ambulance—which I won't take—I could be back in town. If you don't want me to drive, you drive me.'

95

'No. It's too risky. You must see a doctor here.'

'Get one if you want. You'll be wasting your time.'

There was no alternative, so I told him all I had left unsaid. It did not upset him as much as I had expected, because he did not believe me. He reminded me I was a nurse, not a doctor, and he had been told all nurses always took the gloomiest view. 'I am not going to get stuck out of town. I don't mind seeing a Barny's man. I know most of them seem to know their jobs. I'm not letting any country G.P. fool around with my eyes.'

A solution dawned on me. It was not one I cared to use, but it seemed I had no alternative. 'I'm not taking you back to Barny's without a doctor's O.K. for the journey. I may be able to reach one of our men in Astead. If not, it'll have to be a local man.'

He caught my wrist. 'Who is this convenient man in Astead? And why?'

'His name is Robert Gordon. He's off this week-end and, I've heard, visiting Astead. He may be down by now. If he is it'll be sheer luck, as he is doing Eyes at present. I don't know if you know him?' I added, as Robert's name had not been mentioned between us. 'He was at Sister Mary's party.'

'I know Robbie Gordon.' He smiled wryly. 'And you are going to summon him to my aid? Here's a turn-up for the book!'

I guessed from that he had heard about Robert and Sabby Wardell. I did not dwell on it, having other things on my mind. 'Promise not to move, Nick? I'll ring him.'

I could not find a telephone book so I had to ask Enquiries for Mr Norris's number. His housekeeper answered my call.

'Mr Gordon, miss? Yes, he is here, but Mr Gordon and his guest have just sat down to dinner with Mr Norris. My old gentleman does not like having his meals disturbed. Can I take a message and ask Mr Gordon to ring you back later? No? Oh, dear. Very good, miss. What name, please?'

I did not have to wait long.

'Well, Anna?' demanded Robert. 'What's this about?'

I went back to Nick two minutes later. 'He's coming.'

'Did he mind being hauled out on his free evening?'

'If he did he didn't say so.'

He eyed me speculatively. 'Not only pig-headed, bloody-minded, and pessimistic, but intrepid. You are quite a girl, darling. Or was Peter Graveny wrong to advise me not to mention Robbie Gordon to you if I wanted to stay in one piece?'

'Peter wasn't wrong.' I sat on the edge of the sofa to stop him reaching out for me. 'You know Robert well?'

'We've met.' He was smiling. 'This is getting amusing.'

'Why?'

'Your getting him out on a wild-goose chase for me. This I shall enjoy.'

That made sense, and so did his now having totally persuaded himself I was making an unnecessary fuss. I saw that as I had begun to look on him as a patient, and training forced me to view him academically for the first time. Experience had shown me I could sum up the type of patient a person was going to make within five minutes of meeting them—as patients. It was when people were outside of a hospital that I so often went so wrong in my judgment of them. As we waited for Robert and I listened to Nick knocking down my arguments like a card-house, I realised reluctantly that though he might be an amusing patient so long as all was going well, he would not be a good patient. Being a good patient entailed much more than being polite and helpful to the doctors and nurses. It took strength of character, a capacity for standing pain and the discomforts and inconveniences of illness, a sense of humour, and plain courage. That was a formidable list, yet I had found 90 per cent of the human race to possess the qualities on that list when in a hospital bed. I could count on one hand the really 'bad' patients I had come across; the remainder came under the 'difficult' heading. Difficult in that context being synonymous with demanding. And that was the kind of patient I suspected Nick would make.

I did not despise him for this. If anything, it made me more fond of him by making him so helpless. I wanted to hold him in my arms to comfort him like a child. I grew so distressed that I stopped viewing him academically, and, in fact, became so emotionally involved that I nearly succeeded in convincing myself that my months in the eye ward had taught me nothing and I had made the wrong diagnosis—when we heard a car stop outside.

I went to the window. 'Can you come round to the back, Robert?'

Robert came in, apologising for the delay. He had stopped somewhere to borrow an ophthalmoscope.

Nick said he must apologise for dragging Robert across country just because he was seeing the odd star. 'Anna's acting as if I've cracked my nut in three places. I tried to stop her bothering you, Rob. No dice. Tough females, these nurses.'

'They get that way,' agreed Robert. 'As I'm here, let's have a look at that bump. Och, yes, it's only wee. I doubt you've cracked your skull in even one place. You'd better have a picture taken some time to make sure.' He fitted together the ophthalmoscope. 'May as well check your eyes as well. This'll not hurt. It's just a light. Try not to blink.' He bent over the sofa, then found it easier to kneel. 'Right.' He raised one hand behind his head. 'Watch my hand. Fine. Now, follow it as I move it—no, don't turn your head. With your eyes. That's it.'

'Can you see my stars?' asked Nick cheerfully.

Robert sat on his heels to reset the instrument.

'I haven't the gift.' He copied Nick's tone, as if this was an amusing diversion on a normal social occasion. Nick had tensed up since Robert arrived. He began to relax. Robert asked for another look at his right eye. 'Watch my hand again.' He now kept it still. 'That black penny's shifting up, isn't it?'

Nick shook a fist at me. 'Darling, you shouldn't have handed on that nonsense.'

'Don't kick about, Nick.' Robert stood up slowly and began to put away the ophthalmoscope as if he had all eternity at his disposal. 'Did Anna explain why she called me?'

'Did she not! She's been blinding me with science! She even wanted to pack me off to Astead General! That's out for a start!'

'Not if they have a bed—which I expect they will.' Robert then explained exactly as I had done.

Nick flushed. 'You are not serious?'

'Sorry,' said Robert, 'I am, and this is.'

'Then send me back to Barny's; I'll pay for the ambulance—if that's the rub?'

'Barny's is too far. You can't go over the downs with that eye. With the best ambulance in the world there'd be too much movement.'

'You can't shove me into a hospital against my will!'

'No,' said Robert, not ungently. 'No-one can do that. You are perfectly entitled to refuse treatment, and you must by now realise the risk you are running. Unless that retina is stitched back on soon—and the longer the delay the greater the chances against success—you will lose the sight in that eye. You've only got two eyes, man.' Nick's flush had gone, and he was very white. 'I'm sorry to din this in, Nick, but you've got to accept it. You must have treatment.'

'Will they—will they know what to do in Astead? Only a little town?'

'With a very good hospital. You'll be fine there. Their eye specialist is an old Barny's man. He worked eight years under my present boss, Muir. I'll get hold of him.' He lit a cigarette and handed it to Nick. 'You get on with that.'

'Thanks.' Nick glared at me accusingly. 'Women! Why did I have to follow you down here tonight? If I had stayed up I could now be in Barny's.'

Robert said, 'If you had told anyone about your eye. Would you have done that—no, don't shake your head! No? Then it's lucky you came after Anna. Now I must ring Marcus Stock. Where's the phone, Anna?'

Dr Stock, the ophthalmic consultant to the Astead Group of Hospitals, arrived twenty minutes later. He lived the other side of Astead, but had been dining with friends nearer Wylden. Robert traced him with his second call. During the interval Robert went over to The Swan for Nick's suitcase, warned the landlord he was unlikely to use his room, and arranged to have Nick's car housed in the Wylden garage next day. I was glad to have him see to those things and not to see Nick while I waited with him. I was able to calm him to a certain extent. It was not easy.

Dr Stock was a tallish, stout man with thick white hair that made him look older than he must have been to be Mr Muir's junior. He looked more like a successful farmer than a doctor. He spoke medical jargon. 'Right, lad, we'll patch you up. Just a few stitches in the right place, eh? Nothing to worry about.' He nodded to Robert, who removed himself to do some more telephoning, and talked to Nick and myself about the weather. 'Only the fruit farmers are grumbling. Best hay harvest in years. How's London? Like a furnace, eh?'

Robert returned to say an ambulance was on the way and a bed waiting in Dr Stock's ward in Astead General. Dr Stock said he would follow the ambulance in his car. Robert offered to come along in the convoy to drive me back. 'I expect you'll want to go along in the ambulance, Anna?'

I was back holding Nick's hand. He had not let go of me since Robert made his first phone call. 'Yes, please—if it's all right with you, Doctor?'

Dr Stock had been watching Nick and myself. 'Forgive me asking, but am I correct in assuming you two are engaged?'

'That's right, Doctor.' Nick answered for me, and his handclasp tightened. 'That make a difference?'

Dr Stock said, 'Well, yes, one could say that. Of course, fiancées do not have the established rights of wives, but one is always prepared to make allowances for them. And though I appreciate your desire to be with Mr Dexter, Miss Rowe,' he went on reluctantly, 'I would rather you remained here. That tablet I gave you to suck a few minutes back will shortly make you rather drowsy, Mr Dexter. You may be able to get a little nap in the ambulance. The men will look after you well. I would prefer you to be on your own, and will arrange for your fiancée to be allowed to visit you tomorrow. Will that do?'

'You know best, Doctor,' said Nick. 'What do you say, darling? Deal?'

Robert had been studying the fireside wall. He glanced round as Nick waited for my answer. I had no time left for working anything out. I was too distressed over Nick to think about anything but his need for me. 'Sure, Nick. Deal.'

'Good,' said Dr Stock. 'Sensible girl.'

Nick sighed contentedly. 'Thanks, pal,' he murmured, so softly that I doubted anyone but myself heard. Dr Stock walked over to the window to look out for the ambulance and Robert returned to studying the fireside wall.

CHAPTER SEVEN

ROBERT MAKES TEA

THE ambulance men were called John and George. They were youngish, muscular, neat, and very kind. They were Astead men and knew Dr Stock well. When they discovered Robert was in medicine and I was a nurse they made mild little jokes about busman's holidays, and when Nick was in the ambulance and Dr Stock in his car George assured me privately I did not have to worry about my young gentleman as John would take care of him lovely and Dr Stock would do a real good job on his eye. 'He knows his trade, miss. You'll see.'

Dr Stock overtook the ambulance before it was out of Wylden. I said, 'It was nice of him to wait with us.' Robert nodded. 'How much was off?'

'About half. Marcus Stock should be able to fix it back on.' He did not add unless the retina was wholly detached by the time Nick reached the theatre, and had deteriorated beyond hope of saving, which could happen very quickly once it was right off, as we both knew that danger, and he was not a man to waste breath underlining accepted facts. I used to find his habit of silence irritating and callous. Previously, when I had a problem, I had wanted to talk about it, to go into every possible aspect, to scare myself with the worst that could happen, in the hope that the person to whom I was unburdening would be able to produce the right soothing answers to prove I did not have to worry at all. Having been, as I now realised, exceedingly lucky, I had never had to deal with any problem of this present nature. No-one close to me had ever been more than mildly ill. I was accustomed to seeing great anxiety for a patient at second-hand, or feeling the kind of anxiety I had for Tom Elkroyd, but nothing had affected me personally as I was now affected by Nick. I felt hollow with anxiety, and the last thing I wanted to do was discuss it. I did not know if Robert realised that or not, but his silence no longer irritated me. It was restful.

He followed me round to the back and into the kitchen, I assumed to collect his borrowed ophthalmoscope and leave. Instead he looked in the cold teapot, which was still with the other tea things on the table. 'What's the tea situation, Anna?'

'Oh—good, the caddy's full. Why? Want some?'

'Yes, please. Don't you?'

I raised my eyebrows. 'Treating me for shock?'

'If I was I wouldn't use tea; you know that's aged therapy. I just want some. I always do. You must remember that' —he filled and plugged in the kettle—'after the quantities you, Dave, and I drank together.'

'I remember.'

He could have been being unnecessarily tactless, yet in a peculiar way I found his reminder comforting. It made me remember we knew each other too well for me to have to bother with entertaining him. He neither expected nor wanted that. He wanted to make tea, so I left him to it and sat down watching him wash the cups. It was all I felt fit for. The last few hours after my difficult day's work and hot train journey had left me physically and emotionally exhausted. The tea when ready began to revive me. 'May be aged therapy,' I admitted, 'but it still works.'

He sat down. 'The Health Service would have crumbled years ago if it didn't.'

'And the industrial economy. No tea-breaks and every factory worker in the country would be out on strike.'

He smiled faintly and fell silent, which again suited me. It was some time before he asked, 'Had supper yet?'

'No. I'm not hungry. I'll get some later.'

He refilled our cups. 'Would you care to come back to Astead with me for tonight? My godfather's got five spare bedrooms. Mrs Lane'll be glad to get one ready. She enjoys having visitors, and though the old man isn't over-fond of surprises, he's very attached to Sister Mary, and as you are here to help her he'd be genuinely pleased to put you up. I've already left him entertaining one guest to dinner. Why not join the party? I can ring Mrs Lane first to let her know we are on our way.'

It was nice of him to ask, even if the idea appalled me. I thanked him and refused. Then, as he had reminded me of his guest, whom I had completely forgotten, I apologised for wrecking his evening and suggested he ought to be on his way.

'When I've finished my tea.' To my relief he did not press his invitation. 'They'll have finished dinner, and Mrs Lane'll be keeping mine, so there's no hurry.' He saw me look at my watch. 'They won't have reached Astead yet.'

'No.' I looked at the apple-tree outside the window. I did not really see it. My body was in that kitchen; my mind was in the ambulance with Nick. 'Robert, why is Stock "Doctor" not "Mister"?'

'He's got the double.'

'Membership plus Fellowship?' He nodded. 'Why isn't he on the Staff?'

'Muir's only forty-three. He's good for years. He got there first. Stock could have had another pundit's job in one of the rival firms, and I've heard a couple dangled for him, but he turned them down.'

'Why?' I asked curiously. 'Most men would give their souls for the job.'

He said, 'I don't know him well, but, from what the old man has told me, I should say that there was one particular reason why Stock opted out. He detests back-stairs politics —and you know how much of that pundits have to put up with—he doesn't like teaching, or London. Also, at the time these offers came up, he needed to make much more money than he could at a teaching hospital. Out here he gets his consultant's pay and enough time for a private practice. He's got a big private list. This is an affluent county, and he is very good with eyes. The word has got round. He must now be making at least twice as much as Muir, if not more.'

I thought this over. 'He doesn't look like a money grabber.'

'I didn't say he was. I said he needed the money.' He went on to explain how Dr Stock's decision to leave the teaching hospitals must have been affected by his having, at that period, to support elderly parents, a widowed sister with a small child, and a younger brother, to whom he was devoted and who had leukaemia. 'His brother had died first, then both parents a year or so later. His sister married again, and well, last year.'

'Robert, I am sorry! No wonder that poor man has all that white hair and looks so much older than he must be. Yet he looks so cheerful'—I stopped myself as a thought struck me. 'My father says it's always the people who have known great grief who end up looking the most cheerful of individuals. I guess that's because, having known the worst, they've got a sort of yardstick against which to measure all petty problems.'

'You've got something there,' he said. 'I felt something like that after my parents died. I was at school, and everyone was very decent to me. But just after, and for some time, when I heard the other boys getting worked up about Common Entrance or some match, I thought they were all daft. I couldn't follow how they thought such trivial things mattered. It took a while for that "nothing can hurt me any more" feeling to wear off. Saved a lot of worry.'

I did not say 'At what a cost,' but I thought it, and was ashamed it had not occurred to me before to understand why he had seemed happier to stand around watching life rather than join in. 'How old were you when your parents died?'

'Eight.'

I looked at my cup. 'Road?'

'Plane.'

I said, 'I'm sorry—but that sounds so inadequate.'

'I know. There are no words for the things one really wants to say.' He got up for the kettle.

'That'll be cold,' I protested, so he plugged it in again, and added fresh leaves to the drained pot.

'They'll be in the theatre now,' he agreed, as I squinted once more at my watch. When the tea was ready he sat

104

down and began talking more about his childhood, and how much he had enjoyed living with his cousins in Caithness. 'They had four kids of their own, two of each, and I was the youngest, which gave everyone an excuse for spoiling me, which suited me well. The old man fixed that up.'

'Are you related to him at all?'

'No. He was a great friend of my mother's family. He was her godfather, and asked if he could also be mine. He collects godchildren.' He smiled to himself 'At the last count there were ten of us.'

'Ten! Wonderful old man.'

'He's that all right. Incidentally, how did you know I'd be with him this evening?'

'Tom Elkroyd told me.'

'I thought he probably had. He told me you were coming down here to clean up. Which reminds me, I owe you an apology—'

'Forget it. Think what I owe you for Nick. I couldn't get him to take this seriously until you arrived.'

'That's reasonable. You are too close to him.' He flicked open the writing-pad that had been lying on the table where Nick left it. 'What's all this about? Nick redesigning this place for Sister Mary?'

'I thought he was just doing sums.' I had a look. 'He's made sketches. This one must be how he thinks the sitting-room could look without that false wall.'

'What false wall?'

I took him in to show him, and then he wanted to see all round. He seemed as fascinated by the place as Nick had been, and suggested I showed Sister Mary the sketches. 'Nick's an expert, Anna, as one only has to look at Mary Block to appreciate. His advice is worth having.'

'If Sister Mary—or, rather, Jill Collins—will take it. Sister'll probably be happy to leave it all to Jill, and her passion for pastels appals Nick.'

He looked round the sitting-room. 'When do you intend painting this?'

'Not this week-end. This will be all cleaning—when I get started.'

'Then there's time for Nick to work out colour-schemes? That'll keep him busy after his op.'

'You think he'd want to do that?'

'Why not?' He looked over the sketches again. 'This looks to be his hobby as well as his job. Good post-op. therapy.'

We went back to the kitchen. He felt the teapot and poured himself another cup. 'Robert! You can't drink any more of that stuff! It must be horrible by now.'

'I like it. Good for my kidneys.' He reached for the ceiling as Nick had done. 'And this is another fraud?'

'So he said.' I was trying to pay attention, but my thoughts kept darting off to that theatre. 'If Stock succeeds, how long before Nick can use his eyes for drawing? I should remember. I can't.'

'If Stock follows Muir, a few weeks.'

'Stock won't be using the old sandbag routine?'

He shook his head. 'I'm sure he won't. Muir chucked that out five years ago. He'll probably put on a double bandage for a day or so but by next week Nick'll have his good eye free. He'll have the stitches out around the tenth day, the shade off around the twentieth. He'll have to go quietly. They'll give him a telly to watch. Muir swears by the telly. He says there's nothing to touch it for its benefits to ophthalmic surgery as it keeps the eyes still and patients happy. It's far less disturbing than reading, or even watching the nurses rustling round. I'm sure you'll find Stock's in line with Muir. Nick'll be safe with him.'

I said, 'If he can get that retina back.'

He looked at his watch now. 'Shall we find out? It should be over now.'

I had been dreading this moment. 'Is this why you stayed?'

He said, 'They'll tell me the truth. They may not tell you. We know what hospitals are like. I thought I might as well hang around as ring you later. Let's get it over.'

Jill Collins left London at seven next morning. She arrived as I was cooking breakfast. 'Rowe, my poor child! What an evening you must have had! Thank God Marcus Stock got at it in time!'

I gaped. 'Sister, how do you know?'

'From Sabby Wardell.' She put down her suitcase, re-

106

moved her gloves and the jacket of her brown linen suit. The suit had good lines, but the colour accentuated her sallowness. 'I was working very late and got back just as she was arriving back from Astead. Her room's next to mine. She told me all about it.'

'Sabby—— Sister Observation?' I echoed unnecessarily. 'She was down this way last night?'

'Yes, dear. Robbie Gordon drove her down. Didn't he tell you?'

'No. I wish he had.' I sat on the table. 'He was here ages. It must have wrecked her evening. I hope she didn't mind too much?'

She said briskly, 'My child, one has to expect these things if one dates doctors. Robbie probably felt he had to stay and see you were all right before leaving you here alone. Now, tell me all your side of it. And what's the news this morning? Rung the hospital?'

'Just now. I spoke to Nick's ward sister.' I grimaced. 'She said he was comfortable and as well as could be expected.'

'That bromide! Not that there's more she could say at this juncture. And when will they let you see him?'

'Today. Dr Stock said he'd arrange that. He has. The sister said I could come along for a few minutes this afternoon. She didn't sound too happy about it, but good old Marcus Stock seems to be boss in his own ward. He's rather a pet. Did you know him?'

'Oh, yes! Well—this won't do! I'll go and change into working clothes while you eat, and then we must get started!'

I had not had much of an appetite before she arrived. Her news left me with no desire at all for food, so I switched off the frying-pan and settled for tea. Had I used my intelligence, since I had known Wardell had a free evening yesterday, I should have guessed she was Robert's dinner guest. Remembering the time he had left me, he must have gone back to Astead with only a few minutes to spare before putting her on the last train to London at eleven, unless he had driven her back. In either event, God help me in Observation on Monday.

Jill reappeared in a lilac cotton shirt and blue jeans that

would have made Nick shudder. She saw I was not eating, insisted on scrambling some eggs, and then stood over me while I ate them. 'No-one can work without food, dear! And I'm going to make you work! There's nothing like it for worry!' Her voice softened. 'The poor boy! What a dreadful thing to happen to him of all people!'

I was grateful for her concern for Nick and, as the morning unwound, to have her organise me as well as the cottage. The reaction had really hit me, and I felt as if my brain and bones were made of cotton-wool. I stopped brooding about Wardell, as there was nothing I could do about last night, and there was no point in facing Monday until Monday. I almost stopped worrying about Nick. Only almost, because, though his op. had been an initial success, he was going to have to be very careful about that eye for some time, and, unless last night had shocked some sense into him, I could not see his being that. I tried to kid myself that now we were engaged I should have much more influence over him. That was not much help, as I kept remembering how useless my influence in that direction had been last night. Yet he loved me. I was as sure of that this morning as I was that I loved him. I kept reminding myself that was the one very bright spot. I felt that should have put everything right, and when it did not, decided that must just be another side-effect of delayed-action shock.

Sister Mary rang before lunch. She was staying in Hayhurst for the next week or so to nurse her friend. She was very apologetic about leaving us to her cleaning.

Jill assured her we were having a high old time and she was not to worry about us at all. 'Do you need help in Hayhurst? Is there anything we can do? You will need more clothes, of course. If you tell me what you require I will pack a suitcase and put it on the Hayhurst coach. There'll be one through Wylden early this afternoon as it is Saturday.'

She suddenly reminded me very much of Robert dealing with Nick's affairs last night. It struck me those two had a lot in common. Robert was much quieter, but he was as good as Jill at getting on with a job, remembering details, and showing a, to me unexpected, sympathy with other people's problems. I could write off this attitude to Tom Elkroyd as part of his job, but I could not stretch that to cover his behaviour last evening. He had been very nice to me, I realised in retrospect. The strain of waiting would have been even worse without him. When we had our next row, which on past showing was inevitable, in fairness I must remember last evening, and Robert swigging cold stewed tea and talking interior decorating and his childhood to keep my mind off Nick. Jill said he probably felt he had to stay, and probably she was right. It was still an unexpectedly nice gesture, even if it was going to have the most lamentable after-effects on my working life.

We washed the ceilings, walls, windows, and scrubbed the upstairs floors during that morning. Over lunch Jill said she would get on with the sitting-room and study while I was in Astead.

'Sister, won't you come with me? I wish you would!'

She said she refused to do anything for me if I persisted in calling her 'sister' outside Barny's as it was making her feel in Sister Mary's age group. 'You can't possibly want me along this afternoon.'

'I do! I'm nervous.'

'Nonsense! You are used to hospitals!'

'Not from this angle. Please. Then we can both attack the downstairs when we get back.'

She was obviously very reluctant. 'I'll come and hold your hand if you insist, Anna. But this is such a good opportunity to get the work done——'

'We'll only be away for a couple of hours. It'll be a nice bus ride! Do come.'

Eventually she gave in. 'I'm still not clear why you want me.'

I could not answer that as I was not clear myself, the reason I had given her being only a half-truth. I was nervous, but by the thought of seeing Nick again, and not because of a strange hospital. Yet why I should suddenly feel nervous of Nick and need her moral support was beyond me. It remained that I was and did.

We left Sister Mary's suitcase at the village bus station before getting our own Astead bus. To rationalise things to myself, on the way to the hospital I told Jill of my anxiety that he would do fresh damage to his eye during his convalescence.

'You'll have to be firm with that boy, Anna!'

'He's no boy. Thirty-two.'

'But one of those men who always have a touch of the little boy in them. You'll have to look after him. Isn't that part of his great charm? I would have thought so? And, of course, he is so very talented. One couldn't fairly expect anyone with his gifts to be a solid, sober citizen.'

'That's true.'

She looked at me keenly. 'You don't sound very happy about it.'

'Probably because I'm not exactly a solid, sober citizen myself.'

'Then you'll have to change, dear. It's always the woman who has to change, I've noticed. Men don't.'

Astead General Hospital had two hundred beds. It looked like a toy in comparison with Barny's, and the whole place would have fitted into one of our blocks. Dr Stock's six-bedded eye ward was like a miniature Observation without our finer ultra-modern points. There was no air-conditioning, wholesale barrier-nursing, and there were no cornerless rooms, but every bed was in its own small ward with its own equipment for use only in that room.

The sister in charge was a Sister Dawson. She was a pleasant, middle-aged woman with a North Country accent. She did not talk too much. She said, 'You'll not need me to warn you to be quiet, Miss Rowe. Dr Stock told me Mr Dexter's fiancée is a trained nurse. Only a few minutes, mind.' On hearing Jill was a fellow ward sister she invited her to sit in her office. 'We'll not keep you long. I'll take Miss Rowe.' She asked me to wait outside Nick's room. 'I'll warn him.' She disappeared, then was back. 'You can come in now.'

There was plenty of light in Nick's room as both his eyes were bandaged and there was a felt blind over the bandage. He had only one pillow for this first day, and lay on his back. His hair looked very yellow against the pillow and in contrast with the dark double-eye blind. I had seen other patients in this condition. I might have been looking on it for the first time. When his hands groped blindly for me I wanted to weep.

Sister Dawson had a hand on my elbow. She said evenly,

110

'Miss Rowe is on your left, Mr Dexter. She is going to touch your left hand—now.' She nodded at me. 'That's it. Now, don't forget what I've told you, young man. Keep your head still just for today. You'll have that double bandage off your good eye by tomorrow afternoon.' She gave me a chair, had a good look at us both, then removed herself.

I held both his hands. 'She's gone, Nick. How are things?'

He sighed. 'God, darling, I don't know. Everyone keeps telling me I've been bloody lucky. I suppose I am. I don't feel it. I feel bloody awful.'

'Eye hurting?'

'No. Haven't any pain at all. Not even a headache. Is that right?'

'Perfectly.' My opinion of Marcus Stock shot higher. 'Feel sick at all?'

'No. Should I?'

'Not if you've had a good anaesthetist—which you obviously have.'

'Then when will it start hurting?'

'It won't.'

He could neither understand nor believe that; he had never been in hospital before. 'What about when the stitches come out?'

'Stocks won't let it hurt. Honestly.'

'That's what the Dawson woman said. I thought it was all part of the patter.'

'No. It's true.' As he was clearly unconvinced, I changed the subject to tomorrow. 'You'll be much less glum without that double bandage. They make everyone glum.'

'Guess so.' He sighed again. 'Do they know their stuff here, Anna? They are talking of giving me a television by Tuesday. Are they nuts?'

'No. That's the modern technique.' I repeated Robert's words about Muir, and, as that did not cheer him, took Robert's advice about the cottage being good post-op. therapy. I had discussed his ideas with Jill while we cleaned that morning, and shown her his sketches. I said now, 'She loves your white-and-orange scheme for the kitchen. Don't wince, but she had wanted it pale blue.'

'God! Blue for a room facing due north! There's no

111

colder colour. But she likes my ideas?' He brightened. 'Good old Jilly. Have you left her spring-cleaning?'

'She's here with me. In Sister Dawson's office—and here is Sister with Dr Stock,' I added as the door opened.

Dr Stock apologised for disturbing us. Sister Dawson said firmly, 'Miss Rowe's time was well up, Doctor.'

Nick tried to persuade her otherwise, but, as I knew the sound of a ward sister with her mind made up, I said goodbye and promised to be in again tomorrow. 'If I may?' I looked at Sister Dawson as well as Dr Stock.

The consultant said he did not see why not and held open the door for me. Nick asked, 'Couldn't I just say hallo to Miss Collins? Please.'

Sister Dawson looked at Dr Stock. He looked rather startled, then smiled. 'Just for one minute.'

I went for Jill. She was standing at the office window with her back to the door. She turned very slowly. 'He wants to see me?'

'Yes. Stock said he could.' She had gone pink. 'Jill, do. He's so glum. Maybe you can cheer him up.'

'I'll try,' she said, and hurried off.

We were both very quiet on our return journey. Later, in the sitting-room, Jill stopped scrubbing engrained soot off the mock-marble fireplace and sat on her heels. 'I had thought of shell-pink for this room. Your young man insists white is the only possible colour. I can see now he's right.' She looked up at the ceiling. 'Those dark beams will look much better against a white background, and white will make the room bigger.'

I said, 'He seems to have as big a fixation for white as he has for knocking down walls. Was there time for him to get on to this wall here while you were with him?'

'He did! I said it would have to stay *pro tem.* as Sister Mary couldn't possibly afford the extra expense. He tried to persuade me it wouldn't cost all that much if Sister Mary wouldn't object to his being around to keep on eye on things and the expense down, but I vetoed that one too. If not, as soon as they let him out, he'd be in here swinging a pickaxe himself!'

'That's what's worrying me. How did he take your veto?'
'Like a lamb.'

'Jill!' I put down my string cloth and carton of abrasive powder. 'You must have handled him wonderfully. What's your technique?'

'Not sure.' She attacked the fireplace again. 'Probably long experience. I've had to handle midder clerks for the past three years. Before that I had two as a Cas. senior staff nurse handling Cas. dressers. And long before I came to Barny's, having four younger brothers and no sisters, I got in a lot of practice on them. My brothers always said I was born to be either a hospital sister or a Regimental Sergeant-Major. I'm happy to have made the former.' She went into the kitchen for clean hot water. On returning she said, 'I didn't realise you two were officially engaged, but how very pleasing that you are.'

'It's not at all that official'—and though I knew she disliked personal discussions I had to talk to someone; so I told her Nick's proposal had been prompted by Marcus Stock last night. 'Nick didn't mention it this afternoon.'

'And that's upset you? Anna, that's foolish! He was still pretty heavily sedated when we saw him. I doubt he yet remembers all that happened last night. That'll come back as he begins to pick up. You must know he's devoted to you. Even I have heard that, and I don't hear much gossip as listening to it is something I try to avoid. It always seems to me both impertinent and boring.' She held out a hand. 'Let's have that powder. If it doesn't shift this soot I am going to use wire wool.'

I took that as a straight hint to keep my private life to myself, and did not intend mentioning Nick again. Then a few minutes later she said he had told her one of the upstairs cupboards had a false back, and must at one time have been an old powder closet. We went up to investigate, and when our taps echoed hollowly she was jubilant. 'That clever boy! We'll have that back out ourselves in the morning! Sister Mary won't mind! Like every woman, she'll be delighted with the extra cupboard space.' She looked round the bedroom. 'I wonder what colour he wants this? Where's that pad?'

At supper she brought up Nick's name again, and said what a mercy it was that there should be an eye man of Marcus Stock's calibre on hand. As Stock was an old

Barny's man whom she had admitted knowing, I asked if she knew about his family background?

'He had a lot of trouble, I believe, poor man. But it's over now. More cheese? No? Then let's clear up.'

I watched her intent, shiny face and untidy hair as she washed up. Her features were not at all bad, and though she looked angular that was mainly because she would wear the wrong clothes. She had the kind of slimness that could have looked dreamy if only her clothes fitted in the right places and had been the right colours, as Nick's more discerning eye had spotted at sight. Her face had more colour than usual now, and as she went on to talk of Nick's work on the new Mary she looked more alive and almost good-looking. A sudden, wild idea hit me so unexpectedly that I dropped a plate. I had laughed myself out of that idea before I collected the pieces. I did not remember it until we were leaving the cottage next evening.

Jill again went with me to visit Nick, and this time without protest. She wore her brown linen suit, but as she had for once made up her face the colour seemed much less drab.

As yesterday, she waited in Sister Dawson's office while I was with Nick. He was much more cheerful. His good eye was free. 'I like,' he said, 'to see a girl when I kiss her.'

He did not mention our being engaged. He said, 'I've got a sort of blackout about Friday, my sweet. Is that because Stock filled me up with dope?'

'Yes.' I hesitated to say more as I only then realised that his proposal could have been as much prompted by drugs as Marcus Stock. 'It'll come back.'

He said honestly, 'I'm not sure I'm all that keen on recalling the gory details, love. It must have been a bloody awful evening all round. By the way, did you know Rob Gordon looked in here this morning? Rather decent of him, I thought.'

'Yes. Very.'

'And how's the cottage going? You haven't let old Jilly slap on the wrong paint?'

'My dear man, we've done nothing but clean! Don't my hands prove that?'

Before I left he again asked to see Jill. 'Tell old Mother

Dawson I asked Stock myself this morning and he said I could! And when are you coming to see me again?'

'I've a half-day on Thursday. I'll try and get it changed for an earlier one, but Sister Observation isn't very keen on changes.'

He smiled. 'Darling, you ought to know by now that you don't have to be tactful and avoid Sabby's name. You may not believe this, but I can't even remember what she looks like.'

I believed him, as that was how I felt about David.

He stroked my face. 'I have such a weakness for red-heads.'

'Anything you want me to do for you in town?'

'Tell Peter Graveny to come and see me. Stock says I can entertain from tomorrow during normal visiting hours. I want lots of visitors. I am addicted to grapes.'

Jill was with him longer than yesterday. Later she told me she had promised to visit him on her next half-day. 'You don't mind, Anna?'

'Of course not! As his parents have returned to Majorca and both his married sisters are abroad, and he's a stranger to these parts, he'll have no visitors unless his London friends rally.'

She locked the back door and said she would ask Sister Mary to keep an eye on him when she got back from Hay-hurst. 'I could let Professor Ferguson know. Then Mrs Ferguson might go over.'

'Jill, you are bright. You think of everything!'

She blushed. 'Your young man's a nice boy. I think he's going to be a great help to Sister Mary. I'd like to help him if I can, and if it's all right with you?'

'Fine with me!'

'Splendid! Then how about our joining forces here again on our next free week-end to get down to the painting? You can then spend as much time with him as they'll let you, and, as Sister Mary should be with us, we ought to be able to make real progress.' She patted the cottage wall affectionately. 'Little house, I like you. I can't wait to get back to you.'

She could have meant only what she said, but it was then I remembered the idea that had made me drop that

115

plate. It still seemed crazy, but no longer at all funny. She looked younger, neater, and almost pretty. She had done her face with rare care. She had done a lot for the cottage, but not her face. I found that interesting, and rather sad.

CHAPTER EIGHT

SISTER MARY MOVES IN

HELEN ADDY went on holiday at the end of the following week. I took over her job as Sister's stand-in, but as the promotion was only temporary I stayed with my own team and patients. Jean Hutton, a relief staff nurse, joined us during that week, and worked three days with Addy before taking over her rooms.

Addy gave me some very useful advice before she left, including the suggestion that I carried three spare handkerchiefs on duty. 'I have never worked in a ward with so many weeping juniors,' she said. 'Observation must now be like Barny's in the thirties. Mother says when she trained here no ward was complete without a weeping pro behind the sluice door. I wish Wardell would snap out of her mood —or we knew the cause and could do something about it! I hate to leave you holding the baby, but I expect you can cope. One thing's clear: it's nothing to do with you. You are now the only person she can be civil to!'

Oddly, that was true. I was still trying to fathom out why.

From Monday, Sabby Wardell had been as unexpectedly nice to me as Robert last Friday night. She had called me into her duty-room to sympathise about Nick's eye, openly referred to him as an old friend, said she thought it very good of me to have given up an entire week-end to help Sister Mary, and showed no sign of resenting my removing Robert from the dinner table and then letting him stay so long at the cottage. She even apologised for not being able to bring my half-day forward as the ward was too busy.

As the days went by I came to the conclusion that I

owed this mainly to Jill's putting in good words for me in the Sisters' Home, and a little to Robert's tactful handling of the situation on Friday. I guessed he had told her I was engaged to Nick, which would have stopped her worrying about him and myself as nothing else could have done. As I now knew she was interested in Robert, I understood why she had previously seemed unmoved by my relationship with Nick. She might even have been feeling rather guilty about him and grateful to me for taking him off her hands. Yet her continued indulgence towards me and general toughness to the other girls did continue to puzzle me, as it struck an uncharacteristic note. It seemed so unfair, and whatever Wardell was like as a ward sister, as Addy who knew her better than myself agreed, she had always previously been scrupulously fair in her dealings with her nurses.

Addy said, 'I've told you, she likes you, and she doesn't like people easily. It must be that.'

Robert was also puzzling me. Having known and disliked him for years, I was now beginning to wonder if I had ever known him at all. Either he or I had changed utterly, since the more I saw of him these days the less cause I found to dislike him. He seemed to have lost his old desire to scrap with me at sight, and though I did not realise this in a flash, I slowly discovered I no longer braced myself instinctively whenever he appeared.

When we met on duty, if Wardell was around we ignored each other by a sort of unexpressed mutual consent. If she was not there we talked exactly as I talked with the other registrars. When we met in the grounds, instead of pretending we were both invisible as of old, we stopped briefly and talked the latest news of Nick, or Observation shop.

Nick's progress was very good. I rang Astead General nightly for first-hand news, and collected a good deal at second hand from Peter Graveny, who drove down to Astead on Monday, from Jill and from Nick's secretary, Mrs Blake, who visited him daily and left a message for me on her return.

Mrs Bird's bed in Matilda Ward had become vacant sooner than expected, and, as she was doing very well, she

117

left us on Wednesday. I was off that morning, and got back to Observation as she was being wheeled off in a chair. 'Nurse Rowe! I am so glad! I did want to say goodbye and thank you.' She shook my hand briskly. Her face was still too thin, but it now had some colour, and her eyes were bright. 'I'll tell you now, my dear, I never expected to leave this ward alive. I shall not forget you. May I ask you two favours? Can you send a message to me in Matilda with your home address? And Mr Elkroyd's? If my little book ever gets into print I want you to have a copy, and I think it might amuse his children.'

Mrs Bird and Tom had never met, but they had struck up a firm friendship through the messages they sent each other via ourselves, and the long chats Mrs Elkroyd had had with Mrs Bird's sons in our flat. When I asked Tom's permission to give his address and told him the reason he looked very pleased. 'Oh, aye. She's welcome to it. Gone, has she? That's all right, then.'

He had no more acute pain since his injections had been put up, and was sleeping and eating better. In consequence his general condition had improved slightly. His X-rays and spinal pressure results showed no improvement. Brown-plus-E was an optimistic man, but he shook his head over each new plate and report, and Mr Muir made bright conversation in broad Scots in Room Ten. In the corridor and duty-room he talked unaccented English and was openly gloomy. 'Put a knife in now and it'll be straight murder.'

Mrs Elkroyd had had to have the truth. She had taken it with great courage and calm, and agreed that until an operation was possible the facts should be kept from her husband. 'He'll not learn them from me, Doctor.' To save Tom from guessing indirectly, though she longed to stay with him, she was still returning home during the week to look after the children, coming south every week-end. She left the children with her parents.

Tom said, 'There's nowt like a gran and a grandad for spoiling kids. My Betty has her hands full sorting that lot out.'

'A grandparent's privilege. Wait till you're a grandad, Tom.'

'Oh, aye.' His dark glasses hid his eyes, but his square jaw tightened. 'That'll be the day, then.'

He had long stopped asking about his condition, when he would be returning to Henry, or when the endless tests would be finished. He talked about the future when his wife was present, never with us alone. His attitude did not worry me as Mrs Bird's had done. There was no resignation about it. Tom Elkroyd accepted his illness because he had to, but it had not yet defeated him; he was a fighter saving his strength until necessary. If he had to die soon he would not die easily.

Now I knew him so well, I understood his language. 'It could be worse' meant 'This hurts as much as I can stand, but I'll put up with it if it's going to do any good.' 'Nicely, ta,' stood for 'I am very comfortable and feeling better.' 'That's all right, then,' was his top expression of joy and approval.

On Thursday morning Mr Muir was delayed by some meeting from arriving on time for his round, and Robert was waiting for his boss in Tom's room. When I looked in to say Mr Muir had telephoned and he would be another ten minutes the two men were working out a chess move. A pawn slid from Tom's grip. Then it happened again. 'Butterfingers,' he chided himself.

Robert and I looked at each other over his bent head. I shook mine slightly in answer to Robert's unspoken, 'This happened before?'

He said, 'If my boss is coming soon I'd better do some work or I'll get the sack. May I have another look, Tom?'

'Help yourself.' I drew the curtains, Robert fitted together his ophthalmoscope, and Tom removed his dark glasses. 'Better than a turn on telly, is it, then?'

'Much. Until they get colour television.' Robert altered the focus. 'Does this light worry you?'

'Could be worse.'

'Won't take long. There.' Robert switched off the instrument light. 'How's the head?'

'Nicely, ta.' Tom narrowed his eyes against the dim light. 'Happen you've been giving me stronger injections.'

'They're quite good,' was all Robert said. He helped me turn Tom's pillow and straighten the sheets, then handed

119

him his glass of lemonade, and Tom took it as if that was what he had been expecting.

I found it interesting to watch them together. It often gave me a queer 'I have been here before' sensation. I placed it now as Robert passed that glass. I remembered David, years ago in the canteen one evening, when he had been worried about an exam, and Robert had come over from another table, put a cup of tea in front of David, and walked off without saying a word. I had asked, 'How did he know you wanted that?' and David said, 'He knows me.' At the time I had resented Robert's insight. It had made me feel an intruder. I did not feel that now. I did not know why not.

Robert came out into the corridor with me. I asked about that pawn. 'The new stuff?' He nodded. 'So it could be a good sign? He could soon be operable?'

He removed his glasses to polish them, and blinked as short-sighted people do on those occasions. His lashes were very long, thick, and dark as his hair. I had never noticed them before, or that without his glasses he looked much younger and oddly vulnerable. 'Possibly. Dead risky.'

'I know that. But he's such a tough. A mental as well as a physical tough. I think he'll make it.'

'I hope to God you are right.' He put back his glasses to add a note to the bed-ticket.

'But you don't think I am?'

He said slowly, 'My instincts are with you, but I can't get round the facts. They are stacked against him. Muir won't touch him yet—if ever.'

'If this stuff is having that side-effect how long will it last?'

'It should reach maximum in, say, two weeks.'

'Then it'll be now or never?'

'Yes. By then he'll have had the full course. He can't have more without a long break. Too long for him. Brown-plus-E'll probably decide in the next ten days. The decision'll be his, for, though Muir may assist, it'll be Brown-plus-E who goes into his skull.'

'Yes,' I said, 'yes. It will. Robert, if you were going in, what would you do?'

He took his time. 'Risk it.'

'You would? You'd back your instincts against your judgment? Like me?'

His smile was self-derisive. 'And since when has lunacy been a female prerogative?' The lift had stopped. 'Here's the boss.'

After nursing for years I was normally very good at switching off my job when out of the hospital, and switching off my private life when on duty. I had been relieved to discover, this last week, that I was still able to forget Nick wholly in Observation. In the train that afternoon, for once that old mental habit failed me. Tom and my conversation with Robert were so uppermost in my thoughts that by the time I reached Astead General, smelt the old familiar hospital smell on the stairs and in the corridors leading to the eye ward, and was shown into Nick's room by Sister Dawson I was quite startled to see the wrong man sitting up in the bed. I recovered myself at once, but, for once with Nick, I did not feel weak at the knees. I remembered that later.

He had a black patch over his eye. He looked rested and well. 'How do you like me as a pirate, darling?'

'Very dashing. How do you feel?'

'Great! You were right. It doesn't hurt at all. Old Marcus Stock comes in every day and says h'mm, h'mm! The nurses say that means I'm cured. I'm in love with at least three. No objections?'

'So long as it's only three, how could I?'

'Haven't I always said you were the most understanding of women? What's your news?'

'Not much, I'm afraid, as I've been buried in Observation. I saw Peter after he saw you, and Jill rang me, but I haven't seen her all week. I haven't even seen Harriet. She's on a two-to-ten Cas. shift and sleeps all morning.'

'But not all night! Peter says she's living it up with one of his housemen. Stan Someone.'

'Stan Peabody? He her latest? Tell me more!' I begged. 'There's nothing like coming to one hospital for gossip of another.'

Nick said there was now nothing he could not tell me about Astead General, and though he was not all that up on Barny's grapevine he was putting his mind to it. 'This place is agog today with a fine rumour—which Sister Dawson

121

mustn't hear so keep it dark. You know old Marcus? Get this! The girls say he's very thick with some fashion model.'

'Marcus Stock? At his age?'

'The poor old man's only forty, darling. The dangerous age! I can hardly wait!'

'Is she really a model? A real model? What's her name?'

'They wouldn't tell me. I'll get it out of them. Now, what else can I tell you? Ah, yes! You know old Jilly was down? With some colour cards? I've told her she can buy the paint, but she's not to use it until I can get a look at it. She's coming down again next Tuesday, and after dropping in here she's going on to Wylden to go into a huddle with your Sister Mary.'

'Will Sister Mary be back by then?'

'She's moving in on Sunday after packing dear Edith off to spend a few weeks with a married niece in Eastbourne. And on Monday'—he smiled smugly—'she is coming to see me.'

'Nick,' I said, 'is there anything you don't know?'

'One thing, my love.'

'What's that?' I asked, guessing the answer and suddenly turning nervous.

'What has happened to my car? No one seems to know.'

'Oh, didn't Robert explain? It's at the Wylden garage. That all?'

'I think so.' He turned his face to look straight at me with his good eye. His expression was untroubled and only mildly curious. 'Is there anything else I've forgotten?'

'No.' My voice had answered before I had time to think whether that was the answer I wanted to give. 'Are they letting you up now?'

'One hour in the morning, one in the evening. I take little walks with my nurses. And they are already talking about my pushing-out date.'

'That's splendid! When? And where are they sending you?'

'I'm not letting them send me anywhere! Can you see me settling for a convalescent home? I thought of going back to Italy, as Stock's against my working, and I know what'll happen if I go back to my flat in town. But he's not keen on Italy, and, like a mug, I told Jilly. Know her bright idea? She wants to ask your Sister Mary to take me in as a P.G.! Crazy, no?'

'Not crazy! Perfect, if Sister Mary'll have you.'

'Hey! How about me? Don't I have any say in the matter?'

I smiled. 'What did you say to Jill?'

'Darling,' he spread his hands, 'I did try. Old Jilly wasn't having any! She gave me such a stern "my dear boy, we must be sensible" pep-talk that I did not dare argue. May not be too bad. I like Wylden, and it'll be amusing to fix up that cottage,' he added, as if he needed to explain things to himself as well as to me.

The ward orderly came in with his tea, and wanted his advice on a new dress she intended buying for her daughter's school's Open Day. 'Isn't he a one, miss? I never heard a young gentleman talk like he does about clothes! Ever so artistic, he is!'

The ladies with the library trolley put their heads round the door. Though finding Nick was still forbidden to read, they came in at his invitation to be introduced to me. He did not introduce me as his fiancée.

'Another nurse from St Barnabas' Hospital, Miss Rowe? Your hospital seems quite to have adopted Mr Dexter!'

'Mr Dexter has not only adopted us, he's building us a fine new hospital.'

'Really? You clever young man!' they clucked.

Nick was grinning when they left us. 'Popular, darling, that's me. I am beginning to like it here. Everyone spoils me. But everyone! Jealous?'

'Green-eyed.'

He blew me a kiss. 'When are you coming to see me again?'

I had intended staying some time longer, but guessed from that he was growing tired. Being visited in hospital was fun for a short time, but I had seen too many patients left exhausted by their nearest and dearest to feel anything but sympathy with his desire to be alone.

Sister Dawson called me into her office for a little chat on my way out. She said Dr Stock was very satisfied with Nick, and she said he was a most amusing patient. 'Naturally he found life a little difficult at first,' she added, which also told me she had found him 'difficult'. That did not surprise me, nor did his not yet having a total recall of that Friday evening. In the train going back I amused myself picturing the scene between us when he eventually remembered we were engaged. 'Why the devil didn't you tell me, darling?' he would demand. 'Afraid I might have second thoughts?'

Was that it, I wondered. Or was I having second thoughts?

That last thought left me disturbed and guilty. I could not get it off my mind until I got back to Observation next day, when the pressure of work again pushed Nick into the background of my thoughts.

Without Addy my job was even more responsible than previously. Sabby Wardell's natural aloofness had always made the girls wary of bothering her with minor problems. Now she was so constantly 'tetchy' that appeals to her were only made as a last resort. The habitual Observation cry, 'Where's Nurse Addy?' turned into 'Where's Nurse Rowe?' Officially I was only in nursing charge of my own team; unofficially I was now nursemaid to Trimmer's and Hutton's. I did not dislike that, but, as it meant I was making decisions for other people all day long on duty, I had no energy left at the end of the day for making any decisions about my private life. Nick seemed happy to let our affair drift for the present, so I just drifted with him. It was the same with the cottage. I fell in with Jill's plans when I could, slapped on paint approved by Nick with her and Sister Mary, when she at last moved in, visited Nick in Astead General, and very thankfully left all Nick's convalescent arrangements in Jill's capable hands.

Sister Mary was enchanted by the prospect of having Nick as a P.G., and Jill, one lunch time, went scarlet over this. 'Dr Stock gave me a lift back yesterday. He had to come up for some pundit's lunch. He's all for it.'

'You went down just for the morning? That was good of you, Jill.'

Her colour went from scarlet to puce. 'I had a long morning free. I thought I might as well.' It could have been imagination, but she seemed to be avoiding my eyes.

124

'Forgive me, Anna. I'm due back in Elizabeth.'

I was going back to Observation, and we were walking the same way. I let her streak on ahead and watched her back thoughtfully. It looked as if she had finally discovered why she found Astead so attractive. I should have liked to rush after her and tell her I quite understood and did not blame her at all, but, as I was the last person from whom she could have borne to hear that, I slowed my steps until she was right away.

She was out of sight before I remembered it was Friday and her free week-end. It would have been mine had Addy's holiday not caused me now to be out of step with Jill. Sister Observation was off this week-end, and I was having my days off during next week to compensate. So Jill had gone down yesterday morning, even though she was due in Wylden this evening for the whole week-end. Oh, dear, I thought rather wearily, poor old Jilly. What a mess! Then I wondered if Nick knew. I guessed he did. Jilly was no actress, and Nick, though often crazy, was no fool. I wondered if that was why he liked her so much, and then, inevitably, whether he only liked her or if history was going to repeat itself. I held out my bare left hand as I climbed the block stairs. At least this time I had no ring to hand back. That struck me as amusing in a wry sort of way, and I was still smiling when I reached our landing and found Nurse Vint, my team-leader, waiting for me.

'Nurse, "our Linda's" here. She says she's been given the afternoon off from work to make up for all the overtime she's been doing, and wants to sit with Frank to give his mother a free afternoon for once.'

Frank Sands in Room Five was still unconscious. Linda was his girl friend. She and Mrs Sands had not liked each other until Frank's accident, but they were now great friends. At Brown-plus-E's suggestion, ever since Frank's admission his parents and Linda had taken turns to sit with him, or be close at hand in our flat. Mr Browne said, 'In my opinion, if your boy can see a familiar face amongst all our strange ones when he comes round it may prove most beneficial.'

Mr Browne habitually talked about 'when' and not 'if'

when discussing his patients, which was one of the many reasons why I liked nursing his cases, and was so constantly anxious about Tom Elkroyd. Our cranial consultant was a brave as well as an excellent surgeon. The two qualities did not invariably go together. If an operation was the only hope, and there was the smallest chance it would succeed, Brown-plus-E never hesitated to disregard his statistics and take that chance. The fact that he was still holding back told me as much about Tom's prognosis as his keeping the Sands and Linda at their long vigil showed he genuinely believed there was some hope, however slight, that Frank would eventually recover.

The Sands and Linda lived within easy walking distance of Barny's, which helped them a little. They needed all the help they could get. Frank had been in a coma seventy-three days.

I said now, 'A break would do Mrs Sands good; she's missing all this wonderful summer. Why didn't you send Linda straight in?' Vint's expression changed. 'She hasn't a cold?'

'She swears not, but she sounds a little thick. I asked her to wait in the rest-room until you got back from lunch.'

'Sister gone already?'

Vint looked at the floor. 'No. She's waiting for you. I thought Linda wouldn't mind waiting a few minutes, and as Frank's in our team ...'

'Quite. I had better tell Sister I'm back, then I'll come along to see Linda with you.'

Sister left a few minutes later. Vint was hanging around in the linen-room. We went along to the relatives' flat together.

Linda was nineteen and very pretty, with masses of eye make-up. She hotly denied having a cold or feeling unwell. 'Me voice only sounds queer because me glands is up. Me mum says I've always been a one for glands. Tell you what—let me have two masks.'

I looked down her throat and felt her neck. 'Sorry, dear.' I explained the rules she already knew. 'Your glands aren't up for nothing. You must have some sort of germ, and it doesn't matter how mild I'm afraid, I can't let you near Frank or the patients' end of this ward. I really am sorry,

126

Linda. Mrs Sands'll understand. You go and get some sunshine yourself.'

After she had gone we sprayed the whole flat with our special disinfectant air-spray, chucked away the gowns and masks we had been wearing, scrubbed up as if for the theatre, then re-dressed ourselves in clean gowns and masks. Vint apologised for putting me to the trouble. 'I hope you didn't mind my waiting for you, Sister Rowe, but thank Heaven I did. Sister would have taken me apart for letting Linda out of the lift.'

I copied Addy's placidity. 'Sister has to take a strong line on imported bugs.'

'No-one would mind if it was only on bugs! But Sister's bit—I mean takes a strong line on everything these days! Why has she got like this? She never used to be.'

Again I fell back on Addy. 'She must be overtired. She works so hard.'

'Then why will she never take her proper off-duty?' demanded Vint reasonably. 'Why does she insist on staying on when you are in charge? And not only you. She was doing that to Nurse Addy before her holiday. Can't she bear handing over? Or does she feel she must work, as she's worried about something and work keeps it off her mind?'

'I don't know. You could be right, Vint.' I should have liked to give that more thought, but Linda had delayed us, the work was piling up, and the enigma of Wardell's behaviour had to slide.

I went first to see Mrs Sands. She made a homely, bulky little figure in her too-long gown. She was too fat to fit comfortably into a shorter gown, and generally wore one that would have fitted Robert Gordon or Henry Todd, our two tallest residents.

She nodded amiably over her knitting. 'Our Linda don't have to worry, duck. I'll do nicely till his dad comes up after his tea.' She lowered the knitting to look at her son. 'Looks a little brighter today, don't he, duck?' she added, as she did every single day.

I slid my arm through the armlet valve of the oxygen tent to take Frank's pulse. The beat was the same as this morning, as yesterday, and all the other yesterdays.

He was a short slight young man with sharp features

and narrow shoulders. Now his head bandages were off and his brown hair was growing again, it was growing curly. He looked younger than twenty-three, and his artificially lowered temperature made him the colour of a wax doll. He lived in that tent. He was fed by a constant drip. At first he had breathed through a tracheotomy tube, as his natural airway had been damaged as well as his head. Since the removal of the tube he had breathed naturally, but a spare iron lung was waiting in the surgical stockroom across the corridor. It did not take long to put in a fresh tracheotomy tube, but in Barny's that had to be done by a doctor, and Barny's was a big place, whereas fixing a patient into a lung was part of our nurses' training. It was not a part I enjoyed. Iron lungs are life-savers, but they look to me so like coffins.

We changed Frank's position constantly. He might be more like a log than a man, and when he came round his head injuries might prove to have done such permanent damage to his central nervous system as to leave him mentally crippled for life. A lay person might be justified in wondering if we were right to work so hard at saving his life. That question did not occur to the juniors in my team, simply because they had as yet little experience of the possible after-effects of these long comas. It was something Vint, the residents, and myself often discussed among ourselves, and then had to shelve along with all those other unanswerable questions that crop up daily in any hospital ward. It was our job to save life and not make judgments, so we saved Frank from hypostatic pneumonia, from urinary infections, from starvation, and from bedsores. There was not a quarter-inch of redness on his whole skin surface. Had there been, my team would have been sent to Matron, and I should have lost my Observation job. A bedsore in Barny's ranked, as a nursing crime, with making a major drug mistake.

Sister should have gone off at four that afternoon. It was Robert's free week-end. He had worked through the last two, I guessed to get his in line with hers. He came up to Observation at five to say he was off and one Mark Francis was taking over his job for the week-end.

'Who's Mark Francis? Don't know the name. Should I?'

128

He shrugged. 'He's about two years behind me. He's just come back from doing eyes. I think Muir'll keep him on as a permanent J.R. [Junior Registrar] when Joe Yates gets back.'

I had forgotten Joe Yates. 'What's happening to him? He can't still be in Jude?'

'On holiday plus sick leave.' He looked over my head. 'Sister still here? Excuse me——'

'Sure. Have a good week-end.'

He did not hear. He was already half-way to the duty-room.

I expected, and hoped, he would take Wardell off with him, but she was still in the ward when she sent me to early supper.

Harriet raised her eyebrows. 'Why aren't you eating with the upper classes? Aren't you Sister Observation this week-end?'

'On paper. Wardell is still with us.' I took the empty chair by her. 'Haven't seen you in days! How's life? And Stan Peabody?'

She said that life was dreamy and Stan was a dish. He seemed also to be as great a talker as herself. She knew all the news of Nick. 'Stan gets it from Peter Graveny. So the golden boy is settling for the country life *chez* Sister Mary? No wonder you're so keen on that cottage! When are they throwing Nick out?'

'He doesn't know yet. Any moment. Marcus Stock'll probably blow in and say "Out!" You know what pundits are like.'

'Stock? Is he a chubby cutie with lots of white hair and a young face?'

'Yes. Why? See him in Wylden on your scooter?'

'No. But I noticed a strange pundit-type walking through Cas. once or twice. I see him quite often now. Is he a chum of Sabby Wardell? He was on the terrace with her the other morning.'

'You did? Of course! She and Jill are the same set, and Jill remembered him when he was here.'

'You think that's all? Oh, no! I was so hoping we had a nice new juicy romance in our midst!'

I said dryly, 'Hey! I thought you liked Robert Gordon?

Why so anxious to do him dirt?'

'It's because I like Robbie, dear! He's far too nice for that human iceberg! And talking of Robbie, I have one large bone to pick with you, you old meanie! Why have you been holding out on me about him? Peter Graveny says you must have known he was Norris's godson as you hollered for him there for Nick! I suppose Hurricane Jill told you! You might have told me!'

'I couldn't. I only heard accidentally, and promised him I wouldn't spread it. I'll bet he won't like Peter passing it round. Do keep it dark, Harriet, please!'

She stared. 'Whence this new concern for Robbie's feelings?' Then she laughed. 'I get it! There's nothing like the knowledge of all that lovely lolly in the background to open a girl's eyes to a man's charms!'

'Harriet, that's rubbish, and you know it!' I snapped. 'I never could stick Robert, and I still can't! But he was very good about Nick, and for that I must be grateful.'

'Very touching, dear. Very, very touching!' She was still laughing. 'This is going to kill Stan.'

As to say more would make things worse, I kept quiet, and was very relieved when one of the other girls asked Harriet some question about Casualty. I left the meal early and fumed equally at myself and Harriet's chatty tongue all the way back to Observation. I knew very well my rash words were going to give the housemen's sitting-room a good laugh tonight. Instead of now being able to dismiss it as something Robert had coming to him, it had me irritated and more than a little ashamed. Of course it would get back to him, and embroidered, which seemed very hard after he had drunk all that stewed tea and mentally held my hand that Friday evening. Unless I was much mistaken our new beautiful friendship was going to have died the death by Monday morning. Not that it was all that important, I told myself with rather unnecessary frequency, but I just wished it had not happened.

I reached our landing to find Vint again waiting for me. This time she had Mrs Sands with her. Mr Sands had not arrived, and his wife was worried.

'Dad could have dropped off, duck, but it's not like him. He may be poorly. He's not young, mind. I feel as I ought

130

to get home to see after him, but I don't like leaving the boy.' She sighed. 'There's times it's hard to know what's best, duck. What'll I do, Nurse Rowe?'

Vint, standing a little behind her, mouthed, 'No change.' Aloud, she said, 'Sister Observation is with Sir Julius in Twenty-one.'

That made the decision mine. I suggested Mrs Sands should change out of her gown while I got into mine and had another look at Frank. 'I expect he's settled for the night,' I said euphemistically. 'I'll come straight along to the flat if I think you should stay. How long will you be?'

'Only an hour, duck, if his dad can't come up. I left him his tea all ready to heat this morning like as I always do. If he's been kept late down the docks he'll just have to put a match to the oven, and he'll be up soon as he's ate and had his wash. But it's not like Dad to be late for the boy,' she said again. 'I tell you, Nurse Rowe, I been fretting. I knew as you'd know what I should do.' She smiled as she tugged down her crumpled mask. Her smile was very tired. 'Tomorrow may be the day, eh?'

She said that every night. On occasions Mr Sands had given up hope. His wife and Linda refused to contemplate defeat. It had been when Mrs Sands recognised that in Linda that she had stopped referring to her as 'that girl' and changed it to 'our Linda'.

She was between forty and fifty, but her bulk and anxiety made her look older. She ambled heavily off to the flat like an untidy, overfilled bolster with feet. Frank was not her only child. She had three others, all married, and she seemed to love them all in the same undemanding way. If she had a favourite, from her conversation it was her one daughter who was shortly expecting a second baby after having a difficult time with her first. Mrs Sands said, 'I'd like to be with my Joan, duck, but she's got her husband, and the boy needs me. I don't like leaving Dad, neither, but he'll understand. Our Frank's my boy, and I'm his mum. I'll be staying long as the doctor says.'

She was not a particularly intelligent woman. She never looked at more than the pictures in a newspaper, or read anything but the royalty features in her favourite maga-

131

zine, which she called 'her book'. She was hazy about the Government, had no idea who was Prime Minister, and no interest in finding out. She loved the telly and missed it badly. She never complained, or suggested she had cause for self-pity. She was a simple woman, so she had quite simply rearranged her whole life to sit by her youngest son. She never got in our way or questioned us about his treatment. She would have thought that out of place. We were 'they', and 'they' knew what 'they' were doing. Life was a very uncomplicated affair for Mrs Sands, which was probably why she had her priorities right.

CHAPTER NINE

A SUNDAY MORNING IN OBSERVATION

I CHANGED quickly, then went into the empty duty-room and wrote my name, the time, and Frank's room number on the desk memo pad to show Sister I was back and where she could find me. Then I saw the unstamped envelope addressed to me in Nick's writing on the blotter. Peter Graveny or Mrs Blake must have brought it up from Astead. I put it in my dress pocket to read later and hurried on to Room Five.

It was strange in there without Mrs Sands or Linda knitting in the chair against the wall. Frank lay still and colourless beneath his transparent tent; his closed face was blank as a statue's.

I checked his pulse, breathing, blood, and oxygen pressure, body and air temperatures, the flow of drops falling through the drip-connection, and general appearance. My results were identical with the check Vint had made fifteen minutes ago. I charted them, studied the various graphs, then looked down at Frank again, thinking of his mother and Linda, and wondering how such a plain young man could have inspired their kind of love. As I watched him someone dropped a tray in the corridor. I was about to investigate, when I noticed, or thought I noticed, him give a very faint start. I bent closer over his tent. It must have been imagination, but to be sure I took his pulse again, looking at the chart as well as my watch. There was a very slight alteration in the rhythm. It righted itself as I held on, so I let go and clapped my hands hard above his face, then grabbed his wrist. It had altered again. Hearing was the last sense to be affected by any anaesthetic. It could be the first to come back.

I kept my fingers on his pulse for another three minutes. It was no imagination. The rhythm was changing almost imperceptibly, but it was changing. And his breathing was deeper.

I reached for the bell with my free hand and buzzed my team's private SOS signal. Vint appeared immediately. 'Something wrong, Nurse?'

'I'm not sure if it's right or wrong, but something's happening. Get Mrs Sands back, *stat*. If she's gone send someone for her—fast. She may be still on her way out. Then ring Mr Todd and get him here.'

She vanished. The door opened a few seconds later and a junior came in. 'Sister says she is ready to report to you, Nurse Rowe, and can I take over?'

She was my team's second-year and too junior for the present situation. 'Will you apologise to Sister and say I am sorry to keep her waiting, but Frank Sands is growing restive, and I can't leave him until Nurse Vint returns.' As I spoke Frank stirred visibly, then moved himself on to his back. She gazed at him transfixed. 'Tell Sister, please, Nurse.' I had to prompt.

I was altering Frank's air temperature in his tent and did not see her shoot off. His pulse was growing much stronger. He gave a little cough as his mother rushed in white-faced, nervously tugging together the back strings of her gown. 'He's not been too bad, Nurse? He's not took a turn for the worse?' She clutched me. 'I forgot me mask! Did I ought to fetch one?'

'Don't worry about a mask, dear. Just come closer. I don't think he's worse.' I put my free arm round her ample shoulders. 'You'll be better without a mask. Just stand by me. That's it.'

Then she understood. 'He's never going to wake up! He's never—oh, duck! And me nearly gone to see after

133

his dad! Oh, Nurse! Oh, duck! Oh, Gawd!' Her voice rose to a squeak. 'He's a-shifting hisself! You see, duck? You see?' Tears poured down her face, and she mopped them with the skirt of her gown. 'Nurse Rowe, his eyes is opening.' Her voice was suddenly small and controlled. 'Like as that Mr Browne said.' She pressed her face against the tent. 'Hallo, son. It's me. Mum.'

I heard the door open, but did not look round. Henry Todd appeared round the other side of the bed as Frank Sands stared dazedly at his mother's face. Even with his eyes open his face was blank.

Henry said, 'Say that again, Mrs Sands. Louder.'

Before she could say anything her son's face altered. A faint but coherent smile flickered over his features and lingered in his eyes. He mumbled something I did not catch.

'What's he saying?' Mrs Sands grasped me again. 'Did you hear, Nurse? Did you, Doctor? Don't he know me?'

Henry Todd had crouched down with his ear to the tent. He was not really good-looking, but his smile now made him seem so. 'He's recognised you, Mrs Sands. He said, "Why are you wearing your nightie, Mum?"'

Over ninety minutes later Robert appeared in the duty-room doorway as I was writing the report on Frank's altered treatment. 'Sorry to intrude, but is Sister still up here?'

I beamed at him. Everyone in Observation had been beaming at everyone else since Frank came round. Although our patients were in separate rooms, within minutes the news had spread, and sent a wave of new hope sweeping round the entire ward. As usual, over half our patients were on the D.I.L., and there was the usual little group of other anxious relatives in our flat. 'Wonderful what they can do these days!' they told each other. 'Seventy-three and a half days! And you know what his poor mother said about the state of his head when they carried him in! But he knew her! Knew her at once! Just shows what they can do!'

I told Robert Sister had at last gone off for her week-end half an hour ago. 'Poor Robert, have you been waiting for her? You driving her down to Astead again? I see you've

134

got on a fine suit under that white coat—and very chic it looks!' Relief and sheer happiness had me rattling on like Nick in top gear. 'I'm sorry you've had this wait, but I'm glad Sister stayed on. When one of my patients does a Lazarus I don't mind how big the audience!'

He had been watching me from the doorway in mild astonishment. He came in, now smiling widely. 'That chap in Five? Sands? Round?'

'He is.' I gave the details. 'We have been having a ball,' I went on. 'Dad was doing extra overtime and not in his usual dock. I think Sister rang all round the Pool of London before she traced him. Something is not going to get unloaded tonight, as half his mates clocked off to give him moral support, but who cares? You know his girl friend?'

'Linda with the long black hair and eyes?'

'Sounds like the first line of a song, but that's her! She's not on the phone. Sister asked the cops for help, and she rang me ten minutes ago. She let out such a yell of joy it's a wonder my left eardrum hasn't perforated. Since when,' I smiled smugly, 'I have had Mr Browne himself on the telephone congratulating my team for their nursing.' He bowed, so I stood up and dropped a curtsy. 'I have had a few kind words from the Ass. Mat. on her evening round. She said Matron would be very pleased. Sister Observation is very pleased. Everyone is very pleased. We are everyone's little blue-eyed girls, and we will all have to make ourselves new caps tonight to fit our new-sized heads!'

He laughed. 'I see I don't have to ask how it feels. It obviously feels very good.'

'What? Being smug?'

'No.' He stood in front of the desk looking down at me. 'The knowledge that you personally are directly responsible for that chap's being alive to come round. Without great nursing he'd have been a stiff weeks ago. Nice work, Anna. Very nice work.'

I seldom blushed. I did then. 'Thanks. Thanks very much.'

He was silent. There was nothing unusual about that from him, and normally I should have assumed he had

135

said all he wanted to say, ignored his presence, and got on with my report. This was not a normal night. I said, 'Robert, you are taking an awful chance being seen in here in that white coat. If you don't watch out someone'll make you do some work.'

'A calculated risk. I had to come up here, and couldn't do it without the coat. That a new notice?' He walked over to the board and read the many notices pinned there. 'Find Nick's letter?' He asked, without looking round.

'Letter? Oh, Lor'! I'd forgotten! Yes, thanks. Did you bring it up?'

'Yes.' He was still studying the board. 'I drove down to Astead earlier. Marcus Stock was up here this afternoon, and his car croaked in our park, so I ran him back. I didn't seem to have anything else to do.'

As Wardell had stayed on, that figured. 'I wish I'd known!'

He turned slowly, 'You wanted a message taken to Nick?'

'Not that. Jill's off. You could have given her a lift as far as Astead.'

'I did. We saw her leaving the Home as we were driving out of the gates. That's how I saw Nick. She suggested we dropped in at the hospital to say hallo.'

That should have worried me. It did not, for myself. I was not so sanguine about Jill. 'That was nice. How was he?'

'Fine, as you'll see from his letter. It's good news. Stock's chucking him out tomorrow morning. This is your lucky night.'

'That's what it is!' I heard the lift. 'That can't be the night girls?'

He went into the corridor to look. 'Yes. You'll want me to push off and let you finish your report.'

I had to get that report done, but I was suddenly appalled to discover I did not want him to go. Although Frank was not one of his patients, tonight's golden satisfaction was something I could share with him, and I wanted to go on doing that more than I wanted to do anything for a very long time. I did not try to understand why that should be. It seemed wiser not to.

Reluctantly I agreed, 'I must get on. Sorry.'

'Sorry for interrupting.'

'Not at all. Thanks for delivering my letter.'

'No trouble. I'm frequently nipping down to Astead, so any time you want a lift, or something put on the Wylden bus once Nick moves in with Sister Mary, let me know.'

'Thank you,' I said, 'I will.'

Our mutual politeness was as foreign as my unexpected desire for his company. I suspected I owed his side of it to Frank Sands. In general, our men took our work for granted, much as we took theirs, but every now and then, when something like Frank's recovery happened, just for a little while our doctors realised nursing was a skilled as well as a handy profession and treated us with a new respect. It did not last long. It was fun while it lasted.

Robert was in the doorway. 'I'll leave you to it.'

'Duty calls.' I smiled, and picked up my pen. 'Good night. And have a good week-end.'

'Thank you.' He stepped back inside the room to let the night staff go by to the changing-room. 'Too bad Nick isn't up here to celebrate with you later tonight.'

'Too bad,' I echoed untruthfully. I could have explained this was one celebration Nick would have been unable to understand fully, and consequently one I should not have chosen to share with him. I might have explained had he not clearly got a late date with Wardell. 'Actually, if I am finished in time and Henry Todd can get off for an hour and the pubs are still open, he's taking me out for a beer.'

'Henry?' He frowned. 'I thought you didn't like beer?'

'I loathe the stuff. Tonight it'll taste like nectar!'

'I expect it will. Good night, Anna.' He walked away.

The doorway looked extraordinarily empty. I looked at it for a few seconds, then asked myself if I wanted my head examining and went on with my report.

I did not remember to read Nick's letter, or remember my supper conversation with Harriet, until I got in from my date with Henry Todd. By then I was too sleepy to feel more than uncomfortable on those two counts and dropped into bed. The sun shining on my face seemed to wake me five minutes later. I blinked at my watch. Half-past six. If I got up now I could answer Nick's letter before breakfast.

There was a knock on my door, and Jean Hutton's capped head peered round. 'I wondered if you had over-slept. The first breakfast bell's gone!'

'It can't have!' Then I saw my watch had stopped as I had forgotten to wind it last night. 'Thanks, Jean!' I leapt out of bed. 'If Night Super. reads the register before I arrive, say I'm on my way.'

That week-end was my first experience as Acting Sister Observation. By Saturday night I understood why Sabby Wardell so frequently curtailed her own off-duty. I spent so much time chaperoning pundits, making explanatory telephone calls and visits to Matron's office, and dealing with relatives and patients' friends that I was only able to get the daily mountain of paper-work done by shutting myself in the duty-room in my own off-duty. Not having a moment for writing to Nick, I intended ringing him at the cottage that night. It was ten-thirty before I got back to the Home. I decided it was too late to disturb Sister Mary. Tomorrow should be less hectic, as there were no teaching rounds in Barny's on Sunday mornings, the resident's rounds started at ten instead of nine, and if a consultant appeared in a ward, which was seldom on Sundays, it was never before eleven. We had no operations scheduled and, being full, could not admit. Tomorrow there should be plenty of time to think about Nick.

Wardell had put me down to be off from 10 a.m. until 1 p.m. next day. At half-past nine I was in Observation kitchen going through the day's menu with one of the dietitians from the Special Diets Kitchen, when a junior came in. 'Please, Nurse Rowe, Mr Muir's registrar would like to speak to you on the telephone.'

'Mr Francis? Thanks, Nurse.' I excused myself to the dietitian. 'It's all right, Nurse,' I added, as the junior was waiting.

She said, 'Excuse me, Nurse Rowe, but it's not Mr Francis' voice. I think it's Mr Gordon.'

I did not see how it could be as Robert was off, and Mark Francis had told me yesterday he had not seen Robert since Friday night. It was not important, though I could not follow how she could have mistaken Mark Francis' light Australian drawl for Robert's much deeper voice. Perhaps she was tone-deaf?

I took the call in the duty-room. 'Nurse Rowe speaking, Mr Francis.'

'No Mark Francis, Anna. Robert. Sorry to disturb you,' he said, 'but there's something you might like to know. Muir, Brown-plus-E, and Tubby Wallace have just arrived in Cas. together, and at this moment our sitting-room receiver is buzzing for the S.S.O., Henry, Mark, plus housemen. The bosses want the lads to meet them in Observation. Obviously to consult on Tom.'

"Strewth, yes! You coming up?"

'I'd like to. If this is right and you get a chance, ask Mark to ring me.'

'Sure. Thanks a lot.' I rang off and raced for Vint.

'A consultation at this hour? Without warning? Nurse Rowe, how dare they!'

'They make the rules, my dear. We've got about five minutes. Is Ten ready? Then you set in there and the gown trolley in the corridor. I'll clear the duty-room.' I heaved in the portable X-ray-lamp screen. 'Will you warn Tom he's having visitors?' I beckoned a junior and asked her to find Nurse Hutton and to ask the dietitian to join me in the duty-room. It only took a minute to finish our menu discussion, and Jean arrived as the dietitian left. 'Sorry, Rowe, I was doing a dressing. Crisis?'

'Consultation. Will you take over the ward as soon as the pundits arrive instead of waiting till ten?'

She was as indignant as Vint. 'Nine-thirty on Sunday? It's indecent!'

Dr Wallace was a consultant anaesthetist. He always worked with Mr Browne. Thanks to Robert, when the three pundits and our Senior Surgical Officer stepped out of the lift we were ready for them.

Henry Todd, Mark Francis, and the two housemen galloped up the stairs a few seconds later.

'Sorry, Anna,' Henry murmured as he tied his gown, 'but the bastards didn't warn me. Thank God you're on and not Sweet Sabby. This would have been enough to

139

make her take umbrage with me for weeks! How come you're all set? Second sight?'

'Robert Gordon.' The pundits were still scrubbing, so I handed on Robert's message to Mark.

'Oh, my word, I'll ring him,' said Mark. 'He's welcome to join the bloody party.'

Robert had arrived by the time the pundits were ready. Tom Elkroyd greeted the nine men with a laconic, 'Morning, all.'

Mr Browne introduced Dr Wallace. 'One of my distinguished colleagues.' He did not mention Dr Wallace's specific job. 'The Senior Surgical Officer you will remember from your last ward.'

'Oh, aye,' said Tom.

'As it's Sunday,' said Mr Browne, 'we decided to do our round together. Saves the nurses time and much more peaceful without students.'

'Oh, aye.'

'And how are the headaches?' Mr Browne sat on the locker-seat. Mr Muir and the S.S.O. perched themselves on the windowsill. Dr Wallace took a chair round to the other side of the bed. The residents propped up the walls. I stood by Mr Browne.

After the briefest of medical examinations it could have been a social occasion. The conversation was mainly on Tom's trade, bricklaying.

Dr Wallace had lived in China as a boy. He said, 'Their builders used the same hods as you chaps here. They were using them two thousand years ago.'

'Happen there's nowt to beat a hod, then.'

Mr Muir, rolling his 'r's', put in some remarks on traditional building methods in his part of Scotland. Mr Browne said there was one question he had long wanted to ask an expert. 'Why does one frequently observe an improvised flag flying on top of an unfinished building?'

The room was still darkened. Tom had his glasses off, and his slow grin deepened the creases at the corners of his narrowed eyes. 'That'll be for "topping-up", Doctor. Soon as roof's done, up goes flag to show guv'nor it's time for beer all round. The lads'll take it right poorly if there's no sup of beer.' It was a long speech for him. Some of his words were slurred, and while he was speaking he had turned his head carefully towards Mr Browne, then back to Dr Wallace on his other side, as if he found it easier to move his head than his eyes.

It was several minutes later that Mr Browne stood up and announced he had wasted quite enough of the staff nurse's valuable time enjoying this pleasant little chat, and he supposed he ought to move on and do some work. 'Very nice to have seen you, Mr Elkroyd. Your good lady here today? Keeping well? And the children? Good.' He waved at Tom, nodded at me. 'Thank you very much.' He led the procession out.

Vint had been waiting outside to settle Tom. The S.S.O. stood outside to let me out and her in, and as he was senior resident present, the others were still in with Tom. I heard him ask, 'On double time, are you then, Mr Gordon?'

I did not catch Robert's reply, only the quick ripple of laughter and Mark Francis', 'Too bloody right!'

It was the ward sister's prerogative to be present during consultations on her patients. I had been in on several in other wards but not before in Observation.

Most of the talking was done by Messrs Browne and Muir. Dr Wallace asked a few questions. The S.S.O. made an occasional remark, but spent most of his time scowling at the various plates on the lighted screen as the pundits went over Tom's case from his first visit to his firm's doctor. Henry Todd switched on the plates as required. His houseman at first tried to keep Tom's many notes in the right order, until Mr Browne told him to stop that damned fiddling.

Mr Muir said, 'We've dealt with the known risk. What's the possibility of those unknown?'

'No possibility, Ian,' retorted Mr Browne. 'A probability.'

I listened intently as they tossed the subject backward and forward at each other like a ball. Sister would want as near a verbatim report as I could manage. I found it deeply interesting and as deeply distressing. I tried to achieve the correct professional detachment but only succeeded outwardly. I was constantly aware the brain we were looking at belonged to a man I had come to know and like as a great friend. I could not forget Betty Elkroyd; the three elder children at primary school; the baby son who was too fat to crawl and got round at the double on his seat. Betty said she had to patch every pair of pants he possessed. She said he missed his father. 'He's right young —but he knows.'

I knew as much about her parents. Grandad was a passionate supporter of their local football team. He said our Tom must be home by start of season and not let United down. Gran had a weakness for Bingo and potted plants. Gran had right green fingers and could get anything to grow. She had recently won a rose-patterned tea service with her prize pelargonium, and was keeping it to use when our Tom gets home.

Henry fixed up another plate. The S.S.O. said, 'On the move again. From that I'd say a few weeks.'

I grimaced involuntarily and stared at the floor. Robert was watching me when I looked up. He did not look away immediately, as he had already done several times. He looked as if this was hell for him also, and he did not mind my knowing it. Perhaps irrationally, I found that comforting.

The desk was littered with notes, with path. lab and X-ray reports, huge X-ray envelopes, and the X-ray lamp was growing hot and smelling faintly.

Mr Muir began sorting the notes. 'Well, Charles?'

Mr Browne stared long at the most recent plate, now on the lighted screen. 'I think we should do him. I still don't fancy it. I don't fancy it at all. But I fancy the alternative still less.' He spun round. 'What's he got? Two months? Maybe much less. You agree, Ian?'

Mr Muir hesitated. 'From my angle, I'd prefer to wait another day or two. Otherwise, my opinions are the same as yours.'

'Right. How about you, Tubby?'

'If you're willing to risk it,' said Dr Wallace, 'I'll go along with you.'

Henry Todd and Mark Francis had already produced their bosses' theatre booking lists. Mr Browne turned to Henry. 'I want a clear day for this lad. Have I got one clear in this week?'

142

'No, sir. Unless you can do that girl from Catherine next week? She's your only one on Wednesday.'

'She can't wait, and I'll want the best part of a day for her. Elkroyd can't wait more than a few more days. I'd say he'll be ripe around the week-end. Let's have that.' He studied his list. 'Saturday's clear, Henry. That's six days. All right for you, Ian?' Mr Muir nodded. 'Saturday'll be it.'

Henry said, 'It's your free week-end, sir. And Bank Holiday.'

'Is it? It would be! Can't help that. See you book my theatre straight away, as all the others will be busy with road accidents. I'll start at nine. Suit you, Ian?'

Mr Muir had been looking at his list. 'Very well. How long do you expect to take?'

Mr Browne had another look at the X-ray screen. 'Around seven hours. Maybe a little less. Probably longer. Right.'

He switched off the light. 'I'll talk to Elkroyd on Friday. No man should be asked to face more than one night with the knowledge he will then have. Until then he is to be told nothing.'

In Sister's place, I asked, 'And Mrs Elkroyd, Mr Browne?'

He frowned. 'Yes, I'll have to see her. I'll want her here on Friday. But that poor girl already has quite enough on her plate. I don't want to burden her with this today. Let them have today. I'll get in touch with her later. Will you ask Sister Observation to remind me of this in the next couple of days?'

Matron arrived for one of her invariably unexpected rounds as the men were leaving. Mr Browne assured her they would see themselves out.

Matron waited until the corridor had cleared. 'Should you not be off duty, Nurse Rowe?'

I explained about the consultation. She wanted all the details, and, as I was already so late off, said she thought on this occasion I could remain to escort her round. She always spent a few minutes with every patient. By the time she had seen all twenty-eight first lunch was being served. It was not worth my while to go over to the Home,

143

and I went straight to the dining-room.

Harriet was already eating. 'I've just seen your ward sister walking through Cas. looking as if she had stepped out of a fashion magazine in a dream of a pink linen dress.' She helped me to water. 'Is her home near Astead? She told Sister Cas. she was on her way there.'

'I don't know where she lives. I expect Robert was driving her down.'

'Could be. I saw his car in our yard. I know she and Robbie are supposed to be very thick, but she surely can't always be visiting Mr Norris? With his allergy to visitors?'

'He can't be allergic to Robert. He often nips down to Astead when he's off——'

'Oh, sure, but when is a registrar off? One half-day a week with luck, and every other week-end!'

'Which is roughly all Wardell gets, as she never takes her full off-duty—and, baby, do I understand that now!'

'Tough at the top?'

'Tough on my private life.' I explained why.

She went for another helping of apple pie. 'Nick tried to ring you?' she asked, dousing her food with sugar.

'Not as far as I know. Jill's bound to tell him I'm busy, and he may not like to run up Sister Mary's phone bill.'

'No.' She laughed suddenly. 'I can't imagine the three of them together!'

'They'll get along. They're all chums.'

Her round brown eyes glanced at me. 'Talking of chums, I expect you've heard Sabby Wardell used to be chummy with your golden boy?'

'Sure. First from Nick. Later from others.'

'Nick told you?' she echoed, surprised. 'I wonder if she's told Robbie?'

'If she hasn't,' I retorted sharply, 'someone else has! That's for sure!'

She nodded casually, helped herself to more sugar, and promised herself she would start another diet, tomorrow. Then she said, 'If Wardell only goes down with Robbie, why should Sister Cas. tell me Sister Observation must be a great favourite with Dr Beeching for using the railways so much? Do you suppose the attraction could be that old boy—what's his name—Marcus Stock?'

I remembered Nick's rumour then. Anyone seeing Wardell out of uniform and not knowing her job might well describe her as a fashion model. 'Harriet, you could be right!'

'Aren't I always? Or nearly always?' She reached for the cheese. 'Pass the biscuits, Anna. Be a break for Robbie if I am this time.'

'He may not see it that way.'

She glanced at me again. She did not comment on my remark. 'Do pass those biscuits, duckie! I'm still starving, and I'm due back in Cas. in five minutes!'

CHAPTER TEN

A QUIET AFTERNOON IN EYES

In Barny's any ward sister off for the week-end was given a private ward report in her room in the Sisters' Home on Sunday night.

I went over with the Elizabeth senior staff nurse. The Sisters' Home was forbidden territory to nurses unless there for official reasons, but as our two sisters lived next door to each other I hoped to look in on Jill after seeing Wardell to ask about her week-end. The Elizabeth nurse told me her report was not very long.

Sabby Wardell was wearing the pink linen dress Harriet had admired. She looked wonderful and was in a rare matey mood. She gave me coffee, and when my report was over kept me talking another hour about next week's ward arrangements. Jill's light was out, and it was again far too late to ring Nick when I got away. I eased my conscience by writing him a long letter before going to bed. I posted it on my way to breakfast next morning, and then wasted a lot of time that day wondering if I had said too much or not enough.

Observation was a different ward that Monday. On several occasions Sister was seen smiling. Her staff sighed with relief and smiled with her. The new atmosphere continued until she returned from her first visit to Matron's

Office on Tuesday. From the way she swept back up the corridor, it was obvious, despite the readings on our many wall thermometers, the temperature had dropped degrees.

The Office wanted Jean Hutton in another ward a day earlier than Sister had anticipated. Then she heard Jean's team-leader sneeze in the sterilising-room. She reacted as if the poor girl was intentionally spreading bubonic plague. She lined us all up and warned us that the next nurse to come on with a cold would never return to her ward again as long as she was Sister Observation.

'That a promise?' Vint mumbled behind her mask to her neighbour. Luckily, Sister did not hear.

Sister added Jean's team to mine for the rest of the day, which meant a last-minute change in my off-duty. I was off from two till five instead of from five onward. 'I trust you've no objections, Nurse Rowe?'

'No, Sister,' was the only possible answer. I did not object for myself, but in my letter I had told Nick I would be in that evening, and if he did not ring me first I would ring him between seven and eight. I rang the cottage twice while I was off, but got no answer.

Addy was back from holiday and waiting in my room when I got off that night. I was so pleased to see her, I forgot to look and see if there had been any phone messages from Nick until after she had gone. There were no messages.

Harriet looked in as I was getting into bed. 'How's the golden boy?'

'Don't know.' I explained. 'Been out with Stan?'

'Not tonight! It's Tuesday! Julian! I must wash my hair. Is there time?'

'If you do it in your room. The bathroom lights'll be out in ten minutes.'

'Not if I'm in the bath first!' She vanished.

Sister altered her off-duty next day. She wanted that afternoon and evening free instead of a half-day on Friday before her holiday. She was discussing this with Addy and myself when my patient in Room Four had a second coronary. He was barely over it when Sister sent for me. 'You must move Mrs March from Room One to Florence Ward immediately. The Cardiac Unit are sending us an emer-

146

gency. His name is Leslie John Barry, aged nine. As you are off from ten till one, Nurse Vint must special him.' She gave me the child's notes.

Leslie had been a blue baby. The hole in his heart had been repaired eighteen months ago by our Cardiac Unit, and his heart wired to a pacemaker battery that controlled the beat. 'A fault in the time, Sister?'

'Presumably. His pulse-rate is falling, and he is growing cyanosed according to the telephone message I have just received. His father is driving him from Hampshire with the usual relay of police escorts. He should have gone to the Cardiac Recovery Ward, but they have just had to fill their last bed. He should be here soon.'

Leslie had arrived, and his timer was being repaired before I went off. The battery was a little larger than a packet of ten cigarettes. The fault had been caused by one of the external wires breaking.

His father, a farmer, was drinking tea in the corridor when I got back on duty. 'He's having a good sleep now, Nurse—and I wouldn't mind one myself! I've never pushed a car the way I did this morning! We changed cops at every county border, and each lot seemed to step on it harder than the last! It was like a bad dream at the time!' He mopped his face. 'I've got to take my hat off to them! I don't know London well and how they got me through all that traffic and down side roads was nobody's business! God, was I glad to see this place! There were moments when I didn't think we'd make it.'

His son's lips had been dark blue and he had been gasping pathetically when he was carried in. Vint was sitting with him in the room. She stood up, smiling with her eyes. 'Isn't he a poppet?' she whispered.

He was a dark-haired little boy and small for his age, but his chubby face was healthily tanned and serene. Asleep he looked three, not nine. I thought, poor little baby, and then remembered a few years back he would now be a dead boy. He looked a happy child, and his father had a kind face.

'Nurse Rowe.' Another of my team was at the door. 'Could you come? It's Tom Elkroyd.'

It was the first attack of acute pain Tom had had since

147

his injection dose had been increased. We gave him another injection, but this time it was a very long while before it took effect. When the pain had gone Tom was more exhausted than I had ever known him. While he was asleep I took his bed-ticket along to the duty-room. Sister and Addy were at lunch. I thought things over, then asked the switchboard to buzz Mr Todd.

'Sorry, Nurse, Mr Todd's operating.'

I had forgotten that girl from Catherine. 'Then will you try for Mr Gordon? Thanks.'

I waited by the telephone. Robert rang from the canteen a few minutes later. 'Gordon. Yes?'

I told him about Tom. 'He's so weak. I'd like someone to see him as he is now. Could you call up before your afternoon eye clinic?'

'Yes.' He rang off.

I replaced the receiver thoughtfully. He was never loquacious, but it was some time since he had been so terse with me. He had sounded like the old Robert.

That was how he looked when he arrived. We looked at Tom without waking him. He was still too limp with exhaustion. His face was unnaturally swollen, and the skin had an unhealthy shine. His pulse showed that the pressure in his skull was rising.

Back in the corridor, Robert asked, 'As bad as before?'

'It's hard to tell. Perhaps not quite, but it gave his heart a much worse beating. If he starts having these between now and Saturday . . .' I left my sentence unfinished.

He frowned at the bed-ticket. 'This'll have to be stepped up. I can't do it without Muir's O.K. as both he and Brown-plus-E specifically said not to. He's due in Eyes this afternoon. I'll talk to him.'

'Thanks.' I sighed with relief. 'Sorry to have dragged you back.'

'That's all right.' He tugged at the back strings of his gown, and one string snapped.

'Let me.' I got behind him. 'You'll break the lot if you fight them like that.'

He said softly, 'The way I feel right now, Anna, I could break this whole bloody place with my two hands.'

'I know.' I took his gown. 'Cap, please. And mask.'

148

'Sorry.' He handed them over. 'I'll talk to Muir before the clinic if possible. If not, as soon as I can.' He added another note to the case history. 'Talking of talks, though this isn't the time or place, it's the only place I ever see you, and I want to talk to you. When are you off today?'

'I've been.' I was curious and rather disturbed. He was not trying to date me for fun. He had never dated me—and it was Sabby's half-day. 'Why? What do you want to talk about?'

'I can't go into that now. I'm due in Eyes. I'll be there till four. I hoped you'd be off this afternoon and we could have tea somewhere. Mark's on, so I could get out for an hour or so. Tonight's out as I'm on Cas. call in the A.R.R. [Accident Recovery Room] from eight. We'll have to fix something tomorrow.' He walked away before I could tell him tomorrow was out as I was going down to Wylden after lunch and would not be back till Friday night. Sister Mary had invited me for my this week's day and a half at my last visit. She was expecting me for early tea, as I had explained in my letter to Nick. Of course, I could say I had been delayed in the ward and stay on to learn what Robert had to say to me, and Sister Mary would believe me. That was why I could not use the excuse. I then realised it was Sister Mary and not Nick I was bothering about, and had another of those guilty pangs the thought of him kept giving me lately. Fortunately I was on duty, and so the pang was short-lived.

Sister and Addy returned. Sister asked why I had re-called Mr Gordon. She received my answer coldly. 'You did not, I hope, allow Mr Elkroyd's notes to leave the ward? Then you had better go down to the Eye Department now and wait with them for Mr Muir's opinion.'

I had not visited Eyes since the night Robert and I had talked in Sister Eyes' office—the night before my first week-end in the cottage. The department looked as different in daylight as my private life looked since that particular night. Momentarily I wondered which had been the catalyst? That talk with Robert, Nick's detached retina? Then Sister Eyes came out of her glass-walled office.

Mr Muir was with the Dean. 'Wait by all means, Nurse Rowe. He shouldn't be long.'

149

I waited just inside the clinic-room doorway. It was very quiet, though the clinic had started. Eyes had the best appointments system in Barny's and its staff had the best reputation for punctuality. The two housemen were already seeing their first patients, and only three others waited their turn on the bench against the far wall.

The registrar's desk was empty. It stood near one window, between a piebald rocking-horse and three tropical-fish tanks. Then Robert came out of the dark room pushing an old man in a wheelchair. 'That's fine for another month, Mr Brunton. The nurse will push you along to join your wife in the canteen. Mr Yates should be back from holiday by your next visit.'

'You done me nicely, son,' said the old man jovially. 'And that Mr Yates done hisself nicely having his sick-leaf and his holidays in this weather. Lovely bit of sun we've had this year.'

Robert handed him over to the Eyes nurse, then walked up to me. 'I haven't seen him yet.'

'Sister said he's with the Dean. She said he won't be long.'

'I wouldn't bet on that. I forgot the housemen switch round next Tuesday when I was up in Observation just now. If Muir doesn't like the Dean's candidates he'll be there all afternoon. Shall I ring you?'

I hesitated, then shook my head. 'Sister Observation told me to wait. I'd better do that.'

'Please yourself.' He went over to the patients' bench. 'Sorry to delay you, madam. Will you come over here, please?'

The junior ophthalmic houseman took his man into the dark room. Sister Eyes gave two newcomers their cards and showed them to the bench. The nurse returned from the canteen, took a look around, then began embroidering 'Eyes' in red on a new sterile towel. I went on waiting, and watching the clock and the back of Robert's dark head alternately.

His new patient was a middle-aged woman with dyed blonde hair, a nervous giggle and a coy manner. Her multi-coloured shift would have looked fine on a teenager. It accentuated her age.

She had already been seen by the houseman and asked to wait for the registrar. 'I don't know why the young doctor had to fuss, Doctor,' she confided. 'It's not as if there's anything really wrong with silly little me! I expect you think I'm having you on about seeing two of everything!'

'No.' Robert was squinting into his ophthalmoscope. 'I don't think that, madam.' He had been moving his hand behind his head. It was now stationary. 'Just look at my hand. Try not to blink. Good.' He lowered the instrument and glanced over his shoulder. 'Will you now look straight at that nurse by the door? And keep looking at her.'

'That tall pretty nurse with the lovely red hair you were talking to, Doctor?' She slapped her knee archly. 'She your young lady?'

'No,' said Robert. 'But she's the one I want you to look at.'

The Eyes nurse caught my eye. She was in Vint's set. When Robert escorted his patient, now giggling delightedly, into the dark room she came over to me. 'Do you think Sister Observation would like me to go in there and chaperon him, Nurse Rowe?'

I said primly, 'Won't that depend on Sister Eyes?'

She shot me the sort of glance a well-trained fourth-year would give a staff nurse who had suddenly turned very senior and went back to her sewing.

I wanted to kick myself. It was not her fault that truthful monosyllable should have so irritated me. Naturally she knew about Robert and Wardell. Vint apart, it was common knowledge. I had known it for weeks, so why let it rile me now?

For once I had time to stand and think. I was still doing that when Robert and his lady reappeared and went back to his desk. She was less coy now, rather scared because he wanted her to stay and be seen by Mr Muir, and he was being very nice to her. When she moved back to the bench to await Mr Muir and he asked for his next patient he glanced round again to see if his boss had arrived. That time he looked through me as he had done hundreds of times in the past. I had never minded that at all. I minded it so much now that I saw the astonishing truth. I could not conceive how, after so long, this could have

151

happened to me. The fact remained it had. I had no doubts, no confusion. It was so simple, and so senseless.

I looked round the room as if expecting other people to notice some outward change in me. I might have been invisible. The housemen were looking into their patients' eyes; Robert was taking notes; the nurse was intent on her sewing; Sister Eyes was writing; the waiting patients were reading magazines. The rocking-horse was staring belligerently out of the window, and even the tropical fish in their tanks were swimming away from me.

Mr Muir was another twenty minutes. Then I rang Observation. Addy, now in charge, told me to return via the dispensary.

Later, Tom savoured the flavour of his new medicine. 'What's this, then? Run out of needles?'

Next morning he said he felt a new lad. 'Happen that'll be a tonic? That new mucky stuff?'

'Something like that.' I felt like Sapphira, wife to Ananias.

I had had no chance to talk to Robert on personal matters since after lunch yesterday, and though I could have left a message for him at the lodge or with one of the other men, knowing our grapevine, I decided to break a few rules and leave it with Tom.

'Oh, aye. I'll tell him. Doing more painting?'

'That's right. Thanks, Tom. See you Saturday.'

'Aye. Sh—Sh—Shaturday.'

Sister was at first lunch. She had deputed Addy to take my report and tell me to go to second lunch and stay off. I met Jill coming up as I was going down our block stairs.

'The very girl I wanted to see! Off now, Anna? Go and have lunch and change at the double, and Dr Stock'll give you a lift as far as Astead. He's come up to collect his mended car and is calling for you at two! Hurry! He has to be back in Astead General by three-thirty.'

'Jill, that's awfully nice of him.' We cantered down together. 'And thank you for coming up. You ask him to give me a lift? Thanks a lot. How are you? And how did the week-end go? I haven't seen you to ask, and I've kept meaning to ring you, but there's never time.'

'Do I not know it! Elizabeth is hectic!'

'And how did the week-end go?' I asked again.

'Perfect! We've finished the kitchen. You'll love it!'

'I'll bet. How was Nick?'

She had been smiling radiantly. Briefly her smile vanished. Then she turned hearty. 'Making a textbook recovery. Marcus Stock is most satisfied.'

There was something different about her. 'Jill, you've cut your hair.'

'No. Just had it done for a change!'

'It looks terrific!' It did, but it was not the only alteration in her appearance. She was wearing face powder, which she never wore on duty, and though only a trace, a definite trace of eye shadow. 'You had a facial, too?'

She flushed. 'I had to do something, my child! I mean —well—oh, dear! There's the Ass. Mat., and I must see her. Have a nice time, and give my love to Sister Mary.' She sailed down a side corridor to the Assistant Matron. 'Sister, may I have a word with you?'

I walked on with my head over my shoulder and straight into Peter Graveny and two other registrars. Peter asked where I was going so fast.

'Wylden. Marcus Stock is giving me a lift.' I polished my nails on my apron bib. 'That's the kind of girl I am! Pundits give me lifts!'

'To Wylden?' He seemed almost startled, and exchanged an odd glance with his companions. 'Nick expecting you?'

'Lord, yes! Have you been down to the cottage yet!'

'Er—yes. On Monday.'

That surprised me. He had stood me a coffee on Tuesday. I asked why he had not mentioned it then.

'Didn't I? Surely. No? Oh, must have meant to and forgotten. Nice little place, that cottage. Just the thing for Sister Mary.'

'Ideal.' I was beginning to wonder if there was something wrong with my eyesight. Now Peter seemed to be looking different. 'Peter, was Nick all right?'

'Great!' He was as hearty as Jill. 'In very good form and being shockingly pampered by Sister Mary. Trust old Nick to have the luck of his namesake.' he added dryly. 'But I expect you want to get on, Anna. You won't want

153

to keep your tame pundit waiting!'

Everyone seemed so anxious I should not keep Marcus Stock waiting that I skipped lunch, bought myself a couple of sandwiches in the canteen, and ate them in my room while I changed. I was ready by two, and had time to face the fact that I had gone into the canteen to see if Robert was there. He had not been.

I enjoyed my drive to Astead. Marcus Stock did not talk or act like a pundit, but neither did he behave as if we belonged in the same age group. We talked about Nick, Sister Mary, the cottage and the great changes he had noticed in Barny's after an absence of several years. He entranced me by having been a student when Matron was training, and a junior houseman when Brown-plus-E was our youngest S.S.O. ever. He laughed at my reaction. 'I'm from the dark ages of medicine, Nurse Rowe! I remember the no-touch technique, and life when penicillin was in powder form and had to be made up fresh for each injection! I even saw the old M and B 693 in constant use—and heard the patients warned off onions and eggs while on it!'

'What happened if they ate them, Doctor?'

'It was supposed to turn them navy blue—but that I never saw!' He laughed again. 'Face it, Nurse Rowe! You are driving with history! What else do I remember—ah, yes! The present Sisters Elizabeth and Observation as raw P.T.S. juniors!'

I could not visualise Sabby Wardell as a raw anything. 'I'm sure Miss Wardell was as neat and calm as she is now.'

'Very true. And Miss Collins used to blow round like a gust of fresh air, with her cap on the side of her head and a forgotten mask round her neck.'

'So Miss Collins hasn't altered either?'

'Also very true,' he agreed, and asked a question about Observation. 'It must be most interesting to be using so many of the new techniques. I gather you often use high-pressure oxygen on your patients. Sister Elizabeth showed me the pressure chamber. It looked to me like the interior of a spaceship. Doesn't all that apparatus worry the patients?'

'Luckily, not at all. And the women love the tasteful pink paint covering it all.' Our pressure chamber had been in use this morning. 'Did you look through the peep-hole?'

'No. I saw it empty one day last week.'

As we neared Astead the conversation went back to Sister Mary. He said he was delighted to have her as a nearish neighbour. He had been asked to tea last Sunday and had helped with the kitchen painting. 'I fear I was more hindrance than help. Jill—that is, Miss Collins—had to chase me round with a paraffin rag. Our young expert Dexter was not pleased with my handiwork! The shoe-maker should stick to his last. Now then, which is your best bus stop?'

I did not enjoy the bus ride. I no longer had any excuse for avoiding thinking about Nick and what I must say to him some time in the next thirty-six hours. Remembering David, the thought made me squirm. I knew exactly how Nick was going to feel, unless by some miracle he had changed as much as myself.

I thought of Jill this afternoon. In retrospect I saw it was not only her appearance that had changed, it was her whole manner. She had looked so happy. As happy as a girl looks when she discovers she is in love and loved.

The corn was golden, the hops were shooting up their poles, the apples were turning pink, and every garden we passed was blazing with roses. The Garden of England was living up to its name in this most perfect of summers. I admired it absently, as my thoughts drifted from Jill to Sabby Wardell on Sunday night. Wardell's appearance then had had something in common with Jill's this after-noon. Was that happiness? Then I got it. They had both worn the same faint aura of triumph. In Jill's case, no doubt because I liked her very much, I was convinced that had been unconscious. I wanted to be fair to Wardell, even though I knew that was now practically impossible for me, so I did try to persuade myself her triumph on Sunday could not possibly have been intentionally directed at me. She had no reason for rejoicing in scoring over me. She held all the aces. She was far better-looking, she held the better job, and she had Robert on a string.

Then I remembered Jill was one of her oldest friends.

And Peter Graveny was a friend of Nick's. It was more than odd he should not have mentioned seeing Nick when we had that coffee. After his previous visits to Nick he had made a point of bringing me up to date. Jill had always managed to do the same after her visits, either on the telephone or by leaving me a note. Yet since last weekend no one, Nick included, had volunteered any news of him at all. Was it merely a coincidence, or did it tie up with the impression I had long had that Jill was falling in love with Nick? If Nick had discovered it was Jill and not me—and in present circumstances I was the last person to blame him for that—he would certainly have told Peter. I knew Jill's dislike of discussing her private affairs, but there were some things a girl just had to tell someone or burst. Since yesterday I had been aching to unburden to Harriet, and had only managed to keep things to myself because she was such a talker and my situation was so hopeless. Had there been no Sabby Wardell and had I suspected Robert was growing interested in me, not even Harriet's chatty tongue would have kept me quiet. Sabby was no talker, she was Jill's old friend, and she lived in the room next door. If Jill confided in her she would not have been human had she not found the news pleasing and amusing at my expense. She might, as Addy insisted, like me, but our relationship was very superficial. Jill belonged in her original set, and we all had a family feeling about our old sets. I had to be honest. If one of my old set looked like Jill and managed to remove a man as attractive as Nick from a girl years younger than herself and—still being honest—who was much prettier, I should have been enchanted. I was enchanted now, having quite made up my mind I was right. My spirits soared as the bus turned into Wylden.

Nick and Sister Mary were waiting for me at the bus stop. Marcus Stock had rung them from Astead.

'Such a dear man,' said Sister Mary, kissing me affectionately, 'and as thoughtful and cheery now as when he was a hefty midwifery clerk bounding round my nurseries with a baby under each arm and a much-stretched nursery apron round his waist. His hair was then as golden as yours, dear boy.' She slid an arm through mine, the other through

Nick's as we walked slowly towards her cottage. 'You must be as delighted as we are with his pleasing news, dearies!'

'News, Sister Mary?' I looked at Nick. He wore dark glasses with blinkered side-pieces like Tom's. He smiled at me in silence.

'You've not heard, dearie? You don't know Dr Stock is engaged to be married?'

'And that it's all my own work?' Nick put in. 'Isn't that so, Sister, my angel?'

'Dear boy, have I not been giving you all the credit ever since you first opened my eyes to the situation when I visited you in hospital? Just think'—she squeezed my arm —'it was this poor boy's eye that brought those two nice people together again!'

My God, I thought, Harriet was right! I nearly exploded with relief. 'I heard a rumour. Several rumours. I never guessed there was anything really in them.'

'Nor would there have been,' said Nick, 'had I not had the brilliance to spot the truth, albeit with both eyes bandaged, and start asking tactful questions of one and all! You'd be surprised how much I learnt, darling!' He blew me a kiss over Sister Mary's head. 'You may think you know our Jilly! I'll bet you never even guessed time was when she and Marcus Stock were very very good friends!'

'Jilly . . .' My voice cracked. 'Jill Collins?'

They laughed at my surprise. Sister Mary said we must have a nice cup of tea and they would tell me all about it. Nick held open her front gate and said I could call him Cupid. 'I may say Cupid with his one good eye saw a damn sight better than you with your two, my love! You, my precious redhead,' he added almost accusingly, 'go round with your big blue eyes wide, wide open—seeing nothing! Nothing at all!'

CHAPTER ELEVEN

THE GROCER DELIVERS THE GOODS

SISTER MARY looked years younger. She said, 'My old friends keep writing to ask what I find to do in my quiet country village. When I have time to draw breath, dearie, no doubt I shall give that problem my full attention.'

Nick said, 'If you don't watch it, Sister, the district nurse'll be complaining to her union.'

'Nonsense, dear boy! That charming and most sensible girl works long hours even by midwifery standards. She was very sweet about the help I was able to give poor Mrs Ferguson.'

I said, 'You've not been nursing the Prof.'s wife as well as Nick and your Matron, Sister?'

'No, no, dearie. She was only unwell, so I saw to her household.' She smiled. 'I had forgotten how children eat! I rang our dear Mrs Evans for advice, and she told me catering for teenagers was simple. She said allow for each child "as for two healthy men on manual work!" I looked up the correct calories in one of the Professor's books and acted accordingly! It was barely enough. Those children cleared every meal, and half an hour later needed buns and apples to support their flagging energies. And the noise!' She smiled affectionately on us. 'My dears, I am rather thankful you are both past the "pop" age. But I am now an expert on the subject and can discuss at length the Top Ten and the strange magic of the Beatles. I fear dear Edith was very shocked because I looked at those —I believe they are known as pop programmes—on her television. But, as I explained, the Ferguson children all promised to visit me, and have done so, and I want to be able to understand what they are talking about.'

'Sister,' said Nick, 'no excuses! You are as big a fan of the Mersey Beat as any of those kids!'

'Naughty boy! You mustn't tease me! What ever must Nurse Rowe be thinking?'

They got on very well. She treated him as a cross between a pet patient and a pet nephew, and was clearly delighted to have him to fuss over, even though his presence inevitably meant a lot of extra work for her. Housekeeping was still a novelty to her, and she was taking a very active part in her interior decorating, but that had not stopped her keeping open house for Jill and myself, and all her local friends.

Over tea she reminded me of our long search pre-Mr Martin. 'Remember all those terrible barn-like places we looked at, dearie?'

'And that place the house agent called a "quiet little house" that was right next to the sawmill on one side and the forge on the other? Harriet Jones took me to see it on her scooter, and there was so much noise, even on a Saturday afternoon, that we couldn't even hear her engine.'

'What about that "period cottage of character" on the marsh! Dear Jill took me in Mrs Evans' car, and we found it without water, drains, electricity, or a whole roof! Jill put the period as late Roman!'

Nick said, 'One thing I can't understand, ladies, is how, with all this scouring of the countryside, you never seem to have run into Marcus Stock.'

Sister Mary reproached herself for the opportunities wasted in that direction during the years Jill was one of her staff midwives. 'But a maternity hospital works under constant pressure. We were always in a hurry, on and off duty. I was aware Dr Stock worked locally, but he was no longer on our staff, so we had no occasion to require his services. My party was our first and last purely social occasion.'

I asked, 'Did you send him an invitation, Sister?'

Regretfully she shook her head. 'He was included in my general invitation to all old Barny's men, but I believe he was unaware Jill was at Wylden House.' Nick nodded. 'I never knew they were acquainted, or I would have made a point of sending him a personal invitation. You are a remarkably astute young man, Nick!'

He coloured slightly. 'Sister, my angel, I am all for hogging the credit, but, remember, I did ask a lot of questions, and, as I told you, my stroke of luck was seeing someone in Astead General who remembered the past and had known Stock and Jill way back.'

'Why did it break off? His family problems?' I asked. 'Then why didn't he ask her to wait?'

'Because she's the type who would wait unto death, and he's a very decent old boy and wouldn't dream of holding a girl to those terms. So he backed out. My stroke of luck was of the opinion they both took it hard. That's why I decided to move in.'

I snapped my fingers. 'Sister Dawson! I'll bet you had this from her. She told me she had known the Doctor a long time, and he was always sweet to Jill. Am I right?'

'Beloved, as I seem to recollect telling you previously, you mustn't expect me to divulge my sources of information.'

That took me back to his first telephone call and the effect it had had on me. It seemed so long ago, but not, from the way he was watching me, to Nick. I had to change the subject. I asked to be shown round.

It was over two weeks since my last visit, and the ground-floor rooms were now ready. The furniture was wholly free of dust-covers and it was brushed and polished and arranged as neatly as only a trained nurse would arrange a room. Sister Mary had few pictures, but literally hundreds of photographs. They lined every available space. There were rows and rows of babies. Of mothers and babies, of 'old babies' as school-children, 'older babies' in their wedding groups, second-generation babies on their mothers' laps, groups of old pupils and clerks, of nurses in Barny's old uniform, one of which included our present Matron as a plump, rather untidy second-year.

Nick's colour scheme had transformed the kitchen from a poky, dark slit of a room into apparently twice its size. Even in electric light that night the white and orange made it as gay and bright as a summer morning. He had also doubled the size of the front hall. It was now papered in a plain, soft apricot. Sister had papered it herself yesterday morning. 'Dearie, it was so easy—with an expert to advise me at my elbow.'

When she moved on ahead of us Nick kissed me quickly, then asked why I was looking old-fashioned. 'Do you not dig apricot, my sweet?'

'It's not that.' I used the first excuse that occurred to

me. 'I'm just surprised, knowing your views on pastels.'

'There are pastels and pastels. This one has character. It's alive.' As ever, when discussing colours or anything vaguely connected with his work, his attitude changed. He spent the next half-hour lecturing me on colours. 'There are those that give, and those that take. Before you choose any colour you should first decide what you want it to do for you. If you want stimulation you need a strong colour —say, one wall red—something like that. If you want to keep a room cool—blue. You want rest—green. Why do you think all your operating theatres are green?'

'Because green gives no glare? Easy on the eyes and so on?'

'More than that. It soothes the nerves without having the dreamy effect of this pink I want for Sister Mary's bedroom.' He took me into the scullery. 'This'll be your job tomorrow, love, when I have the shade right. We couldn't get what I wanted, so we got a selection, and I am going to mix it myself.'

He began his mixing on the newspaper-protected scullery floor a little later, and was still at it when Sister Mary got ready to go to a Parish Council meeting in the village hall at seven. I offered to cook supper in her absence.

'Nonsense, dearie! You will be doing quite enough for me tomorrow! I'll see to it when I get back. You have a nice little talk with the dear boy.'

I said, 'Sister, if I know the dear boy he'll still be playing with paint when you get back, and he'll start throwing things if I interrupt him.'

'I can see you two are old friends! Well, dearie, if you insist ...'

I thought over her comment later as I peeled potatoes. Through the open scullery door I could see Nick kneeling on the newspapers and whistling to himself as he worked. The day had been very hot, the evening was still warm, but now it was August the evenings were beginning to grow visibly shorter, and through the tiny scullery window I could just see the sun going down.

I remembered the last evening he and I had been in that cottage together, and then Robert sitting at the table drinking all that tea. I looked at the electric kettle with a quite astonishingly absurd rush of affection. When I glanced back at Nick he was watching me. I had to look away briefly.

He sat back on his heels. 'Our cherished Sister Mary gone?'

'Yes.' I gave the potatoes more attention than they required. 'Didn't you hear her say goodbye?'

'Expect so. Forget.' He juggled a large paint-tin as if it were a cocktail-shaker. 'Sister Mary really lives with her meetings! She had the W.I. on Monday, Darby and Joan on Tuesday, something—I forget what—yesterday, and there's something big on tomorrow afternoon. We've already fixed on the hat she's wearing. Sister Mary has a very snazzy line in hats.'

I smiled. 'I'm glad you two are such chums.'

'I adore her, darling, and she adores me!' He shook his tin violently. 'Let's face it—I'm a lovable type!'

'What else? Hey, Nick, don't bounce! I know all your stitches are out, but give your eye a break. Can't you just stir that paint?'

'Not if I want it properly mixed. Stop fussing, Anna. You aren't on duty now, and I know what I'm doing. Back to your cooking, woman, and leave a man to do his work.'

'Sorry,' I said. 'But, Nick, it isn't all that long.'

'Guess not.' He slammed down the tin and stood up. After washing his hands at the scullery sink he came into the kitchen. 'I've still got a partial blackout about that evening it all started in here. I vaguely recollect Rob Gordon materialising and then old Marcus. And you were with me, darling. That I do remember.' He came close, but did not touch me. His blue eyes were as steady and as honest as water. 'I remember your freezing up on me—and then you wouldn't let me knock down any walls. Jilly was just as bloody-minded. And even my favourite Sister wouldn't let me take down this monster of a ceiling.' He reached up. 'Absolute nonsense! As if I'd join in the demolition!'

'The last thing you'd do! But you have done the hell of a lot for this place, Nick. I know Sister Mary is helping you, but this is still very big of you.'

'Darling,' he drawled, 'we know I've a noble nature, but

I could have an ulterior motive.'

That was something else he had said before. Last time it turned me into jelly. Now I again had to change the subject. 'What I've never been able to follow is how old Martin tolerated the place as it was. He was an art-master. How could he live with such dreadful colours?'

He grinned. 'You know what they say: those who can, do; those who can't, teach. Maybe that's not always fair, but it was in his case. He could draw fairly decently, but his colours—ugh! Ever see his pictures?'

'No.' I was curious. 'I never knew you had. I didn't even know you knew him?'

He helped himself to a glass of water. 'He sometimes brought his stuff over to that pub across the road when I was there. Didn't I tell you?'

'No. Did you ever meet his miserable nephew? The one in medicine?'

'A doc.?' He turned. 'I didn't even know he had one in the family. Why "miserable"?'

'The wretch nearly stopped Sister from having this. He wanted him to wait for a better offer or something. She nearly lost it!'

'Who wanted whom to wait? Take this slowly, love. That red hair of yours is having a shocking effect on your grammar, but never mind, we love you the way you are. Sister Mary is in possession, so why worry?' He rinsed the glass. 'I'm all for forgetting the past, unless it suits me to do otherwise, as with Jilly and Stock.'

I forgot my indignation. 'I can't get over that! You might have let me in on it! Instead you lead me astray with that "fashion model" lark!'

'Don't blame me. That was the tale current in Astead General. I only handed it on. I couldn't hand on the other as I had sworn a great swear to keep it dark. Forgive me?'

'Sure.' I waved that aside. 'Nick, do you suppose any-one in Astead General saw Stock with Sabby Wardell? Harriet thinks she must live near Astead. Does she?'

'Sabby?' he echoed as if it was hard to place the name. 'No, her home's—where? I know, Cumberland. Like old Peter's.' He sat on the table. 'Seen much of Peter lately?'

'Not much. Occasionally in the corridor or canteen. I saw him this afternoon on my way out.'

'You knew he was down here on Monday?'

'Only today.' I explained my hurry, and carelessly knocked an empty saucepan off the table. 'Nick, don't dive like that!' I protested as he lunged for it. 'Think of your eye!'

'Anna, for God's sake stop fussing!'

'Sorry. I know it infuriates you. I'll try not to. Snag is, old habits die hard with me.'

'Don't let it keep you awake.' He stood up. 'I think I should remove this sweet scent of paraffin. Have I time for a bath? And how's the hot water?'

I checked the boiler. 'Fine. You should have forty minutes.'

'Then I will love you and leave you.' He twisted me round and kissed me. 'Old habits die hard with me, sweetie,' he said softly, 'and you are very sweet.' He went up to his room, and did not reappear until Sister Mary was back.

My bed in the spare room was comfortable, but I did not sleep well that night. I woke with the light, and lay listening to the birds and trying not to listen to my thoughts. I got up directly I heard Sister Mary moving. We had breakfast alone. She had thought Nick looked very tired when she took in his early tea, and had insisted he stayed in bed until mid-morning. She gave me his profuse apologies and detailed instructions for the painting of her bedroom. She was moving into the spare room until her walls dried.

Nick joined me directly he was up and blew me a kiss from the doorway. 'Take that to go in with as my electric razor has fused. Do I look like a scrubbing-brush?'

'You're too fair for one night's growth to show,' I replied, and we both smiled over-brightly.

His razor also gave him an excuse to go out to the village ironmonger, who dealt with everything from broken razors to broken combine harvesters. I did not hear him come back, and was unaware he was watching me from the doorway again, till he asked, 'Why so grave, sweet maid? Problem?'

I blinked. I had been thinking about the Elkroyds.

Brown-plus-E was seeing Betty privately at noon. Now. 'Yes. A big problem, but only mine indirectly. It concerns the wife of one of my patients.'

'Why? Is he in love with you, darling?'

It was not his fault it jarred. 'No. It's a little more serious than that.'

'And you don't call that serious? Ah, well! No doubt it all depends on how one looks on these things—which reminds me I've promised Sister Mary to look in her oven.' He removed himself and stayed out of my way until Sister Mary called me to get ready for lunch.

She sent us into the sitting-room to drink sherry while she dished up in peace. Nick was now looking as strained as I felt. We talked about the weather, and, as we had never made small talk together, we were very bad at it. Desperately we agreed it had been the most wonderful summer we remembered, that the forecast was excellent for Monday, and the Bank Holiday traffic and accidents were bound to beat all records. The sitting-room door was ajar, and we could hear Sister Mary in the kitchen. Her hearing was not perfect, but it was good enough to prevent my starting the conversation we should have to have before the day ended. She joined us as Nick was saying he thought I should leave fairly early for my return journey as the trains were bound to be crowded.

'I don't think the dear girl need worry too much, Nick,' she protested. 'She will be travelling against the main stream. Ready, my dears? Come and eat!'

Her meeting was in the early afternoon. As we sat down I made up my mind to use that time to straighten things out with Nick. I could no longer go on leaving our affair in the air. I had seen that since yesterday he had been as worried about us as I was myself, if, I was afraid, for a very different reason. I hated the idea of hurting him, but to keep up a pretence would hurt him much more in the long run.

I noticed Sister Mary studying Nick several times during our meal. After we had eaten she said he must take a rest before tea. 'I have allowed you to do far too much. You are looking worn out.' She turned to me for support. 'Do you not agree, dearie?'

165

Nick protested hotly, but I had to back her up, and he had to give in, grumbling. 'I've hardly seen anything of you, Anna.'

Sister Mary said he must not be so impatient, as she hoped I should pay many more visits while he was with her. 'You young people are always so impatient. You have to reach my age to discover the young are the only people who can afford the time for patience. Off you go, dear boy! No—no clearing! We can see to all that.'

I helped her with the dishes, and then went back to my painting. As my immediate personal problem had to wait, I let my thoughts go back to Barny's and the Elkroyds. Browne and Muir were seeing Tom together at two. I looked at my watch. Another ten minutes.

Sister Mary looked in to say she was off and Nick was asleep. 'Rest is all he needs, dearie. He has had so many visitors apart from yourself.'

'Have I tired him, Sister?'

'At this stage all convalescents tire very easily, as you must know. You mustn't blame yourself, dearie. It's my fault for allowing him so much excitement since his discharge. We had Jill the whole week-end, then that tea-party on Sunday. Dr Graveny was down on Monday. Nick's Secretary and one of his senior partners called on Tuesday. On Wednesday afternoon he would go alone by taxi to his follow-up clinic and was so late back! He most thoughtfully rang me from Astead to say he had met an old friend and would be out to supper. That worried me for his health, but he's not a child, so there was nothing I could do. He sounded so happy and cheerful, and he did look very well on his return. Tch, tch, tch.' She clicked her tongue against her teeth. 'It is always so hard to steer the right course with convalescents. If one lets them do too much they grow over-tired; if one keeps them too quiet they grow depressed—which does no good at all!'

Having her take full responsibility made me feel hollow with guilt. 'Sister, you have been wonderful to him. I'm afraid this really is my fault——'

'Nonsense, dearie! He is so fond of you, and you have been so good! I only hope all this hard work on your day off is not going to overtire you as well. Miss Wardell told

166

me how busy you all are in Observation and with some very distressing patients.'

'That's certainly true, Sister.' I had another glance at the time. Five to two. The pundits would be with Wardell now. Then I realised what else Sister Mary had said. 'You've seen Miss Wardell lately?'

'Oh, yes, dearie. She was here to tea on Sunday. And I have met her in Astead recently on several occasions. I believe she has friends in the town. Now I must be off. I shall be back just after four.'

I finished the last wall mechanically. My mind was wholly occupied in darting from Tom Elkroyd to Sabby's visit here on Sunday, and why neither Nick, Jill, Peter Graveny, nor Sabby herself had mentioned it to me.

Next I thought about last Wednesday, and how my ward sister had changed her off-duty to have that as a half-day. Robert had been in Eyes that afternoon, and on call in the A.R.R. that night. That was the afternoon he had asked me out to tea and said he had to talk to me after seeing Wardell in the canteen.

Outside the village church clock chimed the half-hour. Tom should know by now.

My thoughts were shooting backward and forward some time later when they were interrupted by a knock on the back door. I went down at once to prevent Nick's being woken. It was the village grocer's vanman with Sister Mary's weekly order. He carried the box into the kitchen and waited while I checked the contents, as he wanted his box back.

'All there? Ta, miss.' He picked up the empty box and surveyed the kitchen with an appreciative air. 'Never looked neat like this when that Mr Martin was here. And how would he and his new lady be doing, miss? Got to Australia, yet?'

'I'm afraid I haven't heard. I hope they are doing very well.'

He seemed surprised. 'Isn't that young Mr Dexter still here, miss? I thought I saw him up the street, and Bill, over the ironmonger's, said as his eye was getting along nicely. Shocking business that, eh, miss?'

'Very.' I was amused by this new example of the efficiency of the Wylden grapevine. 'He's been very lucky.'

'Like as they say, miss—the good are lucky! But I reckon as Mr Dexter can't be doing with much letter-writing yet, and that Mr Martin never was a one for writing more than a postcard—and the fuss he'd make about that! You'd not credit it, miss! He never had a stamp in the house, and would he remember to buy one up the post-office? Not Mr Martin! He'd always step across to The Swan—I used to work there afore I took on delivering for Mr Greenstreet—"George", he'd say, "let's have one of them whatsits. I got to write to thingummy if I can put my hands on his address."' He smiled indulgently. 'Never got a word nor a name right, he didn't! I reckon as now he's probably forgotten his nephews and the address! And what with young Mr Dexter's being poorly, he'd not be up to writing to his uncle. Miss! Them's eggs! Careful!'

'Sorry. All safe.' I put down the carton. 'Mr Dexter's uncle is Mr Martin?'

'That's right, miss. Didn't you know?' He found that very funny. 'Mr Dexter must be another absent-minded gentleman like his uncle, seem'ly! That Mr Martin'd forget his own name! He never got mine right. I'm Bert. There, it takes all sorts as I always say.' He made for the door. 'You might remember me to Mr Dexter, miss. He'll know me—Bert from over at The Swan. Always had a chat and a laugh we did when he came down—not that that was often, mind. But a real cheerful young gentleman is that Mr Dexter, and they say as he's ever so clever. Mr Martin was real made up with his job he's doing building the new St Barnabas'. You'll be from the hospital, miss? Thought as much. I remember you when you was up at the House. Used to see you on the back of another young lady's scooter. She keeping nicely? That's good. Fine hospital, St Barnabas', they say. But that Mr Martin—do you think he could ever remember the name? "that hospital place, St Whatsit" he'd call it. I dunno! It's a good thing he's got his new lady to look after him now—but I mustn't be keeping you, miss. Much obliged. Good afternoon!'

I sat at the kitchen table and stared at the groceries. I wondered if Sister Mary knew. I suspected she did, knowing the village. She would not let it worry her any more than it now worried me. Once it would have worried me a great deal, and that, of course, was why Nick had never told me. Nor, I remembered, had Robert. He must always have known since he had acted for Mr Norris in the sale. He had seen Nick with me at Sister Mary's party. He had never said anything to make me connect Nick with Mr Martin. That was, I thought carefully, very good of him.

I was still sitting there when the church clock struck four. Sister Mary would soon be back. I put away the groceries, filled the kettle, then went up to wake Nick before plugging it in.

He was too sound asleep to hear my knock. He lay on his side on top of his bedclothes, his fair hair was untidy, and his unguarded face had a faint flush and looked as young as a schoolboy's. In sleep his mouth still curved good-humouredly, and the rather weak lines of his jaw, which I had always tried not to see, were more apparent. Watching him I felt no more annoyed than I should have done with a child who kept up a 'let's pretend' game too long. He could not help being what he was, and he had some very good qualities to compensate for those he lacked. Unfortunately, at least to me, those he lacked were important.

I did not want to wake him suddenly, as that would hurt his eye. I put a hand on his forehead as if dealing with a patient. 'Nick, wake up. Tea-time.'

He stirred and reached for me, his eyes still closed. 'I like your hand there, Sabby. I always like your hand there. You mustn't leave me——' Then he opened his eyes. His stare was hostile until he forced a smile. 'Angel, I was dreaming. Sister back?'

'Not yet.' I moved away. 'I am about to make tea.'

'Grand.' He sat on the edge of his bed and pushed back his hair. 'How's the painting?'

'Finished.' Enough time had been wasted so I wasted no more. 'Nick, there's something I have to tell you, and don't interrupt. It's just this. I've a hunch you are still in love with Sabby Wardell. If you are—I'm not in love with you, either. No, I'm saying this wrong—what I mean is,

169

whether you are or not I don't love you. I like you enormously, but that's the lot.'

He was gazing at me as if I was speaking a foreign language. He said stiffly, 'Darling, don't pretend; I know how you feel about me——'

'You did. Not now.'

He was quite indignant. 'I wish you'd be honest! It'll be much easier for you.'

It would also be much easier for him to believe I loved him, as apart from soothing his ego, that would help him to explain away his behaviour as a necessary act aimed at letting me down gently. I could scarcely hold that against him when, since yesterday, I had been doing much the same myself.

'I am being honest. I'm in love with someone else.'

'Are you?' He stood up. 'It's that patient chap you keep waffling about! Anna, you devil! Of all the two-timers! What about me? Have you forgotten we are supposed to be engaged?'

'No,' I said dryly, 'but I thought you had. It got lost in your blackout—or didn't it?'

He realised what he had said and flushed with annoyance. Then he saw the funny side and took my hands. 'Hell, no! What's the use? That blackout lark was just bloody handy.' He sat on the edge of the bed, still holding my hands. 'How did you guess?'

'Something Sister Mary said. Why didn't you tell me? Not to hurt me? That's what's been stopping me.'

He drew me closer, sliding his arms round my waist and resting his head against me. 'It's your fault for being so bloody attractive. When you are around you do things to me. I don't know why I'm not in love with you.'

It was not the time to give him a biology lecture, so I suggested he told me about Sabby. 'When did it start up again?'

'My first week-end in hospital. She came to see me. She could only stay a few minutes. She took one train down and the next back. I asked her to come again. She did.'

'How? She was so seldom off.'

'Don't I know it!'

'Was it she who told you about Jill and Marcus?'

170

'Yes. She likes old Jilly. She wanted to do her a good turn. I shouldn't tell you this'—he looked up—'but it made her feel less hellish about you. You've worried her.'

I let that one pass. 'You two engaged?'

He grinned ruefully. 'I asked her last Sunday. She said I must put you in the picture first. I was still wondering how to when your last letter arrived.' He paused. 'She came down again on Wednesday. She said if I didn't tell you while you were here she would. I meant to—I kept putting it off. I loathe fuss—scenes. I didn't want to hurt you. It never dawned on me you were so involved with this man in Observation.' He sighed. 'Poor sweetie.'

That was part of the truth, if not the whole truth, so I let that one go. 'Nick, there's one thing I don't get. What about Robert Gordon's angle?'

'Rob?' His face lit with laughter. 'Darling, Rob Gordon must look after his own affairs, which from the little I know of him he'll do nicely. You don't have to waste any time worrying about old Rob!'

I still had a soft spot for Nick and probably always would, but that I found unforgivable. 'That's a monstrous thing to say! Have you forgotten what you owe Robert? That Sabby's been playing him along? Think what this'll do to him!' I disentangled myself from his arms. 'You called me a two-timer! How about you? And Sabby Wardell?'

He made me angrier by rocking with laughter. 'I'm sorry, sweetie,' he spluttered, 'and I know I've been dumb, but you are the dumbest redhead in the business—don't run away.' He followed me on to the small landing at the head of the stairs and grabbed me again. 'Let me tell you something.' But he was laughing too much to go on. He clung to me, and we rocked together.

I was too furious to use my head and my old tears routine. 'Nick! Let me go!'

'Darling, don't be mad at me!' He controlled his laughter with difficulty. 'You know I adore you, even though I am going to marry Sabby just as soon as she's free, so just listen——'

'I gather Anna doesn't want to listen to you, Nick. Let her go!' Robert's voice directly behind us was as cold

171

as it was unexpected. 'Or Marcus Stock may have another rush job on his hands.'

Nick dropped his arms like stones as Sister Mary appeared at the foot of the stairs. 'You've found them, Mr Gordon? Good. Come on down to tea, my dears! Isn't this jolly? Mr Gordon has just driven over from his godfather with some books for me, and I have asked him to join us. He is going to drive you back, dearie, which will be so much nicer than the train. Isn't this a lovely surprise?'

'Lovely,' I agreed weakly, looking at Robert. He was looking at Nick. Nick was looking at the floor. Both men breathed as if they had been running. 'How do you come to be off this afternoon, Robert?'

He looked my way absently as if he had forgotten I was there. I had never seen him or any other man so angry. He held out his left palm and exposed a broad crisscross of strapping.

'A cut in the theatre?' I asked.

'The poor boy has an acid burn,' explained Sister Mary, removing her hat. 'There was a little accident in Casualty, but it could have been much worse, as you will hear over tea. Come on, children.' She smiled up at us. 'We shall have a really merry little party, shan't we?'

CHAPTER TWELVE

TRUST TOM TO SEE RIGHT

Sister Mary blamed our lack of appetite on the heat. 'London must have been intolerable today! Small wonder that ether bottle exploded. As Casualty is not yet air-conditioned, I am only surprised a great many more did not go up.'

Robert smiled faintly. 'To be strictly honest, Sister Mary, there was a double explosion in Cas. this morning, as while this heat lasts all the ether bottles are supposed to live in the fire sand buckets unless in use. A dresser had taken out the one that burst and forgotten to put it back. I doubt he'll forget again.'

'Oh! Oh!' Sister Mary smiled sympathetically. 'The poor boy! He had to learn! What a mercy no one was hit by flying glass!'

I asked, 'How did ether give you an acid burn?'

'The blast blew open an acid cupboard, and some of the bottles pitched out. The S.S.O. and I were standing near and grabbed them. Unfortunately I chose to grab the nitric upside down, so the stopper fell out. The S.S.O.'s reaction was most impressive. He had emptied a stock bottle of meths over my hand before I'd felt much. I've no more than a second-degree burn, thanks to him. I feel a fraud being off, but he told me to stay off for the rest of the day, so here I am.'

'And very pleased to have you with us, dear,' said Sister Mary.

Nick caught my eye and grinned sheepishly. After tea he tried to corner me alone several times before Robert and I left, but I was still too peeved by his attitude to Robert and refused to be cornered.

Sister Mary had decided dear Mr Gordon was another dear friend who could safely be entrusted with Jill's news. Driving out of Wylden, Robert said he had heard it was on the cards previously, and could see only one snag.

'Elizabeth's going to lose a very good sister.'

'I'm afraid so.' The same thing seemed likely to happen to Observation. I kept that to myself. 'I can't see Jill not nursing. Think she'll work down here?'

'Why not? Till she has a baby. Astead General'll jump at her. Like most hospitals, it's short of trained nurses.' We were stopped by the traffic, so he looked at me. 'You didn't know their affair was brewing?'

'No.' I did not enlarge on that, as to do so would mean mentioning Nick. Remembering how I felt directly after David, I had no intention of letting Nick, Sabby Wardell, or even Astead General crop up again in our conversation. Instead I asked about Tom. 'I suppose you had no chance to hear how he's taken the news?'

'Oh, yes. I saw him before I left. I put on a sterile glove. He took it as expected and has signed his consent form.'

'What ever time did you leave London? The men weren't seeing him till early this afternoon.'

'I don't know. I pushed off after seeing him. There wasn't much traffic then. By the way, Tom gave me your message yesterday. Thanks for bothering, but that talk I wanted to have with you isn't—wasn't—all that important. In fact, not important at all now.' The traffic was starting up, but he was still watching me. 'I expect you can follow why?'

'Yes,' I said and left it at that. Obviously Sabby had told him the whole truth in the canteen on Wednesday, and that was why he had looked so black when I called him back to see Tom. I guessed he had felt that, as no one else in our immediate circle had the courage to tell me Sabby and Nick were engaged again, he had better do it. It would have been much easier for Jill, Peter, or even Harriet. After last week-end Jill and Peter must have been aware of the true situation—which explained their evasive attitudes to me yesterday. And, unless I was much mistaken, Harriet, who heard everything in Cas., and sensed the things she did not hear, must have gathered something was going on from her faithful Stan, if not from Peter himself. With the maddening clarity of hindsight I now saw she had tried to drop me the odd vague hint. I suspect Robert had met with a similar silence from his friends in the Doctors' House. It was all an exact repetition of what had happened over David. People convinced themselves they were keeping quiet out of kindness when what was actually silencing them was lack of courage.

'Sorry!' Robert swerved sharply to avoid an overtaking motor-cyclist who would otherwise have removed our off-side wing mirror. Another shot by. 'Any more leather boys coming up?'

I looked back. 'Five.' They roared past. 'Some Cas. somewhere is going to be busy tonight.'

'Strange how keen people are to get into an A.R.R. Our Cas. was beginning to hot up already when I left. Monday'll see its usual Bank Holiday shambles.'

I said, 'I've detested Bank Holidays since one Whit Monday two years back. I've never seen so much blood about. It was worse than the E.N.T. theatre on tonsil days.'

'Not two years ago; three, if you mean the Whit Monday

174

that coach overturned on a double-decker bus?'

'That's the one.' I winced at the memory. 'Were you there? I don't remember that.'

'I was there,' he said grimly. 'I was one of the A.h-s.'s [Accident house-surgeons] all that jolly week-end. That Monday was the first time our morgue filled up in one day since the last war. Weren't you in Eighteen? With the women? Dave was in Twelve. I was in Eleven.'

Dressing-rooms Eleven and Eighteen stood opposite each other, and the doors were always open, but I could not remember him there at all. Looking back now, I could see rather than remember myself on that occasion, as I no longer seemed to have anything in common with that other girl. I could see David as clearly, and our that-time S.S.O. in his shirt-sleeves with blood on his mask. He had long discarded his stained coat. I could still smell the sweet sickly smell of fresh blood on wooden benches. We had had to use the benches when we ran out of stretcher-trolleys. Yet I could not picture Robert anywhere in that scene.

'You were? Sorry, but I don't remember,' I said again, and again we were silent for miles.

We were in outer London when he broke the silence to say Joe Yates was returning tonight. 'Someone remembered the holiday and wired him. He's booked by Muir for to-morrow. I'm back with Blakelock. I'm hoping the S.S.O.'ll let me back on 'dry' from tonight. I'd rather work than hang around as "walking sick".'

'Yes. That's no joy. So you've left Observation.'

'Uh-huh. Tom aside, I'm not sorry.'

As Blakelock never sent us patients and Observation with or without Sabby would be haunted for him, that figured. But the prospect of Observation without him so upset me that I dared not risk even a formal personal regret. 'Tom'll miss you.'

He glanced at me without comment. He did not speak again until he said goodnight when he dropped me at the Home. The clock outside Cas. struck nine as he drove on.

The hands of the cranial theatre clock stood at nine next morning when Tom Elkroyd was wheeled in fully conscious and holding my hand as I walked beside his stretcher-trolley.

As the double doors shut and sealed themselves a row of dark-blue lights came on over the sinks. They would remain on throughout the operation, as always in any of our theatres when an operation was being performed under a local anaesthetic. The theatre staff were glad of the reminder, since, being so accustomed to working on unconscious bodies, the surgeons were apt to discuss everything from the job in hand to their hobbies, or what would be served for the next meal. We had a few surgeons who disliked any form of conversation while operating, but they were in the minority, and even they sometimes gave vent to a 'Good God! Look at the mess in here!' or 'What the hell can I do with this? It's long past repair!'

The gallery was nearly full, though the intercom was switched off. Mr Browne never lectured on conscious patients.

He had briefed me earlier in the privacy of the theatre duty-room. 'Your job is to keep his mind off what I'm doing inside his head. Talk quietly, as much as you wish. If he wants to talk let him. If he drops off from time to time, which he may, so much the better. The table'll be high enough for him to see you through the cut-away face rest. Sit where he can see you easily, and sit still. It's going to be a long day.'

Tom's condition that morning seemed to me to have deteriorated sharply in the last thirty-six hours. Addy was in charge as Wardell's holiday had begun, and directly the night report was over, until the theatre porters arrived, I was occupied with Tom's final pre-operative preparations. I spoke to Betty Elkroyd for a few seconds before we left.

The smile in her eyes was as determinedly cheerful as her manner. 'We'll have band playing tonight, Nurse! Isn't that right, then?'

'I'll say!' I sounded as hearty as Jill. 'What are you going to do? Sit out on our sun-roof? It's another lovely day.'

'Maybe this afternoon, Nurse. I've got me a date this morning. Happen you'll know that?'

'Not I! Who's your date?'

'Happen you've dropped brick, love,' said Tom slowly,

moving his swathed, shaved head with very great care my way. 'Our Mr Gordon's taking my Betty out to Zoo, seeing as they've taken him off job with that bad hand. He come and asked if I'd mind.' His words were now so slurred they were hard to follow. 'I said I reckoned it was fair——' He stopped as Addy came in. 'Time, then?'

During the earlier part of his op. he told me Betty had always wanted to visit the Zoo, and he had mentioned that to Robert last night. 'The Sister let him come in for chat, late like.' He paused. 'Gone now, has she?'

'For three weeks. You been to the Zoo, Tom?'

'Oh, aye.'

We talked about zoos in general, and then, as he was getting tired but wanted to be talked to, I told him more about the cottage, how it looked now, and then how beautiful the country had looked. 'You can't imagine how many orchards they have down there. In spring there is blossom for miles. It's like a whole world in glorious Technicolor.'

'I'd like my kids to see that. My Betty's had a fancy her and me'd move into country when kids have grown up.' His eyes looked inward. 'We'd not reckoned on this lot. How they doing, then?'

I glanced at the surgeon's hands and wished I had not. 'Getting on nicely.'

A little later a sound puzzled him. 'Don't they have this theatre sound-proofed? I fancy I can hear lads working with drill. Got a building job near?'

Dr Wallace and his assistant, our Resident Anaesthetist, were sitting by me. The R.A.'s eyes met mine. I said, 'I expect you can hear them working on the new children's block. It's just across the way from here.'

'Sounds right close.'

'It does,' I said, 'doesn't it?'

Tom's eyes closed as Mr Browne stopped drilling and Sister Cranial Theatre handed him the special saw. The instruments on her trolley looked more like a set of carpenter's tools. On her second and still covered trolley she had waiting the instruments that would be used inside Tom's brain. He had slid into a light sleep when Mr Browne laid back the skull flap. A theatre nurse removed the first instrument trolley and pushed forward the second.

Tom woke. 'Still at it, are they?'

'Yes, Comfortable?'

'I'm all right, then.'

His head was as open as an egg with the top turned back. Mr Muir had now joined Mr Browne. Joe Yates and Henry Todd were actively engaged in their assisting; the housemen only were momentarily standing back with their gloved hands high. Tom could just have woken from a normal sleep. He knew the surgeons were there, but, as he could neither see nor feel them, he was content to take them on trust. Had he been able to see in the magnifying mirror reflecting the operation to the gallery, phlegmatic and sensible though he was, I suspected the shock might have killed him. Looking in that mirror was like looking at some anatomy text book's pictures of the brain. I could see it easily from my chair. I looked at it from time to time only because that was my job. I admired surgeons and surgery, but surgery had sickened me from my first year, and it still did.

Time stood still. After a lifetime it was noon; another lifetime and a few empty spaces in the gallery showed it was the lunch hour. When I next looked up Robert was sitting at the end of the front bench. I told Tom. He was now desperately tired, but his eyes lit up.

'Back from Zoo, eh?'

About twenty minutes later he began blinking. 'What's up with lights, then? Power cut?'

The lights had not changed.

'Could be. I hope not. It won't matter if it is, as this theatre has its own emergency lighting. That may not give us much light, but it'll give Mr Browne and Mr Muir enough.'

Mr Muir was listening. He said jovially, 'A wee bit dark, isn't it, laddie? Why not try and have another little sleep?'

Tom shut his eyes obediently and soon went back to sleep. He woke briefly after a little while. His eyes were very dazed and his speech was almost unintelligible. I bent closer to catch his mumble.

Mr Browne asked, 'All well, Nurse?'

'It's his left foot, Mr Browne. He's got pins and needles.'

178

Sister Theatre nodded to me to stay where I was and raised an eyebrow at one of her nurses. Tom sighed contentedly as she rubbed his foot, and he dozed off again.

By three Mr Muir's work was done, and the final and most dangerous stage of that dangerous operation remained ahead. Word had got round the hospital, as it always did, and though it was Saturday afternoon and the students were free, the gallery had filled up. There was not a spare inch on the benches, the connecting steps, or the gangways. A line of uniformed sisters had appeared on the back bench. I noticed, without its registering, that Sabby Wardell, in uniform instead of being away on holiday, was sitting between Sister Eyes and Sister Henry. Tom's hand in mine was limp, and his face was grey. Dr Wallace and the R.A. were almost constantly on their feet. Then and for another hour and a half, Tom's life was most literally in the small neat hands of Mr Browne.

Later, Helen Addy asked, 'How big was it?'

'This size.' I measured part of one little fingernail. 'It was right down where he said it would be and he got it out intact. I was there and watching, but I don't know how he did it. He couldn't risk feeling around; he was working blind. Directly it was out, Tom changed.' I snapped my fingers. 'Like that! If I hadn't seen it I shouldn't have believed it. His speech picked up, he could see more clearly. . . .' I paused. Then I said, 'When it was all over and old Muir was making one of his wee jokes to Tom about his bonnie white bonnet, Brown-plus-E flopped on to a stool and let his arms dangle, and every bit of him sagged. He looked like a little old man.'

She said kindly, 'He's only in his forties, but he'll be that before his time. Can you imagine the strain of operating non-stop for eight hours and ten minutes, knowing all the time one wrong move could kill a man? Oh, my dear, what a day! And what a wonderful ending! You've seen Betty Elkroyd?'

'Yes.' I was smiling. 'Just now. She looked so happy. She couldn't talk. She kissed me.'

'Bless the girl! She kissed me when I got Sister Theatre's message and told her Mr Browne was on his way up with

179

good news. He didn't mind my jumping the gun. That poor woman has been in hell all day. It was good of Robert Gordon to take her out. He made her have some lunch. Did he get to the theatre?'

'This afternoon.' I then remembered Sabby, and asked if Addy knew why she was not away.

She got up to close the duty-room before answering. 'Keep this to yourself, as it isn't official yet. It will be shortly. Wardell stayed to see Matron—to resign. That's why she had to get into uniform. Matron sent for me after seeing her. She's offered me this ward. Needless to say, I jumped at it.'

I was delighted and said so. 'How soon is Wardell leaving?'

'Matron's letting her go now. She hopes to marry in about a month. She told me this yesterday. She says her future husband refuses to let her work, and, anyway, she didn't think Observation could be combined with marriage. And incidentally'—she smiled wryly—'I have learnt a sharp lesson about listening to tittle-tattle! It's not Robbie Gordon! I actually asked. He's just an old friend. They knew each other as children. You know that?' I shook my head dumbly. 'Her father was an ardent fisherman, and as a child she spent all her summer holidays near his home in Caithness. She gave me the lot yesterday! Like all shy people, once she got herself talking she couldn't stop. The only thing she didn't tell me is the name of her future husband. I just know he's an outsider.'

'Nick Dexter.'

'No! Yes? Good God! What about you?'

I grinned. 'I don't give a damn!'

She studied me closely, then grinned back. 'Well, well, well! So it was him all the time? No wonder she's been so tetchy lately! And this afternoon she made her final appearance in Barny's uniform. Taking it off'll be no mean wrench for her. Will he appreciate that?'

'I dunno; I doubt it. I could be wrong. I generally am.'

'You are not alone, love. Half Barny's is lined up with you.' She opened the door. 'I must now get back to running this ward, and you must get off and have some food. Off you go, and don't come back until tomorrow morning!'

'I'm not off till six. Can't I come back when I've eaten?'

'No, dear,' replied Addy pleasantly. 'Your Nurse Vint is to special Tom until Nurse Carter takes over for the night. I have asked for, and been sent, a relief staff nurse. Everything is under control. Away with you, and have a good evening!'

'Yes, Sister,' I said, smiling. 'Thank you, Sister.' I was not wholly teasing her. I recognised a sister's voice when I heard one. I knew I was listening to the voice of the new Sister Observation. It had a very nice sound. Wardell had been a very efficient sister. Addy was going to make the type of sister who was later made Matron of Barny's. Observation under Addy would be a very happy as well as a very high-powered ward.

Betty Elkroyd came out of her husband's room as I left the changing-room. She said he was sleeping and she had slipped out to ring her parents as she had promised. 'Our Dad's going to be in call-box up road at quarter to six. He said to ring him, whatever. Eh, love—he and our Mum's going to be right glad with news.' Her eyes were wet, and she flicked her cheeks with the back of one hand. 'Our Dad'll know all's well when he hears me sniffling. Always cry when I'm happy, I do.'

'Give them my regards, and tell them from me your Tom was wonderful throughout his op.'

'Aye. He's a good man.' She sniffed. 'Like your chap. He was right nice to me today. Had me all round monkey house and chucking buns at bears! Like a pair of kids, we were. He stood me dinner. Right nice he was,' she repeated. 'You'll do all right with him, love. Like Tom and me.'

I was too taken aback for pretence. 'Betty, you're wrong. He's not——'

'Your chap? Get away, love! You're not telling me you don't fancy him! I can see as you do, though my Tom's not been right certain. Takes a lass to see how it is with another lass, eh, love? And a chap to see how it is with a chap. Trust my Tom to see right even when his eyes were right poorly'—she mopped her eyes again—'and told me from start, he did! That Mr Gordon fancies my Nurse Rowe, he says. Can't see enough of her, he can't. Any time my Nurse Rowe's on job he'll be up for summat, like.

Happen it's as well the Sister's his old mate, my Tom says, or she'd have him out on his ear!' My expression made her eyes widen. 'Hasn't he told you, love? And you've not told him? What you waiting for then?' She nudged me encouragingly. 'Grass to grow greener? Eh—that's daft! And look at time! I mustn't keep our Dad hanging around!'

I went slowly down the block stairs in a complete, but far from unhappy daze. Betty had been right about myself, but Tom had to be wrong. Something as gloriously and unexpectedly wonderful as this could not really happen without my suspecting it. Tom must have imagined it all!

Tom? Tom Elkroyd? Giving way to flights of fancy? Having nursed him, I had to accept that was even harder to believe than his views on Robert.

My thoughts went spinning round as my feet carried me along the ground-floor corridor towards our dining-room. A student came out of the staff canteen as I went by. Before he closed the door I saw Robert sitting alone with his back to the door, at a table by the window. I hesitated momentarily, and then I went in.

The canteen was nearly empty. On this fine Saturday evening everyone free was on the terrace, the river, or somewhere playing some game. I did not even notice the empty tables. I walked up to Robert and said the first thing that came into my head. 'Robert, I've no money on me. Will you buy me a cup of tea?'

His head jerked round. He stood up slowly. 'If you want one. What about food?'

'My lunch is being kept hot. I'll eat some time.'

He looked at me hard, and I was afraid he was going to ask why I had to sponge off him when I could get free tea with my belated lunch. He only said, 'Sit down, then,' and went over to the counter. He returned balancing two teas and a plate of sandwiches.

'Thank you so much. How's the hand?'

'Fine, thanks. I'm working tomorrow.' He sat back and crossed his legs. 'How's Tom now?'

'Flat out, but a new man. Now all we have to do is wait for the path. report. Brown-plus-E told Helen Addy it didn't look malignant to him.'

'So I've heard. How's Betty?'

'Weeping with joy. I gather you had a good morning at the Zoo?' He nodded, and went on watching me thoughtfully. 'She's now ringing Grandad. I'll bet Gran'll be washing that rose-patterned teaset in readiness for Tom's homecoming before today's out.'

'The one she won with her prize geranium?'

'Pelargonium.'

'Pelargoniums are geraniums.'

'They are? I didn't know that.'

He nodded again and stayed silent.

I was glad of the mental breathing-space. There was so much I wanted to say and even more I wanted to ask—if I could get up the courage. And even though I had spent all those hours in the theatre sitting down, I was far more tired than after running round a ward all night long.

He did not let the silence last as long as I hoped. 'What do you want this time, Anna? The tea's obviously an excuse, so can we get to the main issue?'

'Hey! Give me a break, Robert! I've just sat down.'

'And the sooner you get whatever it is off your chest, you can go and have some proper food and get to bed. That, if you'll forgive me saying so, is about all you look fit for.'

I smiled faintly. 'Robert, never say that to a girl! It's just about the most damning testimony to one's looks I can think of!'

'It was not intended as a compliment.'

That took the smile off my face and made me look at him more keenly. 'Just a medical observation?'

'What else would you expect from me?' His smile was derisive. 'After all these years?'

I did not answer. I was beginning to wonder if I had imagined that conversation with Betty Elkroyd. I felt as if the clock had suddenly been put back and any moment David would come into the canteen. I had now recognised Robert's mood, even though it was a very long time since I had seen him in it. I had frequently seen him like this in the old David days, as well as that last week-end at the Mat. Unit. Previously I had put this behaviour down to his dislike of myself, and, having disliked him back, had never hesitated to weigh into battle if we were alone. When David

183

had been present, for his sake I had removed myself at the first opportunity, generally red-faced and fuming. Robert's ability to control his own temper had never done anything to improve mine. He was obviously spoiling for a fight now, and without any trouble I could recollect a dozen major rows between us that had started like this. After those other rows he had ignored me for days, even weeks, then somehow we had got together again and another fight had started.

Until now it had never occurred to me to wonder why history kept repeating itself, or to realise that, as I had never sought his company, he had to have been responsible for our getting together again. He was not a man to enjoy scrapping as some men did. He got on very well with other people. So why pick fights with me? I used to put that down to his resenting my affair with David, but David had not been at the Mat. Unit, and he was not here now.

'Well, Anna? Decided to rival "Old Trypo"?'

I blinked. 'Old—oh, him. No, I'm not asleep.'

'And you've not lost your rare talent for stating the obvious. Congratulations.'

Once that would have made me want to hurl my cup at him. Not now. If Tom was right, such a student-type crack from a most un-student-type man made certain and exciting sense. 'Robert, do stop sniping. As you've guessed, I want to talk to you.'

'Well?'

I took a deep breath. 'First, about that talk you wanted to have with me on Wednesday——'

'Which we yesterday agreed was no longer important? I remember. Why drag it up again, now?'

'Because I thought I understood what you meant in the car. I'm not so sure now.' He was silent. 'Did it concern Nick and Sabby and your discovering they were engaged again? Did you feel someone had to tell me, and then, yesterday, realise I had had it from Nick?' He still did not answer. 'Robert, I would like to talk this over.'

He said curtly, 'Possibly. With Harriet, or even Henry Todd. But you don't really want to discuss it with me, Anna. Let it go.'

'I'd rather not——'

184

'Only because you are very tired. Everyone talks too much when tired, and generally regrets it like the devil later.' He did not often smoke, but he lit a cigarette now. 'Be honest, Anna. You may want a shoulder to weep on, but you don't want my shoulder—as you showed very clearly on our drive back yesterday. Don't say any more——'

I cut him short. 'God, Robert! Don't you give me that "be honest" routine, too! I had quite enough of that from Nick yesterday! The poor man was afraid I'd take to a convent or go into a decline or something! I expect it was my fault. I did lead him up the garden path.'

'You did WHAT?' He sat forward, then pushed the sandwiches at me. 'You'd better eat some more. You're getting low in the blood sugar.'

'My blood sugar's fine, thanks!' I waved the plate away. 'It's true. In a way that's what I did! I'm not particularly proud of it, but luckily, as he did the same, neither of us has to feel badly.'

'I see.' He sat back again. 'Yes. Of course. I see.'

'Oh, no, you don't! You think this is just a good face-saving story! That's written all over you! It's nothing of the sort. It's true. I'll admit I did try to kid myself I was in love with him for a while, particularly when his eye went wrong. You remember that evening at the cottage?'

'Yes?'

'That evening I sort of let my emotions rip. I thought he needed me—I was so sorry for him—he had to be the big thing in my life. I should,' I added more calmly, 'have remembered my job.'

'How the devil does that come into it?'

'This way. Directly anyone takes to a sick-bed I turn soft inside and get all protective. That happens to most nurses, and is probably why we are nurses. It obviously happened to Sabby. She could hold out while Nick was on his two feet, but the moment he was warded—whang!' I slapped the table with one hand. 'She just caved in, and well I understand it! Surely you can, too? I've noticed much the same happens to you with patients and patients' connections. What about your trip to the Zoo this morning? Or how nice you were to Nick and myself that particular

185

evening. When you were alone you didn't snipe at me once. I was very grateful to you.'

'How nice!' He studied his cigarette. 'And that's all there was to it?'

'Yes.' I waited expectantly. When he said nothing I added, 'I wanted you to get this straight.'

He looked at me then. 'I can understand that.'

'How?' I was getting too desperate to bother about pride. 'Because of David? Because I know you've seen me having one jilt and don't want you to suffer under the impression I've just had another?' He nodded reluctantly. 'Did you think I would be afraid your reaction would be to give three loud cheers?'

His face tightened. 'Knowing your opinion of myself, I wouldn't have thought that far off the mark. I know we have seemed to hit it off moderately well in Observation, but we are not in Observation now. So why bother with pretence?'

'Robert, you are so right!' But I could not go on. It was all very well to tell myself I knew Tom, but I also knew Robert. I was not getting through to him, and I had never been able to when he was in this mood. I pushed back my chair. 'I may as well go.'

'I think that would be wise.'

I was about to get up when I realised his tone had altered and he was sounding as dejected as I felt. I stayed sitting. 'Why do you say that?'

He took off his glasses and began to polish them, as he so often did when he wanted to choose his words with more than his usual care. 'You said I was right to dispense with pretence. Why not do the same? You are good at guessing the right answers. You must have guessed the answer to that one long ago.'

'No.'

He replaced his glasses and frowned at me. 'Anna, don't be coy! It does not become you, and it infuriates me.'

'I'm sorry about that,' I retorted, none too steadily, 'as I am not being coy. I don't know what you are getting at.'

'Nonsense! You can't seriously expect me to believe that after all this time you haven't a very clear idea how I feel about you?'

186

'I wish you'd tell me.'

'Why the devil should it interest you?'

There seemed only one answer to that, so I gave it.

He sat very still, and when I had finished he just went on staring at me across the table.

'Robert, now you're doing an "Old Trypo".'

'I was merely wondering which one of us is crazy.' His voice was dazed. 'We both know you've always loathed my guts, but I thought you just said——' He repeated my words.

'That's right.'

He flushed. 'And it happened in Eyes last Wednesday afternoon—just like that?'

'That was when I recognised it for what it was. It had actually happened some time ago, as Betty recognised.'

This was having a very odd effect on his vaso-motor system. He was now white. 'But until you spoke to her just now you never had any idea about me? You have never guessed that I'd loved you damnably for years? Ever since Dave introduced us?'

Happiness was doing odd things to me. I was getting giddy with joy. 'Not until Betty opened my eyes, and even then I couldn't be sure. You always used to be so foul to me. Perhaps I should have worked that out. I didn't—until now,' I said again.

He said, 'It was the only way I knew of dealing with seeing you around as Dave's girl.'

'Did it have anything to do with your advising David not to marry me?'

He grimaced as if I had slapped his face, but his eyes met mine steadily. 'I'd be a liar if I said it hadn't, though at the time I tried to persuade myself I was taking a detached view. I didn't fool Dave.'

'He knew you were in love with me? He never let on!'

'No. He wouldn't have done that.'

'And he wouldn't have done for me, any more than I would have done for him. If we had married it would have been a disaster. So, whatever your motives for giving that advice, it was the right advice. I've realised that for some time. I hope you don't mind my saying this as he was your great pal, but David and Nick are very similar types.' My mind gave one of those mental clicks. 'Nick must have guessed,' I murmured, thinking aloud.

He heard me. 'Probably. The three of us haven't been together much, but whenever we have it's a safe bet he caught me looking at him as if I'd like to throttle him, and at yourself with rather different intentions. Also, Sabby could have enlightened him.'

'She knew?'

'I never discussed you with her, but she knows me pretty well. She knew my leaving Barny's when I did, and the time I fixed to return, was not entirely unconnected with the announcement of your engagement to Dave and then the bust-up. I didn't come down to the Mat. Unit until that last week-end as I thought you'd need the time to get back on balance, particularly as far as I was concerned, being so involved in your affair with Dave.'

He smiled wryly. 'From your welcome you needed a lot more time.'

'Yes. I knocked your glasses off. I'd just met Nick.

'I gathered that later.'

He did not say how, so I told him about the grocer's vanman. 'Why didn't you tell me he was Martin's nephew? Not to rock the boat?'

He hesitated, 'You won't like this——'

'Go on.'

'Well, as you've said, he and Dave are rather alike——'

'You thought he'd rock the boat himself without any help from you? Still, it was nice of you not to give it a gentle shove.'

'If you are going to have the truth you may as well have the lot. It wasn't nice of me at all! It was obvious you'd find out on one of your visits to Wylden, and that when you did you'd realise I was in the know. I hoped that would show you you could trust me, if only a wee bit, and then maybe when the crash came you might,' he shrugged, 'borrow a shoulder. That's why I drove down yesterday directly I found I was off. I stopped in Astead for those books as an excuse. As you've guessed, Sabby had told me Nick had promised to put you straight by yesterday. I was afraid you would be very hurt. I hoped you'd talk about it in the car coming back. Instead you kept me at mental arm's

188

length the whole bloody drive back. We seemed to be right back to square one.'

'That was because I thought you loved Sabby——'

'Anna, no!'

'Robert, yes!' I told him about the grapevine and then what Addy had said. 'David never told me you knew her when you were kids. Why didn't you?'

'I didn't think you'd be interested.'

'Interested! Robert Gordon, I could shake you!'

He was smiling as I had never seen him smile before. 'You have, Anna. You have.' He stood up. 'Shall we go?'

'Where?'

He put his hands in his pockets and looked down at me, still smiling. He waited until a pair of uniformed sisters went by to the counter. 'Anywhere where my kissing you in uniform won't automatically get us both the sack. I love you so much,' he said very, very quietly, 'that I honestly don't know how I've been able to keep my hands off you. After this I'm not sure I can hold out much longer. Will you come?'

We left the canteen sedately, walked along the main corridor, took a short cut across the car park to the Doctors' House, and went up in the lift with a houseman. We discussed the weather with him.

Robert opened the door of the senior registrar's sitting-room. 'If this isn't empty I'll empty it,' he murmured. But it was empty.

Over an hour later Peter Graveny came in and backed out fast, slamming the door.

'Who was that?' asked Robert dreamily, without letting go of me and blinking without his glasses.

'Peter Graveny.'

'A good man. Let's ask him to our wedding too.'

'Let's.' I felt my head. 'Where's my cap?'

'Somewhere with my glasses. We don't need 'em yet. We've wasted a lot of time, sweetheart. I'm wasting no more,' he said, and kissed me again.

Harriet was changing for a date when I went over to get ready while Robert booked us a table for dinner. Inevitably Harriet had already heard from her Stan via Peter. 'I knew it! As I told Stan, there had to be a reason why

189

you and Robbie had so many rows. And why else should you have lost all interest in the golden boy? Stuck out a mile! Zip me up, Anna!' She presented me with her back. 'And how about Hurricane Jill and old Stock, eh! I'll bet the old bags in the Sisters' Home are rocking tonight! What with Jill and Sweet Sabby resigning . . .' She spun round. 'It's Nick for her, isn't it? I thought so! I told Stan it had to be either Stock or Nick, and though he tried doing an old-pals-mustn't-split act, because Peter had sworn him to keep his mouth shut, I guessed! I haven't been sure until now, but I would have warned you about my guess, only I didn't think you'd care. And wasn't I right? Aren't I always? Well, nearly always?' She dived at my mirror to fix on her eyelashes. 'I say, Anna! Wasn't it dead lucky Sister Mary wanted that cottage?'

Betty Elkroyd knew what had happened directly she saw me next day, despite my mask. She told her husband. When I was going off that evening Tom said, 'So you and Mr Gordon'll be getting wed?'

'Yes. Tom, Mr Gordon asked me to give you his regards and say thank you.'

'Oh, aye?' He was still very pale and tired, but there was a new quality of strength about him, and the first pathological report was good. 'How's that, then?'

Robert had agreed I could explain, so I did.

Tom grinned hugely. 'That's all right then.'

I looked from him to the photograph of Betty and the children on his locker. He could now look at it without having to turn his head. I thought of Addy waiting to take my report and wearing a sister's belt and the new lightened atmosphere in Observation all day. It had been a busy day, and until now I had not dared think one private thought. Now it was safe, so I thought about Nick and Sabby, Jill and her old Marcus, and Sister Mary in her cottage. Then I thought of Robert. He had promised to be at the foot of our block stairs in ten minutes' time if he could possibly make it. If it was possible he would make it.

'Oh, aye, Tom,' I said, smiling back behind my mask, 'that's what it is. It's all right.'

THE END

THE PRINT PETTICOAT
by LUCILLA ANDREWS

In the country Maternity Unit of a London teaching hospital Joanna Anthony enjoyed both her job as nursery staff nurse, and her love for the man who had been her 'steady' for five years. Two other young men, one an old friend, one a new, watched, waited and shared her hectically busy professional life.

When she moved back to London to share a flat with her great friend Beth (and wallow in the luxury of 'living out of hospital' for the first time) Allan and Marcus were regular 'droppers in'. And then a serious illness took her back to her parent hospital as a patient, and in a hospital bed she finally faced reality and happiness. . . .

THE PRINT PETTICOAT

was Lucilla Andrews first published novel,
and with it she created what is virtually
a new genre in popular reading.

0 552 11385 9—**75p**

THE YOUNG DOCTORS DOWNSTAIRS
by LUCILLA ANDREWS

'You married?' I asked.
'Not yet. Just as well under the circumstances.'
He sat on the floor as I had the only chair in his fishing hut.
It was the only occupied hut on the island that wild night.
'Mind if I call you Aphrodite?'
My name was Shelley Dexter, but I didn't mind.
He'd just saved my life.
I didn't mind either when I discovered he was a senior medical student at my hospital, St. Barnabas, London.
For I was still in love with Alistair that night.
Extraordinary what a dousing in icy water can do to a girl. . . .
And a man. . . .

0 552 11386 7—**75p**

A SELECTED LIST OF CORGI ROMANCE
FOR YOUR READING PLEASURE